viking voices

VIKING VOICES

The Sword of Amleth

VINCENT ATHERTON

Matador
9 Priory Business Park
Kibworth Beauchamp
Leicestershire LE8 0RX, UK
Tel: (+44) 116 279 2299
Fax: (+44) 116 279 2277
Email: books@troubador.co.uk
Web: www.troubador.co.uk/matador

ISBN 978 1783065 325

British Library Cataloguing in Publication Data.
A catalogue record for this book is available from the British Library.

Typeset in Aldine401 BT Roman by Troubador Publishing Ltd
Printed and bound in the UK by TJ International, Padstow, Cornwall

Matador is an imprint of Troubador Publishing Ltd

the historical context

This novel is set in the Viking world of Northern England, Ireland and the Irish Sea between them, starting with the expulsion of the Vikings from Dublin in 902 AD and continuing until after their return in 917. Those two events define the time span of the novel.

It is a fictitious account of how things might have been, rather than a serious attempt at a factual account. Nevertheless it holds true to the historic events of the period, using actual characters, such as Ragnald, and adding some fictious ones, including Amleth and Aud, and describing how it might have felt to be a Viking living during that era.

The Norwegian Vikings, or Lochlain as the Irish called them, had established a large settlement and fortress at Dublin (Dyflinn) and its hinterland they called the Dyflinnarskiri. It was established as a centre for the slave trade, and they took Irish, British and Saxon slaves, mainly back into the Baltic, there to be traded on. They could not hold onto Dublin though, as in 902 the Kings of Brega and Leinster united to expel them. They were said to have left a great number of boats as the Vikings escaped half-dead, wounded and broken. It is not clear that Dublin was completely abandoned and there is evidence suggesting Norse traders may have continued to work and trade in the city after this event.

Following this setback the Hiberno-Norse operated in several groups, seeking refuge in various places around the Irish Sea. They re-organised and centred on various leaders, including Ragnald, Guthfrith and Sihtric, who were all the grandsons of Ivarr the Boneless, an earlier king of the Hiberno Norse. The latter two were perhaps brothers, but it was their cousin Ragnald who rapidly became the most important and is recorded as raiding the Picts in 904 and 905.

They had left Dublin with all their families, and so it was necessary to find the wives a secure place to raise their children well away from the conflicts. It is likely that they would have founded a settlement or settlements in typical Viking locations on an estuary somewhere on the English or Scottish coast between Galloway and the Wirral.

It is known that another of their leaders, Ingamund, was granted land on the Wirral peninsula by Aethelflaed, the Lady of Mercia after 902. They were controlled by the Angles who sought to constrain and limit their power, but nevertheless attacked Chester (Ceaster) in 907. These may be the people that had earlier attempted to settle in Anglesey (Môn) and were driven off by the King of Gwynedd.

The River Ribble (Ripam) was then on the main trade route from the Irish Sea to the great Viking centre at York (Jorvik) and was a busy and well trodden highway at that time. It was here at Cuerdale, near my home in Preston (Prestune), that the greatest treasure ever found in Europe (outside of Russia) was buried by the Hiberno Norse around 905. It consisted of a great amount of silver, apparently collected over a lengthy time, tied in leather sacks and put into a lead-lined chest. It lay there until discovered accidentally by agricultural labourers in May 1840. Preston itself, situated above the Ribble on a sandy ridge, was the site of an extensive Viking settlement. It is the story of this treasure that inspired me to write this novel.

In 909 the Mercian army made a five-week incursion into Danelaw, across the Mersey. This was not well received by Agmundthe Hold, the Scandinavian lord who held that area. In 910 he and the Danish army retaliated by invading Mercia, but the expedition ended disastrously for him and the Danes. They met with a wholesale defeat at Tettenhall, and Agmund was among the dead. As a result there was a switch towards Hiberno Norse control of the Danelaw.

Ragnald defeated Bardr Ottarson, a rival Norse leader, in a sea battle off the Isle of Man in 912 and secured a Manx base for his community. In 913 another Norse fleet arrived in Waterford from Brittany, and they joined forces with Ragnald providing a turning point in Hiberno Norse power in Ireland. In 917, the Scandinavians took Dublin back from the Irish, and the Angles were left facing an apparently renewed and strengthened Norse presence from the twin and allied centres of York and Dublin.

Nevertheless southern Danelaw, including the large buhrs of Nottingham, Leicester and Derby, collapsed in 917/18, falling to Edward the Elder, King of Wessex and the son and successor to the Danes great foe; Alfred the Great. The fall of the Mercian Danelaw alarmed Ragnald and he conquered York around 919, establishing himself as King of Northumberland, and unifying Scandinavian resistance to Wessex.

Ragnald died in 921.

The languages and the ethnic groups of Britain and Ireland in the 10th century

Anglo Saxons: Germanic people of the seven English kingdoms: Mercia, Wessex, Kent, Essex, Sussex, East Anglia and Northumberland.

Vikings: Scandinavians both Norwegian (Lochlain/Norse), Danish (Danir) and occasionally Swedish. The Vikings held an area known as Danelaw which covered Northumberland, East Mercia, East Anglia and Essex. The Hiberno-Norse also held significant areas in Ireland such as Limerick, Waterford and Wexford, and of course, Dublin for a time.

Brythonic/Welsh (referred to as Britons): British Celts inhabiting Wales, Cornwall, Strathclyde and some other large pockets in Scotland and England, including Danelaw, plus Brittany in modern France. These people had been the original inhabitants of Britain.

Gaelic (referred to by the Norse as Irskric): The Irish living in Ireland and the western part of the Scottish Highlands and Islands.

Picts: Occupying Fortriu, now the Highlands of northern Scotland. A group who were original inhabitants of Britain, with different language and culture from the Britons.

Norse, British, Saxon and Irish place names
used in the novel

Dyflinn	Dublin
Fortriu	Scottish Highlands
Gleawecstre	Gloucester
Jorvik	York
Maes Osfeilion	Llanddonna, Anglesey
Mersam	River Mersey
Môn	Anglesey/Ynys Môn
Prestune	Preston, Lancs
Ripam	River Ribble
Seafern	River Severn
Seafern Sea	Bristol Channel
Trente	River Trent
Vannin	Isle of Man
Wirral	Wirral, Merseyside
Woden's field	Wednesfield, West Midlands

Chapter One

ᴄʜᴇ BᴀᴄᴄLᴇ ᴏF ᴅyꜰLiɲɲ

Even in the midst of a siege it is a lovely feeling to wake up lying alongside your new bride.

Lovely, but this time it is also tinged with a bitter sense of anxiety, so there is not too much of our happy laughter together today. Aud puts her head on my shoulder, too sleepy to speak while we lie side by side together, our naked skin touching sensually under the warm skins that cover us. We feel safe and comfortable here but we are also very conscious of how dangerous and how cold it is beyond these skins.

I am Amleth, Amleth Eriksson, and a proud young warrior of the Lochlain of Dyflinn, the Norse people who founded this town long ago. Alongside me is my darling wife, the tall, blonde and very beautiful Aud Gerdsdottar. I am looking into her eyes but am not very comforted by the anxiety I can see etched on her face today.

It is difficult enough to be afraid for yourself, your parents and siblings, but now there is so much for us both to live for. We envisage such a wonderfully happy life stretching out in front of us but it could all be taken away in one moment of violence. I am frightened of dying but I am even more frightened of surviving if Aud was to die. It is just four months since my father approached Gerd and agreed to pay him ten ounces of silver for Aud his daughter, now my bride. She is typical of the very best of the Lochlain women, with her own special charm. I think she is also capable of enduring hard times if necessary, but I will make sacrifices to the gods to ensure that she never has to.

1

Her personal charm really won me over, a beautiful smile and laughter that sounds like falling water; she has a strong sense of fun and mischief. So it is wonderful to have such a good friend to become my wife and lover, to chat and laugh with and to enjoy life. I know that she has an inner strength that would allow her to survive anything that might come our way. Although I hope she will never need that quality, I know in my heart that she certainly will need it at some point.

We were married just a few weeks ago, and that was such a wonderfully happy occasion, although it seems like a hundred years ago now. Our thoughts have been so occupied since then by our troubles. Aud was so proud and beautiful wearing her wedding crown, and I was so proud to become her husband. It was a privilege to put a silver ring onto her finger, and to receive hers in return. Naturally all of our friends and family attended the ritual and, of course, the feasting afterwards. It was such a joyous occasion and I had never seen Aud so radiant and happy, the centre of everyone's admiration.

Despite today's great anxiety we have been so happy together since, never being away from each other's side. We hope to have our children soon, and to have a piece of land to farm, and lead a quiet industrious life. At present, however, we cannot claim any land in the Dyflinnskari, as it's become just too dangerous to venture beyond the inner fort.

The grey morning's half light is coming onto the eastern horizon, but we can sense that there is a great mass of humanity waiting, somewhere just out of our sight. The Irish, or Irskr as we call them, may live much nearer to the mountains than to our settlement, but those mountains are not far away at all. They may come today or tomorrow, or even the day after but it will certainly be soon now.

Then we hear the distant beating of drums and wild savage screaming, and realisation dawns with a sense of dread! They are coming and they are coming right now! We have very little time and must move fast to save ourselves. We all spring up in alarm!

My first reaction is to get Aud away from the danger. She is my first and my most important concern, so she, like all the women and children, must be put onto a boat and leave immediately; there is no time to lose. After my concern for Aud I also look to ensure that my mother and Aud's mother get away in the same boat as she is in. I am too slow to react though, as my very capable wife has already found them and brought them together. Aud is crying with fear and hugs me tightly, she asks to stay with me, but at the same time she understands what is happening, what she and I need to do, and that there is little time for farewells. She is caring and sensitive but also very sensible and gets quickly into the boat, still in tears.

All of the women of the settlement are now frantically grabbing all they can of our possessions and taking their children, rushing for the boats. There are no warriors to spare to row for them and they must do what they can for themselves. They have been directed to take the big knarr boats which are broader, more stable and more seaworthy. These are the boats which are used for the long voyages of the traders, often carrying larger cargoes. Some of the women understand what is required of them but none have done this task before. It is a skilled task, only previously undertaken by men, and they are struggling to control the boats which therefore leave chaotically. Despite the struggle they are safe as soon as they get away from the river bank and are on the water, as the Irskrs cannot reach them there, and will not attempt to. Fortunately there is a strong ebb tide running which will carry them downstream, and perhaps even out to sea if they can only control the boats sufficiently to keep them off the sand banks.

Having seen our women leave, all of the men including myself are rushing to take up arms and to position ourselves around the palisades. Most of us have a sword or an axe to wield. It is important that every part of the fence is defended; there can be no gaps around the whole circuit. We have little time but we are very highly motivated, our minds focussed by the threat of imminent death.

Down the hillsides and across the boggy fields many thousands of men, resembling small brown woolly bundles, are struggling towards us. They dress all in drab woollen garments, even covering their heads, and only their warrior elite have chain mail. Mostly they carry clubs and knives or scythes, most of them agricultural implements that have now been pressed into military use. The majority are not warriors at all, just farmers who have been required to fight for their Lords in this one great battle. Their great advantage this time is that they are coming in huge numbers.

There are a significant number of true warriors as well though. Both of the Irskr Kings keep their own household guards, several hundred in number. Normally these guards allow them to dominate their own subjects. Today though their arms are all to be turned onto us. They do wear chain mail and are well equipped with swords and battle axes. They also carry shields and have been trained to understand how to work together to maximise their impact in battle. They may even be capable of forming a shield wall if needed though that is unlikely to be required by a force attacking in numbers.

The Irskrs are like us in battle, they work themselves into a rage screaming and howling, biting their shields and swinging swords and axes. They believe that their rage makes them fight more fiercely and they may also be drinking beer to dull the fear, or herbal potions which make them even more delirious! We have these potions too, and many of our warriors are also drinking them. Although they give you courage and take away some of the fear I have noticed that those who take them are more likely to die in the first rush. The difference between bravery and stupidity is always a fine one, and in the heat of battle it disappears, but in the first skirmishes I believe it is better to keep a cool head and I will not drink any of those potions.

They are coming directly at us. Rushing down the hills and across the fields, screaming and waving their weapons, still many with clubs but many more with spears and certainly many more than we expected with real weapons, axes and swords. They are far better armed than ever before, and they come at us in huge numbers, almost beyond our belief. The surrounding fields are covered in them as far as the eye can see.

Now the first group of them arrive and collide with the palisade. We defenders have an advantage, being higher up and so we hack down at the attackers who retaliate, thrusting back up at us. There are many wounded, especially among the Irskr, but few fatalities at this opening stage. Many of those who are wounded now will, however, die over the next few days from loss of blood or from infection. For the present though, they are able and very willing to continue fighting.

Then suddenly a section of the palisade collapses with a great creaking and splintering noise, the timbers breaking under the weight of the bodies pushing against it and the great throng behind them. The crush caused by the men piling up against the fence is too much for the fence, which falls over. Many of the attackers spill through and gathering themselves up from the floor they immediately turn on a group of Viking warriors nearby. This group of brave and desperate Norsemen can instantly see that they are in trouble, and I can see the fear written on their faces as they hack and slash desperately at their assailants, frenzied by the rush of adrenalin. Despite their furious and frenzied reaction they are completely outnumbered and are instantly overwhelmed and they disappear underneath the throng, without doubt they have all been hacked to pieces.

All of the Viking warriors in the enclosure can see what has happened and all rush to save their comrades. Arriving too late, but in even larger numbers than the Irskrs now have on this side of the fence, they can only fall on the assailants and revenge the deaths of their kin. Now it is the Irskrs who are overwhelmed, now it is they who are hacked to pieces. This time I am very close to the action and can see the red spray as blood is spilt. This time I can hear the screams and gurgles of the dying men, and although they are the enemy, I feel sick with horror at their fate.

We move to re-build the gap in the palisade but the Jarl Guthfrith is here and he stops us. He wants the Irskrs to keep coming through in the limited numbers that can make it through the gap, so we can continually outnumber and overwhelm them as they come, and it works for a short while too. Around another twenty or so are killed, but then they realise what is happening and start to pull down the stakes to widen the gap, allowing more to get through together. Now the fortune of the battle swings against us once more.

Having moved to one side of the fortress our defenders have diluted their ability to maintain a defence all around the semi-circle. This is fatal when the whole palisade is under a determined and concerted attack, as a fence is of no value unless there are enough determined defenders behind it. "Enough" is a very large number in a battle of this size. Before long the foreigners have two more gaps in the fence and are streaming through. It is immediately obvious now that the battle will soon be lost; we cannot hold the fence as a defensive line, which was our best and perhaps only chance, and we are heavily outnumbered.

This is the moment that Mael Finnia, the overking of Brega, chooses to appear. He is a huge man, who looks as powerful as his reputation says he is, and he is accompanied by a group of even larger warriors; he is striding through one of the many gaps which are appearing on the side farthest away from me, like a conquering hero. Unlike the Norse Jarls the Irskr Lords do not bear banners, but they do have their own emblems, and he carries the sign of a white stag. He carries a two-handed sword and has no need of a shield as he has protectors all around him. They keep pace with him blocking any attempt to thrust at him and allowing the king the glory of striking out, to kill opponents unopposed. It reinforces the confidence of the attackers there and is a dreadful sight for us defenders.

It brings new energy and confidence to the assailants and they rush towards us screaming and howling to hack and cut at us with new vigour. The energy and confidence it generates is like having a thousand new warriors and the Irskr are re-invigorated and triumphant.

We are Viking warriors though and we cannot be intimidated by Irskrs! Despite their overwhelming numbers I see my brother Kjartan urging a group of our men to rush against them, they are valiantly trying to organise sufficiently to form a shield wall to advance on them and halt their advance. A group of men who organise themselves into a wall share each other's strength and will always have an advantage of a rabble. For a moment it seems that Kjartan and his friends might succeed.

They have created some confusion among the Irskr who have lost several of their number, who flung themselves against the wall and have been stabbed from below the shields by the short swords of our men. Many of them are bleeding profusely from severed arteries in their thighs. None of these men are likely to survive, having sustained such horrific wounds. The Irskr are now paying a heavy price for intruding into our settlement.

Then, just as suddenly, the Irskr are around the back of the wall, and they enjoy far greater success there. There are simply too few of our warriors to turn and form a second defensive shield to protect both sides of the line, and the whole line simply disappears into the Irskr throng, who clamber over their bodies in a welter of waving clubs. We can hear the thud of those clubs crushing skulls and the cries and shrieks of our dying men but are powerless to influence the horror unfolding before our eyes. In just seconds the whole line has disappeared.

Ragnald, normally the first to attack, shows his pragmatic side, decides we must pull back and already has a number of boats in the water to allow our escape. We can see his distinctive red and gold boar's head banner among the boats, so that is the point to rally on. It is already too late for many of our comrades and withdrawing under this kind of attack is more immediately dangerous than standing to fight. None can turn their back on their foe without being cut down and so must retreat facing them with their shields up and their weapons flailing in order to defend themselves.

A few do turn to run in a disorderly panic, and some do get away to the boats this way. They make it even more difficult for the rest of us to fight our way back, and they are breaking their warrior vows to defend their comrades. This will not be forgotten after the battle is over.

Others who turn to run receive more immediate punishment for their cowardice, as the Irskrs strike at the back of their unprotected calves, slicing into the muscles or breaking their legs and bringing them down unable to regain their feet. Anyone falling in this situation is completely vulnerable and immediately falls into the hands of their enemy and therefore has only seconds to live. There are very many casualties on both sides but we are definitely taking the greater losses now because we are retreating under pressure.

We pull right back to the river bank and once there we receive some momentary relief, those already on the boats are hurling spears over our heads, and for a few minutes the attackers hold back, startled by this new barrage. We only need a few minutes and are already bounding through the shallow water and hurling ourselves over the sides of the drakken boats, the long narrow boats we use for raiding. We can each only look after ourselves now, no time to look after anyone else. We must all get onboard as best we can since this is the most dangerous phase of the whole battle for all of us. Many do get on the boats, but some fall in the shallow water where they must recover quickly or fall prey to the Irskrs.

We scramble as hard as we can, and once in the boat we each take an oar and as soon as there are thirty men sitting in position onboard we pull away, though a few more desperate men are clambering over the side even while we are moving off. We are pulling as hard as we can, as though we are rowing for our very lives, which of course, we are! Thank goodness the ebb tide is still flowing and helping us, although it is just a little slower than before. As we are in the hands of a skilled helmsman we are soon moving quickly and consistently towards the open sea, and soon the kick of the first waves hits us.

Once on the water and away from land we are out of immediate danger. So after the terrible ordeal we are beyond the reach of our enemies. I have survived my first battle but I have lost everything that I and my family ever owned, including our home and our home land! As yet I have no news of any of my family, but I know that all of them are at great risk, and Kjartan is surely lost.

As we move out of the river and into the bay I can see there are many other boats around us that pitch and sway under the impact of the increasing waves as we move into open sea. The murky brown water is swirling and turbulent, lots of white caps on the many waves around us, yet I am hardly even aware of the movement of the boat, and the consequent discomfort. I need to keep rowing, partly to keep the boat moving and partly to numb my mind. I have great troubles to occupy my thoughts, but I want to shut them out if I can. I can see yet more boats both ahead and behind us, in a steady stream moving from the defeated fortress mostly going towards Dalkey Island.

Most people seem to know that is the place to gather, though I see others are heading north across the bay. I have taken this course once before, as I assisted Ragnald to carry a large and very heavy wooden chest filled with leather bags full of silver. We took it across the bay to Dalkey Island and buried it there for safekeeping.

Perhaps I am not the only one, who helped to move goods away to safety on that island or maybe another island, and perhaps Ragnald was not alone in foreseeing that this disastrous day was coming. The prospect of this tragedy was certainly extremely well signalled in the days leading up to the attack on our beloved town.

Once on the island we pull the boat on the beach as high as we can, to be above the reach of the next tide, and then rush to meet our comrades. Everyone is frightened and anxious to know who has survived and who has not. After searching frantically for what seems like an eternity among the women who got here earlier I finally find Aud, and hug her close, collapsing in tears into her arms. We are both in tears, perhaps of joy, perhaps of relief but probably mostly of pure hysteria. She is still with her mother Grunhilde and my mother Edda, having been with them all the way on the boat, so they are all safe. There is no sign of my father Erik, my brother Kjartan or of Aud's father Gerd. Naturally we fear the worst for them, so many men have died, and there will be little hope of seeing them again if they do not turn up here very soon.

The sun is above us now, it is just midday. Only half the day

9

gone and already many of our warriors have died, half my family missing and the work of four or five generations lost.

There is surprisingly plenty of good quality food and drink already prepared and cooked as though someone is expecting us to arrive here in such numbers. Although it seems very odd to have good food available in these large quantities, in these circumstances we are glad of that food since we are all very emotional and completely exhausted. There is also the opportunity to wash away the stains of blood from our garments and take away the physical stain of that defeat, though the hurt and humiliation that go with it will not go away. It will be necessary to fight again and to avenge this day. Nothing we can ever do will bring back the lives of those that have died in the battle.

Although it is just noon I am exhausted and fall asleep in Aud's arms, taking comfort from being with her here. It is a shallow, unhappy sleep though and full of the sight, taste and smells of blood and death and is dominated by dark terrifying thoughts. So it is not long before I am awake again, shaking uncontrollably with fear and weeping bitterly for the relatives and friends I have seen brutally slaughtered in front of my eyes. I am horribly aware of my own death having passed so very close by me and I still tremble with fright. Although I have awoken from my sleep the terrible feeling of horror, weariness and misery will not go away from me. We are in desperate straits and facing a very uncertain future in a strange place.

Aud comforts me and tries to get me to talk about it, saying that it will help me cope with the trauma and grief. I cannot cope with talking about it though, as even thinking of it brings the horror back. Not only can I not talk of what has happened but I will never talk about it again. It is sealed away in a compartment of my memory that I will never want to access again. Occasionally it will visit me at nights in the months and years to come, disturbing my sleep and waking me up in a hot sweat, trembling and shaking. It is one of the few things that I cannot and will not share willingly even with my wife, and even less with any other human being. In fact, Aud will become very familiar with the mood created by these disturbed dreams but eventually learn to accept it sympathetically and without question.

By evening it is clear that all of those who are coming are already here, and our last hopes of seeing our men folk ever again are finally extinguished. They must have perished in the battle, and so we will never see them again. My mother and Aud's mother are inconsolable; their grief and the grief of so many other women are all around us, and it is heart breaking to see and even worse to hear.

Now in the midst of this anguish we are called by King Ivarr to assemble for the Althing, an assembly which all free men can attend but obviously not the slaves or women. We are a little surprised to see King Ivarr here in all his majesty and great clothes, brilliantly coloured as befits his rank but perhaps not the situation. Given our terrible circumstances this seems to be out of place, and all of us immediately become fully aware that he has been absent during the battle. Because of that no one is happy with him, and there is a black mood developing among the defeated warriors. They are clearly starting to look for someone to blame. Ivarr's judgement and timing in calling the Althing this evening could hardly be worse for his own safety; he is the natural target of all that blame.

He takes the space at the centre and speaks loudly to us, calling on all of us to respect his kingship over us and asking for credit for having planned our withdrawal in the face of an overwhelming force, pointing out that Dalkey Island was prepared for us. We have food for the whole community for several weeks thanks to his efforts and foresight, and have kept many of the riches and resources of the city. We are now safe away from the threat of our enemies and being on Dalkey will gain us time and will therefore allow us to decide on where we go next and to go there in good order. Most of our boats have also been saved, and will allow us to continue to move and fight in the Viking manner. He calls on us to know the value of unity, and therefore to stay together and remain strong as one community under his leadership. He says that he alone offers the opportunity to stay united under one king, as one group. We should resist the temptation to disperse, or going away with any other leader, as by

11

staying as one people we can best hope to use our strength to restore our fortunes by re-organising to regain our lost city and its lands.

We all expect that it will be Ragnald who will stride forward to respond and express what we are all thinking, and right on cue he does so. Ragnald is always easy to predict, he has little guile and no subtlety, but he certainly knows how to convey anger and indignation very well. It reflects the mood of the gathered warriors perfectly.

I admire Ragnald, and think him the strongest of the Jarls. Like all of them he is a tall, young, athletic and muscular man, well-skilled in fighting and the arts of war. More than most he is decisive and aggressive, if a little inclined to be impulsive and maybe even hot-headed at times. Despite his youth he is very proud and confident, he holds himself superior to the others and with good reason. He has royal blood linking him to the great King Ivarr, and is always decisive and often wise. Although he also has that hot streak which can cloud his judgement he knows this weakness and tries to restrain his impulses and to listen to his counsellors.

He wears a full beard and has a full head of black hair. His most prominent features though are his lively piercing blue eyes, always darting here and there. He seems to observe everything, but maybe this is an outside sign of the internal strife that he is suffering. Certainly it is a sign of the continuous energy that sings through his veins. I never met anyone with greater vigour. When he is relaxed it asserts itself in great good humour, and he is wonderful company and it is a pleasure to drink with him and his comrades in the evening. There is always a lot of banter and laughter around him.

When the black mood settles on him though, he is the most difficult and argumentative individual. In that mood he is very dangerous as he believes in settling all quarrels with violence. No doubt he believes that the strongest people deserve to dominate and to have whatever they desire. All Norse people know that is the will of the gods.

When he leads a raid he is always at the front, in the most dangerous place, taking risks with his own life. He shows great respect for his fellow warriors. And many times he has turned back,

12

at the risk of his own life, to assist others who got into danger. He is always true to the vows we warriors take to aid and support each other. No warrior should turn away in a fight and Ragnald never does. He is true and fair and has a warrior's temperament, so no one gets in his way. We have seen him slice men open with a single stroke of his longsword during raids, and he has brutally split open many skulls. Although he is true to his own loyal warriors he can also be savage to anyone who betrays him. His vengeance is devastating and we have heard stories of his rages and of him strangling with his bare hands those who turned against him. None of us has ever seen that happen but no one doubts that the stories are true.

His record speaks for itself though; he is careful and calculating in his adventures. He does not carry out raids unless he is sure of their success, unlike the unfortunate Sigfrid, who recently disappeared. He only fights those battles which he is confident he will win. As a result of that all of us that follow him are all still alive, but naturally he has carried out very few raids in the past few weeks.

Ragnald speaks boldly and confidently, taking centre stage, like one who has complete authority and the right to command the attention of every one. The role of a Viking king, he says, is not to plan and organise a defeat, it is to fight and lead the battle to gain victory. Why was all this effort and thinking put into getting away from our enemy? This is not the warrior way since we do not want to avoid battles; we want to win the battles. Most important of all, why was Ivarr our king and so called leader not there, in his rightful place at the front of the battle, to lead us and to take his chance, make his reputation as a hero and be at the front of the fighting? It is clear that he has devoted his efforts to getting himself, his family and immediate personal guard away when everyone else was left to take their chance with the battle. This is rank cowardice, unworthy of any king, and especially not a Norse king! He turns to confront Ivarr and spits on the floor in front of him, a gesture of open contempt.

Ivarr knows that he is being confronted and his authority challenged. He reacts like a cornered rat and turns angrily and aggressively on Ragnald, hitting him and rebuking him for his insolence to a king. Ragnald sways away under the blow and then straightens up to look Ivarr directly in the eye, a black angry look, an unspoken challenge to fight.

Both men draw their swords and are circling each other, making desperate and dangerous moves and for each they could easily be fatal moves. Ivarr glances towards his huskarls, his personally selected warriors, hoping for assistance, but they can sense that the mood of the community is against them. None of them take a step forward to protect their king. Now he must protect his own honour alone in single combat, and he has, at least in theory, an equal chance in a fight with Ragnald.

These two are immediately plunged into an aggressive combat to the death, each believing that the winner will be the ruler of this reduced community, and knowing that the winner will take all. We must see who it is that Tyr, the one-handed god of those involved in single combat, will favour.

These are both muscular, large men who have trained as warriors all their lives, but Ragnald is clearly the younger and more athletic and he is also expected to be the more determined and aggressive. Sure enough he is the aggressor; it is in his nature to attack remorselessly. First he forces Ivarr back and the king must know that this is the defining moment of his life. He must win this fight, and he must kill Ragnald to retain his crown or he will certainly be killed himself. He gains huge energy from his desperation too, and finally shows the aggression and determination that we always wanted from him, hitting out at Ragnald and striking the side of his head. Surprised by this sudden and unexpected discovery of courage and fortitude by someone who he has always thought of as a coward and a weakling, Ragnald recoils, stumbles and takes a faltering step backwards.

This is not what is expected and the crowd gasps aloud, giving great encouragement to Ivarr who bounds forward to attack with new confidence. His moment of triumph is short-lived though, as Ragnald has instantly recovered both his poise and his wits. He is able to counter Ivarr's thrusts, and there are several of them, and when they relent for a moment he makes a thrust of his own, drawing blood from a shallow wound on the king's right arm.

Ivarr charges Ragnald again but this time he is ready and moves nimbly out of the way and the king falls humiliatingly flat on his face. He is up again immediately, behaving as though nothing has happened. Nevertheless it is clear to us that Ivarr is not anything like as agile as his opponent and so he is trying to compensate with sheer brute force and desperation. It is not effective this time, as Ragnald moves aside, and slashes at his adversary. This time he opens a deep gash, slicing through the muscle of the bicep. It looks bloody and painful though not too dramatic at first, but in fact, this proves to be the decisive blow.

The king is disabled, unable to hold his sword or defend himself effectively and soon we can all see that his moment has come. I can see that realisation appear in horror in Ivarr's eyes, now wide open. He can only hope for pity from his opponent but Ragnald has a warrior's instincts and spirit, he feels no pity and has no hesitation. He smites Ivarr a terrible blow across his head with both hands on his longsword, knocking him out cold.

Another swift brutal thrust to the throat and then we can all hear the king's last gurgle, his blood forming a fine red mist as it sprays out, then it runs thick, red and hot across the earth, and the fight is over.

It is a great entertainment for the crowd, a hugely dramatic spectacle and with a popular outcome. All of the crowd cheer loudly, enjoying the moment since no one pities Ivarr. We all feel that he had let us all down very badly, and a defeated king is a useless king. Those who have great power and enjoy the great wealth and privileges that goes with it must accept the great consequences if they fail. Ivarr has failed completely, so he has had to face the final consequence as he deserved to. Tyr's judgement has been just.

Perhaps alone in this crowd I look towards Ivarr's queen, Thora and their small children, and feel concerned for their fate. While I have no feeling for Ivarr, it's hard on the family to see their husband or father killed in front of them, and they have little prospect now as their wealth and privilege has also just died in front of their eyes.

Both of the children are extremely distressed and crying, clinging onto their mother, who comforts them though she must know that there will be no likelihood of sympathy, and little help, for her from any of the assembled people.

In complete contrast Ragnald turns to stand in triumph to accept the acclaim of his people, grabbing his personal banner with its red and gold colouring in the shape of a boar's head and waving it aloft. He shouts a tribute to Tyr, to show his gratitude to that god. Clearly he believes that he is now the unchallengeable King of the Dyflinn Norse, even though he will be king in exile. He enjoys his moment and embraces the acclaim, turning around with his arms held high, gloating like a hero, a man who really enjoys the attention of a crowd.

Ragnald swirls the red and gold boar's head above him, loudly cursing the Irskrs, and swears to avenge our defeat and calls on all of us to vow to regain our city. None of us will see Valhalla unless we first reclaim our birthright by throwing the Irskrs out of Dyflinn, the city that we Lochlain created and to whom it rightly belongs forever.

So we all publicly and openly swear before our assembled comrades to avenge our defeat and recover our once proud city. We do so willingly and it has therefore become our sacred task to gain it back for the Lochlain people, living and dead. The pledge is to be a great burden to all the honourable men who took it, though we do not know it yet. Many, perhaps even most of us, will never live to see the great day when the mission is fulfilled.

The assembly is not yet finished, however, as other Jarls have been gathered in a corner muttering between themselves. These men do not look like they are joining in Ragnald's triumphal mood and now Guthfrith steps forward accompanied by his brother Sihtric. They also have a personal group of huskarls, and these warriors are making their presence known, shoulder to shoulder behind the Jarls. Sihtric claims equal status with Ragnald for both himself and his brother. It is clear that they are going to back their demands, not in single combat with Ragnald but, if necessary by civil war among the gathered Lochlain.

Even Ragnald, angry again and with adrenalin running and his blood boiling, can see this is no way to go forward. He accepts tersely and with evident bad grace, a compromise, the suggestion that all of the gathered warriors will have the right to follow whichever Jarl they believe is best equipped to lead them to the goal of reclaiming our city. By far the largest number, including myself, immediately gathers under the red and gold banner around Ragnald and even one of the other Jarls, Ingamund pledges himself to follow Ragnald. The Vikings from Dyflinn are, however, split at least three ways even among those who have gathered here in Dalkey, and others may have gathered elsewhere.

Although Ragnald is content to allow his rivals to leave unharmed he is even keener to claim Ivarr's legacy, and in particular he has taken Ivarr's widow Thora and his children under his care. This seems a surprisingly generous and caring action for such a ferocious and ruthless man. It seems, however, that some part of his generosity is explained by his also taking charge of a very large wooden chest just like the one that we brought leather bags containing silver to fill a few days ago. Or maybe he is motivated by Thora's beauty as she is certainly young and very attractive.

Although I did not previously consider Ragnald as a ladies man it is clear that he is quite smitten and very attentive to his new conquest. It is, however, incredible to me that she can accept a man, apparently warmly; who only minutes before has brutally killed her husband. Thora is clearly a very pragmatic woman, who can put her emotions aside to assist her future fortunes and those of her children.

Perhaps there are actually more than three groups among the dispirited Lochlain now, since a number of the freemen do not gather around any Jarl. There is a distinct group who are not warriors, even in a warrior society, and who have no wish to follow a warrior lifestyle, and that is certainly the life we are all going to have now. These are mostly the tradesmen: iron workers, leather makers and jewellers and even some who just see themselves as farmers. In the main these people have never wanted to fight, never wanted to go raiding, they are peaceful, honest and simple men. Others are old or sick, or perhaps they are just not brave and are therefore content to return live in their city and ply their trades as quietly as they can.

Many of these people are closer than we are to the foreigners, and may even have learnt the language in order to carry out trade with them. Often they have Irskr wives and children and it is therefore their intention to return to the defeated town and take their chance on negotiating terms with the Irskrs. They hope to resume something like their previous lives, though evidently now it will be as subjects of the King of Leinster, rather than as free Norsemen. They must believe in his mercy and goodwill a great deal more than we do, and they are therefore prepared to take their chances.

So a momentous Althing disperses, with each man uneasily moving his family with him into his new group and a very hostile and uneasy truce is held overnight. Surprisingly the truce does hold though, there are no incidents. Perhaps that is because we are all too weary to fight any more, or maybe we realise that we are better fighting our enemies rather than our kin. No one knows what the future holds but we are just a few against a very hostile world far away from any friends and we have made ourselves even fewer and even weaker by splitting among ourselves.

Each of us, having taken our family under the banner of our new allegiance discusses in hushed whispers the drama we have seen unfold, before settling down to an uncomfortable and unhappy night's rest. A light rain sets in just as we settle down to drench us and thus to complete our misery.

In the middle of the night, I feel extremely cold and then suddenly very hot, and move around sweating profusely and seeing images of heavily armed Irskr warriors about to strike my head off, while I am lying on the floor unarmed and helpless. Then out of the mist comes the figure of my father, and I hear his voice: low, quiet and yet eerily harsh as though he has a throat infection.

I can see that I am back on the palisade of our settlement, and still looking out to see if we are safe from the attack as though it had not happened yet. I can see the green fields of the Dyflinnskari and the Irskr's wild lands in the mountains beyond that. I can feel the soft rain brush my face, the touch of the gentle rain that is such a very familiar feeling. It falls so often like this here, it is like an integral part of the landscape. I will never think of Dyflinn again without feeling that gentle rain on my face.

Just along the fence from me stands the lonely figure, a grey man, just visible in the mist of the early morning drizzle although he is not more than thirty yards away. He is dressed all in black leather and his hair and beard have grown long, mostly white now. He looks feeble, old and above all, dispirited. He is Erik, my father, and I am very frightened to see him now like this, and he looks troubled, very troubled. Thoughtful and distant as he is, he appears thin and gaunt as though an already a dead man is still walking. The grey face turns to look at me, I am terrified to meet his dull eyes, but there is no escape, they do meet mine and he speaks.

The eyes remain dull and lifeless, his skin taut, and while his jaw opens his lips and tongue are still, the voice appears to echo from inside the hollow shell of his grey body.

"Don't worry about me Amleth, I have no regrets and am happy to be among the dead. I have no regrets about the spilling of my blood in the land of my father. My time was already spent and I am too weary to carry on any longer. Just look after your mother now.

You are doing the right thing to get out of Dyflinn, it is finished now and the Irskr will trash the place, burn every building since they are savages who have no idea what else to do with houses. It will be many years before it is again fit for civilised people to live there. You must find hope for your family elsewhere, and under new leaders.

I have no time for that arrogant, young upstart Ragnald that you seem so impressed by. He is no more than a hot-headed braggart who has achieved nothing more than fight a few brawls. Nothing good will come your way while you follow him. You might believe that he favours you and honours you but it will never be really true. He only works for himself and much will be happening behind your back, you will never see it and never know about it. All of it evil.

I know you heard that I was a powerful warrior in my time. In a way it is true and certainly I was respected for that among the great Norse warriors who defended this town. I was born here and have lived here through almost all of its history. I can say with pride that I lived my youth under the reign of Olafr the White and his brother Ivarr the Boneless, who were real Viking kings. They terrorised not only the Irskrs but all of the surrounding lands and brought us great wealth and prosperity. Their achievements went beyond fighting, as they set up the farming communities and established trade routes.

You know that I was a fierce fighter, a ruthless killer who never shirked from the most dangerous place at the centre of every battle. As a young boy you often asked me to tell you of my adventures, and I could see that you expected great tales of adventure and of great glory won bravely in the face of terrible adversity. No wonder you were so obviously disappointed to find that you got very little of that from me. I was always extremely reluctant to talk about it all.

I can tell you just a little of my time as a warrior now. I do not see those times as glorious, far from it. I hated every moment of it and wanted nothing more than to run away, to be able to live in peace. All of my memories of my warrior days are of terrible hardship and death, especially of the loss of close friends.

I lived this life because I had no better option than to take my place in the ranks and fight as fiercely as anyone. Being a warrior is what we Norse are born to do; it gives us the highest status in our society and the best living for our families. We are surrounded by hostile people and must always fight them, dominate and enslave them, or be dominated and enslaved ourselves.

Throwing myself headlong into the fighting was my way of coping with it. I blotted out all thought of what I was doing and became an unthinking fighting animal, devoid of any thoughts or feelings. Everything happened in a frenzy, I could hardly see the men I killed, and I rarely had any time to think of how it might feel to be on the receiving end. Well, no time during the battle. Only in that manner could I accept the role I had to take.

After the fighting finished though, all of its scenes and all of its horror came back to me. Then I knew of the hardship and suffering that came from it. I think you will soon know these feelings too.

The death of friends alongside me affected me terribly, especially as they were sometimes hacked to pieces right beside me, covering me in their blood and guts while I still had to fight on and hack the other bastards to pieces to save my own life. No time to reflect, no time to help them, not even time to vomit as my body revolted at the sights, sounds and smells around me.

Even the victories were terrible and hollow as I looked into my opponent's eyes as they died, and often I was required to execute them in cold blood after the battle. Most of them were people who I did not hate and pitied, with no reason to kill except the orders of our cruel kings and Jarls.

Can you wonder that all of this filled me with a horror of war and all that suffering and blood spilt unnecessarily has infected my mind although I tried to wipe it out of my memory?

You were young and naive before today's battle, unaffected by my traumas and proud to be a citizen of the town of Dyflinn, the strongest enclave of our Norse people, alone here in the midst of all the foreigners. You thought it a strong, well-defended place, with that wooden fence built on an earth bank that surrounded the town. Where is it now? It was never as impenetrable as you thought in your youthful foolishness, you were happy in your blindness to the perils that were all around us.

You are cursed now as I was, you will never have that confidence again, you are doomed now to inherit my nightmares and wake up in the night screaming and suffering from the same shakes and sweats that I had. There is nothing I can do to spare you that, I was never free of these terrors. All the power that we thought we had was just an illusion.

Right now all the efforts of many generations lie in ruins! The town that we valued and thought invincible is shattered. All the thought and planning that went into building the very many rectangular houses built in a regular pattern along straight streets, where people come in peace to trade for slaves and exchange goods, are all in ruins. The Irskr have their revenge for the decades of misery that we have subjected them too. It looks like the gods have taken their side against us and paid us back for the great evil we brought to this country.

It was through that cursed trade in slaves that we got all the goods that we could ever need or want. It enhanced our lives greatly, and we were the richest and strongest people in this land. It was the riches from this trade in misery that brought our people here, and that same trade sowed the seeds of our doom. Although we have held this turf proudly for several generations we are far from our own native land and our own people. Even in the old country the Norse do not want us anymore, and they would certainly never give up any of their land to us. So this is the only country I have ever known. Although it was my only home it was always going to deliver us into the hands of our enemies.

There was no way that the foreigners could have just stood by, generation after generation as we plundered their youth. We have been using their children as a crop to be reaped as each of them reached their teen years. No people would take this forever, and neither did the Irskr. Eventually they had to rise up and wipe us off their land, and now that time has come.

I died fighting with a sword held in my hand but I have not seen any of the Valkyrie yet. They must be here soon to carry me to my place in Valhalla. I know I have damn well earned it."

With that the hollow voice ceases and the grey man with the dead eyes turns his back on me without a word of farewell or a backward glance and walks into the mist, his bitterness shown and his message of doom delivered.

He is no longer alone, as there seem to be other figures walking in the shadows which he is approaching. I can see a group of young women are waving him forwards towards them and he goes together with them, disappearing with them into the darkness. I hope he is going to Valhalla now, to live in happiness feasting with Odin and Thor until the day of Ragnarok when he will be needed to fight again, although it is already written that the giants will destroy them all and the world with them.

That is the last I ever saw of him and I awake suddenly. I am shouting in fear to Aud to come and help me, I am shaking and covered in sweat. Of course, she is there immediately to help me and I can see that she is very frightened by my fear.

I must look truly frightful as well as truly frightened.

Chapter Two

ACROSS THE NARROW SEA

As the grey light of the new morning breaks we can see a fleet of around 50 boats sailing away to the north carrying Sihtric and Guthfrith and their followers away. They have left at the very first chance, no doubt feeling insecure and very vulnerable as they are a minority in a hostile situation. We have perhaps around 80 boats left to us, still a large number and perhaps more than we need for our reduced number. They will be difficult to crew after all our losses, but no Viking will ever abandon a longboat if it can possibly be taken with him. We are all sailors at heart; it is woven into our souls and every part of our culture and nothing is more precious than a longboat.

The first business that Ragnald has been left to settle is the fate of the traders who are seeking to return to Dyflinn. He will allow them to exercise their choice as promised, though he tries hard to persuade them to stay with us, and he is especially keen to retain the iron workers as he will constantly need new swords and other arms. He even succeeds in keeping one or two by promising to keep them from the fighting and allowing them some better conditions when we set up our new settlement. What those better conditions will be is not yet clear, but in the short term it clearly means some extra meat, which is very welcome to them.

Those tradesmen and their families who cannot be persuaded to stay with us are not allowed to take any boats back to Dyflinn. They are just taken to the shore nearby, with no food, no provisions and no weapons, and are told to walk back to Dyflinn and take their chances with the foreigners. It is quite possible, even likely, that they will all be slaughtered but they have made their choice and must live with it. They all appear content to do so.

We who remain know that we cannot linger much longer on this island as the Irskrs will soon know where we are and how weakened and depleted we are. They will also know that as we are burning with anger and seeking vengeance, we will always represent a danger to them while we survive, so they will be here to attack us before long. It is a small surprise that they are not here already to besiege us.

It is time to leave this country and look for a safer new home elsewhere, but we will have to return some day in a mighty force, as we are all now pledged to take back our town. It is a pledge we all intend to fulfil, or die in the attempt.

Our fleet, a mixture of the knarr trader boats and drakken fighting boats, carries us east from Dalkey Island in a long, weary and very cold voyage across the narrow sea. We move rather slowly, as we have to travel at the pace of the slowest boat, and can hardly afford to deplete our little community any further. It would have taken even longer if we had not benefitted from a following wind that allowed us to sail all the way. No man ever had to use an oar until the very last stretch that took us into the bay where we have now landed.

That gives me the ability to lie in the bilges of the boat, free from the need to row, and it is comforting. It has left me free to stay close to the little that is left of my family: Aud, my mother and my mother-in-law. We have all been in great distress over the loss of our family members and are deeply consumed by our grief. It is rare that we Scandinavians show our grief but today we are all continuously in tears at this situation.

I try to do what I can to console them, but I am not strong enough and I need consoling myself. I will greatly miss my own father and brother, and am conscious of having lost the opportunity to get to know Aud's father. I spend a lot of that voyage weeping and lying in my wife's arms taking comfort there, drawing on her superior mental strength.

My mother Edda is also an old woman of around forty, and she has acquired a great deal of wisdom through her many years. She is still a very competent gardener and animal keeper and so much respected here. Her expertise has grown and she is very often consulted by many of the community in how best to breed animals. She is often involved in supervising births and in looking at illnesses and diseases in the cattle, pigs and sheep. She has developed a range of herbal recipes which benefit the health of the beasts, and knows how to vary their diet so as to fatten them up before slaughter.

Having set off in the middle of the day we arrive in the middle of the night, which is exactly how we want it for reasons of security. No one is likely to observe our arrival at that time, as both the darkness and the cliffs will shield us from prying view and we are therefore safe from any immediate attack. We will quickly need to search out what people, if any, there are around us here. We now have the sea between us and the Irskrs, but there will be other foreigners here who will also know of the Vikings, since our people will have raided here often in the past. That experience means they will certainly not be pleased to have our company, and we are very conscious of the dangers we face from them. There is some safety in our numbers though and we all carry weapons, so only an army would take us on.

We passed by the large island in the gathering darkness, an island which we had been approaching for some hours. It first appeared in the afternoon as a small peak on the eastern horizon and slowly grew throughout the afternoon. Then as it grew closer eventually it showed some lower land to the north as well. It always seemed to be getting closer, but very slowly, and it took many hours before we finally arrived. Perhaps it is an island or perhaps it is just a peninsula, we have no way to know, and right now none of us care. We arrive exhausted and in almost total darkness onto a pebbly beach on the north shore of a rocky bay surrounded by cliffs. Only the moon gives us a little light to see where we are, and that is only an occasional light as it is often covered by cloud. It is quite a small bay for so many boats and every pebble of that beach and the next bay as well, seems to have a Viking boat hauled high up onto it, every one competing for that part of the beach which is likely to lie above the level of the next tide.

Although we have no shelter we fall onto the stony ground wrapped in pelts and hides and attempt to fall asleep. Some sleep easily and deeply because of their exhaustion, but many others are awake long into the night. They may be conscious of their discomfort or are still troubled by the unhappy recollections and the thoughts of their grief or fear. I sleep very badly again, troubled by the terrible dreams that still haunt me with scenes of the battle of Dyflinn.

Early in the morning Ragnald sends out a large group of well-armed warriors to seek food, and to reconnoitre the hinterland around us. That means raiding nearby farms and eliminating any people that live there so they will not attack us in retaliation, or raise the alarm among any others. This place can be a refuge for us if no one knows we are here, at least for a time, and we need a safe refuge for all of our people more than anything else. Any of the local peasants we come across today are unlucky, as Ragnald is in no mood for mercy. They are all despatched quickly, their throats cut with no ceremony, and all the bodies of any men, women and children encountered are thrown into the nearest ditch.

I have stayed behind with another group of men who are seeking out timber to build some basic shelters, and to light fires. There is often a light rain falling, and so we are again always cold and wet. Shelter and a fire are as vital to us as food, and all are needed quickly.

After a few hours the raiders come back with five cattle. We immediately slaughter the bull and start a large fire to roast his whole carcass. A few hours later there is sufficient meat for the whole community and there will be still more for tomorrow and a few days. We have found our respite, at least temporarily, but we are still an unhappy group of refugees and will need to understand our position better; especially we will need to understand both the attitude and the capability of our new neighbours, before we commit much effort to building more permanent structures.

Ragnald is naturally impatient to make progress and he has already decided the families are safe enough here for the short term. Although he leaves most of the men to protect them he will take a group of four boats to reconnoitre the island, carry out a raid, take plunder, especially food and perhaps some slaves. I am delighted to be among the group he has chosen for the raid as I want to be known as a capable and courageous warrior and am already concerned that my display of grief has been too public for my own good. Among this group it carries a lot of prestige to be recognised as a warrior, even more to be part of the king's inner circle. It is time to demonstrate that my tears are over and that I am still a man to be feared in a fight.

The four boats are launched from the beach and, as we set off, we find ourselves immediately in a very fast flowing tidal stream which takes us rapidly eastwards around the island. The tide is strong and fast, moving like a living creature here; it feels like a collection of serpents are squirming and wriggling under the keel of the boat. Tugging us one way, then the other but always producing a powerful and strange fluent motion under us, a little frightening. I half expect a serpent's head to appear from under the sea and to consume us all. It is all too apparent that we are not fully in control of the boat, which is in the grip of another force. The wind is again at our back too, so we have every element moving us forward and it is exhilarating to travel so fast now we have raised the sails. The great woollen sails swell before the breeze and we can hear the hemp rigging creaking as it takes the strain. For the first time since we left Dyflinn life seems worth living. The sun has even come out at last and is shining on us!

Soon we reach a headland where the coastline turns south, and the cliffs then become lower. As we turn south to follow the coast the tide slackens and the wind now goes across our track and although we can still sail it is at a slower rate. Although the pace is reduced we are still moving well, and are very content with our progress.

We soon reach a very large bay full of red sand stretching out to the west of us, lit for a moment by a shaft of sunshine. We can see the sand close in is very shallow and there will be sand banks, or even rocks there. It therefore makes sense to stay further out to sea, where the boat will be safer. The tide is now starting to turn against us though. If that had been the sole factor we would have been better to be closer in where the adverse current would flow more slowly against us.

On the southern shore of the bay there are high cliffs and we can see smoke rising from their tops indicating the position of a settlement, a nice target it seems. There are clearly fires there, perhaps there are many fires, suggesting a large settlement, and that offers us the prospect of a lot of plunder. As we draw closer we take down the sail, since we know that it may be difficult to see the boat from the shore unless the sail is up. If we row it's likely that they will not see us until we are quite close inshore. If we wait until dusk or even dark it's very unlikely that they will ever see us, and then many will die in their sleep, perhaps never becoming aware of their danger.

Such people obviously get very few visitors, and probably none before who have arrived silently and unobserved from the sea with hostile intentions, so they rarely keep a guard and our arrival will therefore be a very unhappy surprise for them. We all agree that if these foreigners are so foolish they do not deserve to keep their lives and possessions, and we will be happy to give them Thor's verdict on their foolish husbandry. It is any way their fate, as pre-written by the Norn's, the witches who determine the fate of all living creatures.

I have always been fascinated by Thor, the warrior's god, and like most warriors I carry a small amulet of his hammer tied onto a piece of calf skin around my neck. I know that I must take care to placate Thor, the most fickle and perverse of the gods. He may turn against you at any moment even when you need him most, in the midst of battle. Some day he is certain to betray my trust and when that happens I will surely die a sudden and bloody death. I hope that I will have hold of my sword when it happens so that the Valkyrie, the beautiful warrior maidens who find the souls of the bravest warriors who die in battle, might carry me off to sit beside Woden in the hall of heroes at Valhalla.

It's not great fun waiting out at sea. Even in only a moderate swell the waves are rolling us continuously and we feel it a great deal more now we have stopped rowing. We intend to stay motionless so as to await nightfall but there is constant motion. The cold grey water rises and falls endlessly, sometimes higher and sometimes spraying foam across us. Although we are on the leeward side of the island we are getting little shelter from the breeze because we must stay far enough away from the shore to preserve the element of surprise. We can help to steady things by rowing sufficiently to keep the prow facing into the swell, but it's still cold and the rain falls slowly. It steadily drenches us despite the furs that we all wear.

These are the drakken boats, long and narrow with little keel, good to row but sometimes difficult to sail, especially towards the wind. They are fast and able to reach into very shallow waters, and so they are ideal boats for raiding, but evidently a little unstable now they are completely stopped as they have so little keel. Ragnald calls the four boats together and we tie them to each other to form a raft. It's a good call from our leader, who is a skilled sailor, as now the movement in the sea becomes a lot easier.

There is little to eat or drink while we wait. Perhaps we can find a few pieces of dried fish to chew, and if we are lucky there might be a little water left from the voyage, though it is a now few days old and tastes very leathery like the flask that contains it. We all know that if we carry out the raid well though, there will be rich pickings and much meat to eat and good things to drink before we leave. No one comments on the discomfort now, it's not the warrior way, but we all thinking the same thoughts. We are impatient for the time to pass so we can get ashore and carry out our raid.

I pass the time thinking of Aud and how happy she makes me feel when we are together. It's cold comfort as we are not together now, and I feel miserable to be here without her. I tell myself that I must be a good warrior and be sure to bring back great plunder to assist our family. My first experience of battle has done little to encourage me; indeed it has filled me with dread. I have to put these thoughts aside as we ride in the boat.

The time passes slowly. I know it is my duty as the head of the household to provide for the women and perhaps even make us all rich if I can find something really valuable. They are depending on me now that I am the only surviving male in a household with three women to support.

We sit uncomfortably and miserably in our boat, saying little but waiting impatiently. Occasionally a warrior sharpens his sword. Suddenly one swings his axe in practise, and then again, until he is told abruptly to stop. He is in danger of unintentionally decapitating one of his neighbours, none of whom are at all impressed by his stupid behaviour. The mood is tense and everyone is on edge. A sullen silence hangs over the whole crew

The time passes slowly. We have all made vows to protect and support each other in battle, and if necessary to die in order to rescue and protect our fellow warriors. Fortunately we have not sworn to be good-natured or polite to each other, as those vows would undoubtedly be broken in times like these. Tempers are becoming easily frayed. Although fights are common between the warriors on land, no one will break ranks in the boat since these are circumstances where we have to stay united before the raid. There is, however, a lot of muttering and cursing, much of it bad tempered.

Although the time passes slowly, it does pass, and we can see that the sun is a little further along its track, although it is still a long way from setting in the west. There are gulls wheeling around above us, looking for anything that might fall from the boat. We are not pleased to see them, as anything that might give away our position is unwelcome, although we know it would be only a very wary foe that looked for such small signs as thoroughly as we do. We are all trained to look for such signs and to detect the presence of enemies.

Like a few others I take the chance to comb my hair, using the beautifully made antler comb I bought on Fish Shambles Street, when there still was a Fish Shambles Street. It allows me to find a few of the head lice who often live with me, and I crush them under my thumb.

Many Vikings own such items as we place a great value on personal hygiene. Everyone must bathe once a week which is usually a very uncomfortable experience as it is almost always cold water. Maybe in late summer the water can be a comfortable temperature but otherwise it is an unwelcome chore. In winter it is a rare treat to heat up some stones in the fire and then drop the stones into a bucket to give hot water to wash in. We also regularly wash our hair in urine and then comb it to control those lice, which we are constantly battling with.

In the quiet of the fading afternoon, with time passing slowly, and the water lapping gently against the boat my mind drifts back to memories of our lost home. Inside the settlement, the areas were divided by wattle fences with many long rectangular buildings, with walls that were also made from wattle and daub. Externally the buildings had rounded corners and a single door. Around twenty people lived in each house, along with our animals in winter. Having the animals with us was very necessary as they heated the buildings, which were our only refuge from the cold. These were very strong houses with huge timber joists holding their frames together. These frames lasted for many decades, longer with good maintenance, though the turf roof needed to be renewed every few years. No one is likely to do it now.

Our houses lay within a very large d-shaped enclosure with the river as the straight edge, and there was also a brook helping to protect the eastern boundary, with a large tidal pool just before it reached the main river. The richest people lived on the higher ground, and although it did not flood more than twice a year, when it did it was devastating to our lives, and the waterlogged ground made our lives uncomfortable even without a full flood.

Beyond the settlement there were often over 200 longboats drawn up along the banks of the river. It was a spectacular sight and an indication of the size and power of the town. The largest fleet that I have ever seen and maybe the largest I will ever see again. Most of those boats were made there, and only a few remained of the ships that had first brought our people here. These were the source of all our wealth and centre of our hopes, since they often reached Scandinavia or the lands of the Saxons or Franks and brought us wealth through our trading.

In a calm situations like these waiting for action, we have a lot of time to think not just of our past, but it's also a good time to think of death which has already passed so very close to us, and still remains a constant possibility. A warrior's death is a good death though and will let us meet the Valkyrie as Erik did, and sit beside Woden in Valhalla. It is a much better death than those who die of disease or old age as they cannot make it to Valhalla but will be sent to live in the dark, cold and wet world of Niflheim where they will be ruled over by the hideous goddess Hel, who has the appearance of a rotting corpse.

Since we might be close to death all warriors have carefully cut their fingernails. On the final day before the destruction of the world, which we know as Ragnarok, the giant Hrim will sail over the land using a ship made from the untrimmed nails of the dead, to attack and defeat the gods and thus bring about the destruction of the earth. All of us are being careful to ensure our fingernails will not provide him with any more material for his ship if we should fall. That might give Hrim the ability to bring forward the date of Ragnarok.

Not only time is moving on. The tide is moving too and it has carried us further away from the bay. It's not such a bad thing, since every sailor knows that deeper water is safer. Not just because it gets us away from the rocks and sand banks but also as it ensures that we will still stay invisible to the people on the shore.

The time passes slowly, but it does pass. When Ragnald can finally see that the sun is close to setting he gives the order to disengage the boats and the raft separates into the four individual drakken again. We have an hour or more of slow, gentle rowing towards the cliffs with their smoking fires; we have no need to move quickly, and every reason to move quietly.

33

When we stop again, much closer to the cliffs, the light has really started to fail. As we are east of the shore it will not be as easy for us to be seen in the gathering darkness as the sun sets and the cliffs cast their long shadow over us. It is nearly time to attack.

Under the cliffs the wind drops and the sea is much flatter. The long tedium of the afternoon is forgotten now as we prepare for the raid and morale is higher, with excitement mounting. The rowing has already warmed us, and the adrenalin of anticipation flows in our veins as the boat crunches onto the sand. We are ready to go raiding! The Vikings have arrived, and we will soon be dealing out death and will have our plunder, just as Thor intends! I touch the hammer amulet around my neck to acknowledge my need for Thor's assistance.

The group goes across the beach as silently as we can and find a well used path that leads gently up the cliff, and which must certainly lead us to the village. We are more than a hundred strong men but we can still move very quietly, almost silently, up the path in the twilight. No one in the village seems to be aware of our presence and we are covered by the trees branching over the path. There is complete darkness now, really intense on such a cloudy night, there is no moon or stars to cast even a half light on our activities. That lack of light hindered us as we came ashore, but it is very much to our advantage now. We reach the top of the cliff and, glancing back can see across the bay and just make out the boats that carried us beached below. Just four warriors were left to safeguard them, and they are four very unhappy men as they will miss the action with its best chances of plunder.

Ahead of us we can see the glow of fires and hear the contented murmur of happy people chatting over their evening meal. It represents a very placid, happy domestic scene, but as we are clearly very close to them now things are about to change dramatically for them. As we reach the outskirts of their village we are crawling on our stomachs to avoid detection and spread out to allow more of our warriors to get into place before we rush them. We intend to minimise the resistance by taking them completely by surprise.

All of the warriors have reached the top of the cliff and are spread around the perimeter of the village, but Ragnald is still not content with our positioning. I am told to lead ten warriors and we are sent to the far side, so as to rush the villagers from another angle. This will spread more confusion, and make it even more difficult for them to escape. It is difficult to achieve this without being seen and we have to crawl very slowly on our bellies all of the way. It takes time, care and immense patience. Once we are in place another ten go slowly to another side of the village and then yet another group of ten to the other side. Now everyone is in place and we are ready for the assault.

Ragnald rises to his feet to launch the attack with a blood curdling scream, hurling his huge body forward and waving his warriors onward, the terrifying boar's head banner held high above him. That scream even terrifies me so it must really bring sheer terror to the villagers who are not expecting anything to disturb their peaceful evening activities. I rise too and urge my men forward as all of the remaining Vikings then rise together and rush forward, swords and axes in hand and smite out at any and every man they find, killing many in the first few minutes or so. It is chaos and hysteria, but we are brutally and efficiently killing very many of our unarmed victims without any danger to ourselves in return. The women and children are terrified, screaming and running around but they are surrounded and can find no route to escape. We do not want to lose any of them; they have great value as slaves.

The attack is over in only three or four minutes and we have achieved a complete victory without taking any casualties. No man of the village got the time to find weapons or to offer any resistance, which is why none of our men have been hurt in any way. The bodies of the slain are strewn around the village, many still breathing and often groaning in great pain. All are surrounded by great pools of red blood which continues to ooze onto the ground around them. It is a gruesome and horrific sight.

Now it is time to gather the screaming, hysterical women together in a huddle, a few men have survived the flailing swords and are attempting to hide among the women. They are quickly found and dragged roughly out of the crowd by their hair and finished off, despite the screams and resistance of the women. One young boy is protected by a group of young women but to no avail. The warriors strike out angrily at the women with their swords and several receive terrible wounds. The boy is soon dragged off and his throat brutally cut.

One of the girls, a tall and very pretty woman with raven black hair, rushes towards these warriors with rage and anger showing in her wild eyes. I grab her and pull her back and throw her to floor, I would spare her the death that is so close to her now if I can. Any of the others would have simply stabbed her. Her eyes turn on me and she jumps at me, her nails scratching at my face. I throw her down again and hold up my hand to calm her. The other women pull her back; they can see that her actions are futile and that I have helped her by stopping her impetuous rush. Our eyes meet and there is a great deal of confused emotion passing between us.

Maybe she is trying to transmit hatred towards me for being part of the group killing their men, maybe she is accepting that I have helped her survive and is conveying thanks, or maybe it is the heat of sexual attraction moving between us with our blood flowing hot in our veins. I know that I feel attracted to her, and find myself getting an erection in the middle of the battle. I hope no one will notice but I can feel the heat as my face reddens under my helmet.

A number of us are detailed to stand guard over these women; Ragnald picks me out again for this responsibility, which is again the least popular job when the others will be looting all of the huts for food, drink or anything of value. We who are left guarding will get little plunder or even nothing, and it is not an easy job as the traumatised women are very determined to escape if they can! I look for the agitated maiden, although she is not to be seen right now I feel sure that we will meet again. I certainly intend to claim her as my prize when the slaves are divided between us, whatever Aud might feel about that.

Soon there is great merriment among the victorious Vikings as they find a large amount of good food and, even better, a large amount of good mead to drink. All of us, even the guards, get to take part in a great feast with a lot of drink. After the bitter taste of defeat at Dyflinn this is sweet indeed, like a great party and we all take part, eating and drinking our fill. The guarding is soon forgotten completely and we guards also gather our share of the loot, in particular many leather goods and hides.

There is a price to pay for the drunken party though, and it soon obvious that all of our captives have managed to run away. Too late I rally the guards to take care of their captives but the last are already running down the hill. As they disappear I can see the tall and very pretty woman with raven black hair glaring back over her shoulder at me. Is she trying to communicate with me? Does she want me to return to find her?

I am tempted to run and follow her, to try and get her to stay with me, but I know that would be dangerous. We are only safe here, in hostile territory, while we are together.

We will take no slaves this night now and there had been many available to us, mostly young, strong and of good quality too including lots of young girls. The girls, in particular, would have fetched a very good price if we could have got them to our former trading centre in Dalkey and a better price still back in the Baltic in Birka or Gotland. Maybe there will be new places closer by where we can sell them now that Dalkey is finished as a trading centre, though we do not yet know where they are. Realistically we could not have taken many slaves with us in just our four small boats and so perhaps it is not such a huge loss as it first appears.

Slowly and rather unsteadily the drunken warriors carry their plunder down the cliff path. We suffer our first casualties here as several fall and get injured, mostly minor injuries: many cuts, sprained ankles and bruised heads. The unfortunate four guards who stayed by the boat also get to have some of the food at last but obviously there is no mead remaining for them.

It's a long and quite difficult voyage back to the community we left on the north of the island. The tide is with us at first though it runs slowly, which makes rowing easier, but it is difficult to know where we are going in the dark and we seem to be often off course. The helmsmen could have really earned their place this night, but it seems they have a full belly of mead too, and they are not performing well. As we turn west at the big headland we find the tide is now turning against us and runs strongly here. No matter how hard we row we can make no headway into it and have little choice but to turn out of the stream and into a rocky bay near at hand. There we beach the boats and settle down to sleep off the effects of the mead! Those effects together with the excitement of the raid and the long periods of rowing have left us exhausted, and we all sleep soundly. No one even thinks to leave a guard.

As the grey dawn breaks we are awake with a start, having slept only a little, since Ragnald is calling us urgently to action. He has gathered us under his boar's head banner. Further up the beach are a small group of armed men, all staring angrily at us. None of them move towards us, which may be wise for we are more numerous than they are, and we are also well-armed. They have lost the advantage of surprise as we are all awake now and well aware of the threat they pose to us. We might be feeling badly jaded and weary, but faced with a fight we will give a very good account of ourselves, and our bad temper will be taken out on our enemy.

There is no battle though, or at least, not this time. After a lengthy time of fiercely staring at us the foreigners recognise that they are outnumbered, and with our warriors spread out in a semi-circle to face them they can see our strength. We see that realisation spread through them and as soon as it has they start to move backwards and slip away along hidden pathways among the undergrowth, paths which we cannot see. Not that we try too hard to follow, it's our boats that interest us and so we launch them immediately and row off along the coast to rejoin our families, bringing them the remainder of our plunder. Mostly it consists of clothing and hides though there is enough food left for all of the community. That seems to be the most welcome item among them even though it will not go far in this large group.

Although no one says anything about it we all know that the main beneficiary of the night's efforts, in fact the only one to gain anything of real lasting value, was Ragnald. Once again he has collected some silver coins to add to his hoard, and perhaps quite a large amount. It is clearly a real obsession with him to collect silver, and we have all now seen examples of his gathering it and no one has ever seen him spend any. Clearly he has a purpose for this!

Perhaps it is a simple purpose, to gather great riches for himself and his family. We certainly know that he sees himself as a strong king and great leader and has great ambitions. It seems that a great deal of our future is dependent on his leadership too; so we will need to support him as much as we are able, his fate will also be our fate.

A more immediate question for him to consider is whether we will stay here on this island, the first place we have found after leaving Dyflinn. It has the great advantage of being close enough to Dyflinn to allow us to raid the Irskrs regularly, but it would also allow them to raid us. The greatest priority now has to be a safe place for our families, especially our women and children. We do not want them to be on the receiving end of the kind of raid that we mounted last night.

The group of captive women that escaped from us last night will be probably even now be spreading stories of the slaughter of their men and calling for vengeance among their people. I can imagine the unrestrained wrath of that raven haired maiden, clearly a very passionate woman. The group of men who confronted us on the beach were probably there to show us that there are warriors here who are capable of, and willing to, resist us. The question remains as to whether the foreigners have the capability to put together an army large enough and strong enough to resist us, now that we are back in the main group.

We are soon to find out.

Chapter Three

OUR WANDERINGS

After a week we are feeling much more settled in our temporary camp above the cliffs of our exposed and stony bay. There have been no further signs of any interest in us from the foreigners, and we are starting to feel more secure here, though probably with no good reason.

The weather has been a little drier and even a little sunny at times which has helped improve the mood of the whole community. The shelters have been made a little sturdier, and we have been able to supplement our food stocks with a good and regular catch of fish, which are very plentiful here and easily caught in nets and traps. So we are all eating well, feeling better and starting to believe that we can make a home here. It will however, certainly not be on this site.

The reason we are here is that it allowed us to land on an unknown and possibly hostile shore with the best chance of being unobserved. We will need to find a bigger, better and more sheltered harbour if we are to stay longer. This bay will be very open to a northerly gale, and we would lose most of our precious boats in the next big storm if we were to leave them here. Time is not on our side but, as so often, Ragnald is complacent and needs persuading to move on and he has a few advisers who urge him to do so. He even asked my opinion, which pleased me, but also shows that he has so little ability to see the longer term issues.

We have made many short trips exploring the coast from here, and these have taught us of the necessity to go out as the flood tide starts to run and return on the next ebb tide. The wriggling motion under the boat is not really a group of serpents but a very rapid tidal stream here, which is another reason why we would benefit from a different location with a better harbour, and easier access. We are ideally looking for a large estuary, just like Dyflinn, which we can arrive by sea at any state of the tide, but also be far enough inland to be accessible to good land so we are able to farm the valley.

Well to the east of us there is the large sandy bay which is close to the village we have already raided. That might be a better prospect for a permanent base although it would have a small drawback in that it would sometimes be difficult access for boats, since it is all dry sand at low tide. It is not a great problem, though we would need to carry the boats up the beach when arriving at low tide. Not far to the west is a very large sheltered bay with a good site for developing a new longphort. It might have a little less farm land than we would ideally want and, of course, it is already inhabited so we would need to drive the current inhabitants off the site. Neither of these sites are absolutely ideal for us so perhaps we will need to look further afield than we have already.

It is not long before we have a new and pressing reason to look much further away. We have visitors, who have not brought us good tidings. A small group of unarmed men have entered the settlement seeking talks with Ragnald, and this will surely mean that danger, in some form, is coming sooner or later. I am included in the small group of men around Ragnald who are there to listen and advise him, and it seems I might have become something of a favoured adviser of Ragnald's, perhaps he sees me as one of his most trusted and capable warriors now. These people have come to meet him as representatives of the King of Gwynedd, who rules this region, and they have been chosen for this task as they are Norse speakers, a rare thing in these parts.

It seems that we are not the first Vikings to come here and that there have been a large number of Norse raiders and even a few settlers here in the past, so these foreigners have learnt our language from them. One of them is the son of a Viking who settled here many years ago and took a local wife, so he speaks both languages fluently and is the perfect ambassador.

They are not bringing much good news but at least we can understand a great deal more about the land we are in, and especially the attitude of our new neighbours. Not surprisingly, in the light of our recent raiding, that attitude is very hostile towards us. It seems we have arrived at the most northerly point of the Kingdom of Gwynedd, and are on the island of Môn, which is a well populated island with very fertile farming land. It is known as the main source of food, especially grain, sheep and cattle, for the entire region. The people here are Britons and they have already resisted the Angles for a long time, before eventually King Alfred forced them to form an alliance with his Saxons. It is clear that they still hate the Anglo-Saxons more than anyone else, but they have also fought off many expeditions from the Irskrs and have met many other Vikings who came here to raid and even to attempt to build colonies earlier. Often those raiders were our own kin from Dyflinn.

It seems their king now knows of our current plight and is not planning to allow us to take any part of his land even in these circumstances. He is obviously fully aware both of our presence, and our reasons to be here. He already knows a great deal about our strength, our numbers and our plight as well. The raid we carried out on the village, their ambassador calls it Maes Osfeilion, has indeed stirred up great anger and hostility towards us. As a result he is finding it easy to gather a large army together and will be coming to sweep us off the island, they will outnumber us enormously and they will be here in just a few day's time.

Our visitors have come on his behalf to warn us and to give us the chance to leave peacefully and so avoid bloodshed on both sides. They are keen to suggest that we go north to the island of Vannin which they say is already a Norse settlement, and where they suggest we are more likely to be welcome. I have already been to this place, which is only one day's sail away, and traded with the people there. They are indeed Scandinavian, but Danir rather than Lochlain, so it is not at all clear that they will welcome us. There is, however,

probably no better option available to us in looking fc
After all, we are wanderers now, having lost our true ho
few good options in these terrible times. Our opportuni.
limited by knowing too little of the lands and the people tha.
surround us, so it is time to get to know much more.

Ragnald is characteristically unhappy at the threats he is
receiving, and his instinct immediately is to fight, but he is above
all a pragmatic leader and listens to my advice on the subject. He
already knows it is much better for us to avoid a full scale conflict at
this time when our numbers are reduced and our men still
demoralised by their defeat at the hands of the Irskr. Most of all we
have our women and children with us and must find a safe place for
them. They would be in great danger here if we fought and lost.

It is much better to accept the opportunity to move on, which
we must do anyway as we need a better harbour, and find another
location with a better site for our new town. I suggest to Ragnald
that he plans for us to come back to this island later when we have
built up our strength and our numbers, and give the King of
Gwynedd a better answer than our current retreat by raiding him
again, and thus punish him for expelling us. Ragnald feels better
when he thinks of that prospect; vengeance is something he can
readily understand.

So the next day is taken up by our loading the boats and
preparing to leave once more. At least we will move on better fed
and better prepared than when we arrived, but it does feels like
another defeat, and so leaves a bitter taste. Somewhere else we
cannot remain, one more place which will not be our home, and we
are still wanderers! We are still searching for that safe haven for our
people.

Ragnald gathers his inner group of warriors around him and I
find myself among them, we get the awkward task of carrying a large
and very heavy wooden trunk down the beach and into Ragnald's
drakken boat. It is obviously the same one taken from the dead King
Ivarr and is surely his collection of silver. It is impossible to move
such a heavy bulky item discreetly, and it is certainly very heavy.

although we do our best the whole of the population watches this procession in silence, and every one must know that it is Ragnald's personal treasure hoard.

In the morning, at dawn, the fleet is launched and the entire community is taken out across the hostile sea, dark grey but covered in white foam in the strong breeze. Ragnald is taking us to the island of Vannin as the foreigner suggested, and we will go directly north from here.

I have suggested to Ragnald that he sends Ingamund, the other Jarl, eastwards with a smaller group to search out other possibilities there. Ragnald should not be putting all his eggs in one basket this time and we also need to look for contacts in Danelaw or perhaps even with the Saxons. So we will not see Ingamund again for some time, probably some weeks or even months, as it is necessary for him to explore this sea and its various lands very thoroughly to gather full information and draw charts. We cannot wander unguided forever as a safe place for our families is our first need. We might find it in Vannin but this is far from certain and we therefore need to have other options if that should turn out badly. We have no friends in the world and so must fend for ourselves and it is best to do that in a planned and intelligent way.

Even the elements are unfriendly as we row out from the shore into a turbulent current, with the wind going across our intended course, and opposing the tidal stream. We can still use the wind to move us but it stretches the sails and it tries to take us further east and so we will also need to row strongly to keep to our northerly track. We are all battered by the wind and the waves, the families being bounced around in the bottom of the boats, a very uncomfortable journey for them. Most of them will be extremely sea sick on this voyage and many of the men will be too.

Although we hope for brighter weather with lighter winds the opposite happens; the turbulence of the sea heightens and the rain falls steadily on us. It is a good thing that we have many leather hides to cover us and warm us. They do not keep us very dry though and so no one is cheerful, it is a thoroughly miserable journey. Our only consolation is that for most of our voyage we can see the mountains of our destination occasionally appearing through the clouds ahead of us. First they are far away on the horizon, but each time they appear through the gaps in the cloud they are larger and therefore closer. Our next resting place is not far away, and we are moving rapidly towards it. Perhaps this time we will find our true haven. That is the great hope and consolation that we are all clinging onto.

The wind is behind us as we get close and the last part of our journey passes rapidly. Suddenly the clouds have cleared and the island appears large and immediately in front of us, lit up in a great red glow by the setting sun. The last rays of light brightening the western slopes and picking out all the colours. They are the sunlit uplands that promise a happy life to come.

As before, when we arrived in Môn, we make landfall at the island in darkness but this time we come into a large sweeping bay with gently sloping beaches with fields and woods beyond them, leading up towards some low hills. We are close to a small existing settlement and, having discussed our strategy with Ragnald, he has decided that we will not attempt to conceal ourselves this time but will make our presence here apparent to our neighbours. So we sail the boats together right into the bay as a grand fleet, in full sail until we are very close in to the land. In this place we expect to be able to converse with people in our own language and gain ourselves some time to rest through negotiation. It is most unlikely that we will be attacked before some attempt to carry out talks takes place, and we are in a land where we can converse in a common language. We are not simply a group of helpless refugees, but a strong and well-armed group very capable of defending ourselves if necessary. Any sensible leader will take us seriously, and although we are vulnerable and needy ourselves we also represent a serious threat to those who will make enemies of us.

At present we will be content to carry our wives and families ashore and settle them down in whatever shelter we can find or quickly construct from the dismantled shanties that we have brought with us from the now abandoned site on Môn. It is a great relief to me to see Aud and our two mothers arrive safely in this new haven and Ragnald is also seen carrying Thora and her children up the beach in a touching display of affection for such a difficult, aggressive and self-centred man. Perhaps there is a softer, more family oriented side to him after all.

Thora seems to have won his heart completely, and I have no doubt that having lost one king she is very anxious to keep the second one. I think her wise to do that, as few women get one, let alone two, chances to be a queen. Clearly he is a great comfort to her, as she seems to have no grief at all for her first husband, so recently deceased but already completely forgotten. She is always the finest dressed in the community, with brightly coloured costumes made of expensive cloth: acquired in the good times of Dyflinn. Even then they were difficult and expensive articles to acquire.

Her impressive appearance enhances her status and many of our women admire her good looks and rich clothes. Others are less generous about her manner and particularly her ambition. While she is both respected and admired among our women, she is not liked by many.

Aud speaks to her occasionally and has a good relationship with her, they are apparently quite friendly, but in chatting with me Aud admits that she does not really like Thora very much either. My wife can be as contrary as most women in her dealings with her neighbours, but it is difficult to feel much warmth in Thora. Her instant switch of affection from Ivarr to Ragnald without a moment of mourning has left a very sour taste in all of our mouths. No one feels that she is a woman of any depth of emotion and is just coldly looking after her own best interest.

The only credit she is given is for being a very effective mother in looking after the interests of her children with Ivarr. They have been able to retain their privileged lifestyle.

It is not the most peaceful of night's sleep, as the rain and wind continue to drive down and there is little shelter, but we both feel a great relief to be on land again after the difficult crossing, and we are learning to see the best in all the events that befall us. Aud says that we must fight hard, work hard and solve every problem, as that is the Viking spirit.

That Viking spirit, which will carry us through all these difficulties is strong within us, and Ragnald knows his duty is to keep the fiery motivation alive. There is no better man for that job; he has the Viking spirit in great measure, with all its virtues and all its flaws, and he shows his spirit it to all and sundry.

The morning sunshine makes us feel better and the rain has stopped for a while. We can see that we have been fortunate to arrive here as we have indeed found a very favourable site. This is a large south facing bay, which has several different beaches in a broad arc, where we can move the boats to. We can thus gain shelter from storms coming from most directions though our boats will always be vulnerable to a full storm coming directly from the south. It has good flat land for farming near to the coast and extensive woods for timber, so we could build our new town right here, and we therefore intend to do so.

Ragnald strides out to negotiate with our neighbours, as he can undertake the task himself here without any need for translators. As a Jarl, with the backing of a heavily armed force that outnumber the farmers by at least ten to one, he has a very strong negotiating hand, and he is not in the mood for small talk. It is not so much a negotiation as his rapid dictation of terms to them, but he has my advice on the need to be fair or even generous to them.

These villagers may be simple folk but they will be our neighbours for a long time and they will also have other Viking kinsmen who will look at this arrangement, and those kin will be better armed and perhaps also be very numerous. It makes sense to form a pact which emphasises co-operation and suits everyone. We already have enough enemies and too few friends.

Ragnald's terms are that the current owners will take the land to the east of the village, which has the more of the developed farm land, and just a few woods. Our men will cut down those woods straight away as we have need of the timber. This will allow them to easily develop some new land for farming, restoring the amount of land currently available to them, and enabling us to build new houses. We will be doing so right next to the existing settlements on raised land next to the bay.

This will leave us extensive lands to the west of the settlement. Although most of it is now wooded, and therefore less immediately useful, it can soon be cultivated after we clear the woods. So the main task of developing new farm land will fall on us, the newcomers, and this seems to be just to all of us. It also gives us that great source of green timber, which we need for building houses and for fuel for our fires.

It is already late in the season though and this winter we will struggle to feed ourselves. There is no possibility of any crops this year and we will need to live on our wits for some time to come. It will be difficult to feed such a large community and all of us will be hungry for much of the coming winter.

By noon the work has already started. Our axes which were once used in battle or in raiding are now being used to cut down trees. We also have just a few of the Dyflinn tradesmen still in our party and they are the most useful of all people to Ragnald now. Some of them even have saws which are suddenly much more valuable than swords or any other iron implement. The trees are felled steadily and carried over to the site where our new homes have already started to emerge, first using the dry timber that was carried with us from Môn.

The work progresses well over a week, then two weeks, and already the first outline of an enlarged village has started to appear. There will be twelve new longhouses, for our community, with some additional buildings further away for iron working. These are placed at a safe distance away since they are well known for their tendency to catch fire.

Many of the trees have been cut into planks, a long arduous task with so few saws and we are all learning new trades, especially carpentry, as the work progresses. A few are given the task of feeding us while the construction is done, and we are thriving, mostly on a diet of fish and especially shellfish which are very plentiful here. Although there are three surviving cattle brought with us from our last island home no one can imagine butchering them for meat. They are our first, and at present only farm stock, useful for pulling carts and our only means of moving the heavy timbers. It will be necessary to acquire some more, probably by raiding the lands around us later on. For now the first wattle fences will be built to retain the valuable beasts on their new pasture land.

The hard work is purposeful and good for us and therefore morale is high, as we feel very reassured by the apparent permanence of our constructions. All of the community feel Ragnald must be very certain that this is the right place for us, though I feel that there will inevitably be a challenge coming to him soon.

Unsurprisingly it is not long before other parties start to take an interest in us, the new comers. The island of Vannin already has a Danir king who has taken a little while to notice our presence but is now not best pleased by the arrival of several thousand new people who might provide him with a rival. After all, Ragnald is already well known, as is his aggression, fighting ability and ambition, and so the representatives of King Ottar soon come to see Ragnald and to hold talks. We hope and believe that this must be a good sign as they come in peace and want to talk, but we remain quite suspicious of them. We had, however, also hoped that there were prospects for a negotiated peace when the King of Gwynedd sent his ambassadors to meet Ragnald. That had not gone at all well for us in the end. So now I am once more at Ragnald's shoulder, listening to the negotiations.

The talks take many hours and then break up for a time, while we discuss the issues facing us. Ragnald has to consider onerous demands that have been made on him by Ottar the Dane, and is not at all pleased with his choices. King Ottar is prepared to let us stay but only if Ragnald pays him a huge silver tribute. This is not a happy idea for Ragnald, as he is such a proud, fierce man and hates the idea of accepting any one as his overlord. What is more the price will be very high, and Ragnald and this community seem to have so little wealth at present.

It seems that Ottar knows of Ragnald's flight from Dyflinn and has heard stories that he took large quantities of silver with him and is carrying it around in his wanderings. This is the curse of carrying that chest around with us. Many will talk about it and word of treasure spreads faster than any other gossip. Ottar believes that Ragnald is able to pay him off by dipping into the precious silver hoard. Clearly our king hates this idea with a vengeance, and I was standing close enough to hear him cursing and explaining to his personal guards that this money is sacred for him. He says that has not collected it for the benefit of himself or his family, but for the task he has sworn to undertake, that of recapturing Dyflinn from the Irskrs, and gain vengeance for the Lochlain. Therefore no part of this wealth should be spent in paying off a greedy Dane.

This leaves him with a very unpleasant choice, and he has to decide quickly. I know he is very tempted to fight and defend what he has already built here. This is confirmed when I am chosen to lead a group who are sent to go over the hills, to reconnoitre our neighbour's base, and look at what strength Ottar has at his disposal if it comes to a fight. I am delighted that Ragnald recognises me as the warrior who is both capable of and trustworthy to carry out this vital task.

I am to set off at daybreak and Aud wakes me gently with a kiss, that morning as the first light streams onto us, through the skins that are stretched over us, forming the temporary shelter where we live right now. She sends me off with a small supply of dried herring to keep me going through the day.

We have a long walk of three hours over the nearby hills, through the woods and over the mud of the valleys, but it is good to see that this is a green, fertile land with great potential, even if it is not yet extensively farmed. We have only a sketchy idea of where we are going so it is fortunate that we can soon follow the coast, in the sure knowledge that all Viking settlements are built on the coast. We are fortunate to get a dry day, but it is very overcast with grey cloud and not at all warm. The summer has already passed, so we are very pleased to be moving energetically through the countryside. It is probably also wise to move quickly so as to keep the chances of our being observed to a minimum, we are unlikely to be welcomed.

Soon we have arrived on a small steep hill from where we can overlook Ottar's stronghold on the western side of the island. He has a fortress on a small island with steep cliffs on each side, the timber palisades built around the tops of the cliffs. These cliffs make this a formidable site, a natural fortification, almost as good a natural defensive site as I can imagine. Much stronger than the one we lost in Dyflinn and nearly as large. Next to it is a small estuary which is very well sheltered from all directions by the small island which lies across the river mouth, forming a natural harbour. There are around sixty boats pulled up on the beaches around the harbour, and this suggests a community around the same size as our own, now that Ingamund and his people have left us.

It seems there is a considerable town next to the castle as well. All in all this is around the same area as the town that we lost to the Irskrs, though perhaps fewer people in it. That smaller population seems appropriate, as it has much less developed hinterland to provide farming to feed the population.

It has enough defenders to make it secure though and we, with Ingamund's group missing, are now a smaller force than before. There is no way I can see that we can succeed in attacking this site. At best we could harry it by mounting surprise raids. None of this will be the good news which Ragnald is hoping we will take back with us. His great hope was that he can hope to attack Ottar, wipe him out and thus take over his realm. That hope is clearly now unrealistic.

Perhaps we might take the castle if we could all get inside the fortress but it is certain we would lose more than half our force while scaling the cliffs alone. We have all heard the stories of the warlocks who can turn warriors into ravens so that they can fly into the fortress before turning back into warriors, but no one has yet met the warlock that can do that. When I do meet him I hope he is on our side! We will certainly need some sorcery to win this battle.

Apart from my day dreaming, the appraisal is now fully complete and I can return to make my report. Although it is not what Ragnald will want to hear it is important and essential information to allow him to make a sound judgement. Despite his aggressive nature Ragnald will make a calm, considered evaluation before he decides on which course of action to follow, and this is a good reason why we follow him rather than any of the other Jarls. We know that he will eventually choose a wise course, and his decisions will be very much made with the wider interest of the community in mind.

This time when we bring our news I tell Ragnald just the bare facts of what we have seen, and I make no recommendations, although I know the implications are clear. I am not tempted to explain that it means he cannot sensibly attack the Danir. I want him to figure it out for himself and make his own decision, and it is clear that he does understand when he immediately lets out a huge roar of anger and frustration.

We all feel that frustration. So much effort has been made in the building of our new homes, and we desperately need a safe secure place where our families can grow up in safety, but it looks likely that we will now need to leave again. It is even more frustrating since this island is entirely Viking controlled, so there is the minimum danger of attack from Irskr, Briton or Saxon. They would hesitate to attack this island; they know it would certainly be defended vigorously. Although we know that nowhere is completely safe in these dangerous times, especially on a coastal site, this place had seemed our best prospect of security.

Despite his evident commitment to the development of site on the south facing bay, and the agreement with the villagers, Ragnald has decided that he will not pay the tribute and therefore we cannot stay unless he comes up with some clever new solution. None of us, including myself, can imagine what he could dream up that might possibly work.

I discuss the situation with Aud as we lay together that night. It seems that all of the community are asking her what will happen next as, by now, they believe that she will know, as I am seen as

Ragnald's principal adviser. Although she does not say this I am confident that Aud is very happy to be at the very centre of all of the gossip, with every one expecting her to know as much as I do. She is seen as the best source of information in the whole of our group, and her company is greatly sought after among all of the women.

Once I have explained our position and options to her, as I see them, she is strongly of the opinion that Ragnald should pay the tribute and allow us to stay here. Of course, she understands his desire to preserve the silver hoard in order to allow us to attack and regain Dyflinn, but she also sees both the immediate needs of our group and the long term advantages of being on Vannin, rather than further away.

In the short term my wife is right about the need to draw the best advantage from all the time and effort invested into this site. It has great promise both as an agricultural site, and a base to raid or even invade Dyflinn. If Ragnald was patient he might build up his numbers here and, in the long run, could easily become more powerful than Ottar. He will certainly need to do that anyway if we are to be powerful enough to throw the Irskr out again.

I can see her arguments and they make complete sense, but I have no intention of attempting to advise Ragnald to part with his silver. It would certainly be pushing my developing bond with him beyond its probable breaking point.

When the idea comes to Ragnald after two days of dark thought it is not so clever but absolutely characteristic of the man's aggression and courage. He will challenge Ottar to single combat, a fight to the death, with the winner taking the leadership of both of the two communities. It is a fair challenge and Ottar is honour bound, in the Viking code, to accept it. Ragnald is a younger, stronger man though, and much feared in battle, so Ottar will know that he will be in significant danger of losing his life. He could possibly nominate a champion to fight on his behalf but would look like a coward if he did that. Ragnald has already played this card in successfully challenging Ivarr the Younger and he clearly has great confidence that it will work again for him.

53

Again he believes that he has the support of Tyr, the one handed god of single combat who looked after him on Dalkey Island. Even if Ragnald has had Tyr on his side in the past we cannot take that support for granted. He will need to make many blood sacrifices to retain that support. All of the gods are fickle and changeable with their favours. This time he has cut the throat of his favourite hound as a first blood sacrifice, to seek Tyr's further help.

Ragnald's move will obviously create confusion for Ottar and will at least buy us time while he ponders the problem he has been set. I would hate to be the messenger that takes the challenge to the Danir king, who is certain to be very angry at this reaction to his demands. No doubt he had felt very pleased with the misfortune of the Dyflinn Vikings and had fully expected to gain a rich reward in silver at our expense. It must be clear now that he only gained a powerful rival, who will compete with him for control of this island.

We are still using the time to continue to cut down the woods and prepare timbers for the new houses, though no more are actually being constructed as permanent structures now. If necessary we could take these prepared timbers with us and assemble them quickly elsewhere if we have to move on again.

Ottar's answer does not come quickly and it is obvious that he is not at all happy with the dilemma he has been posed. Finally the reply comes back through the messenger that Ragnald sent, and the poor wretch comes back terrified and shaking. He has been held with no food and little water for several days and under the constant threat of being put to death. He has, however, been spared in order to bring back the response to us. Ottar will not fight with Ragnald; he will send his army to wipe us out if the silver is not paid within the week. He has also doubled the size of the demand as punishment for Ragnald's insolence.

Ottar has violated the Viking warrior's code of honour in declining the challenge but it is obvious he cares little or nothing for such ideas of honour. Ragnald has the same dilemma to face as before, nothing has been gained except time, and he knows that his meagre force is still probably insufficient to take on Ottar's army in an open battle.

It is at this timely moment that we gain our first news from Ingamund, who went east from Môn as we sailed north to this place on the Isle of Vannin. The messengers he sent have been searching the coast of the island for us for several days and have now finally found us. For once it contains some positive news, and so perhaps we can hope that our fortunes have finally changed for good.

Ingamund has negotiated with the Saxons and has struck a bargain with Ethelred, the king of the Anglian kingdom of Mercia, who has granted him a small area of land to make a Norse settlement. It is granted on condition that he does not attack any Angle and will also help to protect them from any attack whether it is from any other Norse, Danir, British or other group. He also has to pay tribute to King Ethelred in the form of annual payments in grain or animal meats.

While Ragnald is still not pleased with the concept of paying tributes of any form he is happy to avoid parting with his silver, and can instantly see that this is the best proposition he has available to him. It offers respite from our wanderings, safety for our families and the opportunity to rebuild our strength for future ventures. What is more it allows him to retain his precious silver hoard until he can raise his new army. These last few weeks have given him new enemies to avenge himself on as well as new grievances against his old enemies. He is especially bitter against Ottar, condemning him as a rogue, a tyrant and a coward, and will certainly be back to raid this kingdom at the earliest opportunity. The need for revenge is burning brightly inside his chest and there are now several candidates for his vengeance.

For now, it is time to pack everything we can back onto our boats and leave in good order. The trading boats are very well suited for the task of transporting our timbers, ready cut to be built into new houses. Within a day we are all packed and ready to leave, with little to show that we have ever been here.

Once more Ragnald gathers his inner group of warriors around him and we again get the awkward task of carrying the same large and very heavy wooden trunk down the beach and into Ragnald's drakken. On the other hand, it is perhaps good to know that the silver hoard is still here, safe and sound, and available when we need it to finance our invasion of Dyflinn. That still feels like a very long time off in the indefinite future.

The Danir villagers we have been living alongside are sorry to see us depart, there have been many new friendships formed here as we had all believed we were here for the long term. They are also unhappy and unimpressed by the behaviour of their King Ottar but, of course, must remain loyal to him. Unlike us they must remain here and staying in peace with their ruler is wholly necessary to them. Their lives have been enhanced by having us here and we leave them with much more of the land next to the village cleared and available and ready for farming. It was planned for our use but will now benefit them.

Soon the whole fleet is on the sea again and we are all rowing vigorously out into the swell until we can raise our sails and set off to our next home. We all hope that this time we have the opportunity to set up a permanent settlement, and have some security in our lives again. It seems we are bound for a small piece of land called the Wirral granted to us by the Mercian Angles, between the Rivers Mersam and Dee, which is now uninhabited, unfarmed and undeveloped. It sounds like a desolate, lonely place.

They have promised that it is a good place with a lot of fertile land, good for raising cattle and with the prospect of growing grain, and if it is we will be very content there. It is surrounded by the sea on one side and there are rivers on two other sides, so we only need worry about defending one. In addition, the river estuaries have lots of fish, and shellfish are especially plentiful, which will help feed our people. The Angles are content for us to settle there as none of them live there and they have no use for it.

The voyage progresses well, as it is generally easier go eastwards, and to run before the prevailing west wind. We make fast progress, and the sea seems much smoother than in our previous voyage, so this time only a few are sea sick. Those few are already swearing that they will never set foot in a boat ever again.

As we get closer it is more of a challenge to navigate and there are many sand banks here to make sailing more difficult, especially in a strong breeze. The position of these banks is sometimes visible even when they are underwater; they are shown by a line of white water as the swell breaks on the shallow areas. Naturally we have to turn the boats to avoid those sand banks.

We are heading into a corner of the sea where the coast forms a right angle and a wide river enters the sea. We are told that we must stay on the north shore of this estuary as that is the area granted to us, to land on the south shore might cause conflict. Other people hold that land. Just for today we will do all we can to avoid conflict, get our kinfolk safely ashore and form our settlement in peace.

It is certainly a wide estuary with hills to the south and high flat land to the north. We pass several miles up the river from the entrance to get good shelter and to be more secure away from any sea raiders. We know that this is a waterway for many traders heading to the port of Ceaster. Finally we select an area of the bank with a gentle wooded slope behind it. Here we can build and farm.

Now we pull the boats up onto the sandy beaches before taking our women and children up the strand and onto this new land which has been promised to us. There we find Ingamund and his community, who are expecting us and they welcome us with lots of hot food and drink which is very welcome after the long, cold voyage. It seems that here we have finally found the safety we craved, at last we have our refuge and our wanderings are over!

We can see immediately that place they call the Wirral is a rich fertile land. Although heavily wooded at present it can be developed to make good farms; perhaps the small farm that Aud and I longed for in the Dyflinnskari will finally be available to us here. We have been told that the Angles have kept the better land to themselves but we are happy with what we have here, at least for the present.

Aud and I certainly hope that we can live a happy peaceful life here, just as we planned it before, although we are in a different place far from our home. We have good cause for optimism arriving here.

Once again we have the ritual of hauling Ragnald's silver out of the boat and up the beach, waiting until nightfall to unload it and doing what we can to remain unobserved. All of us are horribly aware of the attention this chest is receiving once more, and I fear that the gossip is likely to spread again and bring unwelcome strangers to our small community. If Ottar could have heard of it then many other hostile people will also get to know about it. We might well find ourselves under attack by those foreigners who come to know of it and want to enrich themselves on Ragnald's treasure. There are very many greedy and dangerous men who will think like this.

Once Ragnald's silver is out of the boat we are directed to carry it up the beach, and into the forest beyond where we leave it to be buried later. Now only Ragnald knows exactly where it will go next. It seems that even we, the inner group of friends, are not trusted enough to know its final place. Thora is still there so she will be his only confidante in this matter.

For now though, we have happier issues to concentrate on and can lead our families to their third new home in a matter of weeks. This time there is an important difference: we have the permission and agreement of the people who rule this land to live here. That gives us a much better chance of remaining undisturbed to build and farm.

We should certainly be safe from any immediate threat of attack here, and our spirits are higher than they have been since we left our homes in Dyflinn. That seems such a long time ago now; and so much has happened and so much changed since we were there.

The most important thing is still the same. That Aud and I are together and very much in love, our adventures have had the effect of binding us closer, always supporting, comforting and encouraging each other. We were always able and inclined to discuss everything and identify the threats and possibilities. Now we can look to build a new life together, providing protection and help to our mothers, who have faced their trial with great courage. These two wonderful old ladies have, however, visibly aged under the stress of these events and they now deserve a period of peace.

Aud and I hope and expect that we are about to enter that period of peace. Not just for ourselves but for our mothers too. My own little household with its three women.

Chapter Four

A HAVEN OF PEACE

The next day we recognise that there is an enormous amount of work to do in order to create a home here. We had achieved so much in a short time in Vannin, but it has nearly all been taken away from us, and now we must start again and do it with just as much energy as before. It is hard to face setback after setback with the same energy as we met the first one, but we are Norse people and take great pride in our resilience. That inexhaustible Viking spirit will be needed yet again.

We start by unloading the timbers that were brought with us in the knarr boats from the island of Vannin, and the effort spent in preparing them is now paying off for us. The houses are almost already built and are just waiting to be assembled. We only need to spend some time levelling the land where they will be built, and have already chosen a site on the slope above the beach. It is well drained and sheltered from the worst effects of the wind and rain, and with a fine south facing view across the river to the hills beyond. We need to dig level patches out of ground from the slope to allow the houses to stand almost level, though a slight slope has an advantage; we want to keep the animals in lower ground within the house, and need their slurry to drain away out of the house and down the hill.

The land above the slope has woods which will soon be stripped away to provide pasture or fields for growing grain and vegetables next year, and provide yet more timber this year. I am sure we can buy some cattle and the seed grain we will need, or if not, we can acquire some by other means. Although we cannot raid the Angles, who are our hosts, or the Danir, our fellow Scandinavians and potential allies, there is still plenty of opportunity to raid the Britons, who are not far away along the south side of our estuary, and further west. Further away but still within reach are the Picts, and of course, our old enemy the Irskrs.

The beach allows us access to the river to fish and soon we will be using the boats to trade again. There are extensive sands exposed at low tide which allows us to gather as many shellfish as we could ever need. Whatever happens there will always be shellfish to eat here, and in such great abundance that we will quickly be sick of eating them. We can be sheltered, well fed and content here within a short time. It really does seem like the haven of peace that we have been seeking ever since we were expelled from our own city. Few people come here, there is nothing here to attract them, and so it gives us some security as well. We just need to ensure good relations with our neighbours so we can stay without threat or harassment.

The frames of our first houses have been built in just a few days and in little more than a week the whole village has taken shape, with the shapes of the twelve new houses jostling against each other up the slope. Of course, they are not fully finished but they do already afford us some shelter from the rain and the cold with temporary roofs. These houses are very crowded though, as there are so many of us now that we have rejoined Ingamund's group, and we will need to cut many more trees, trim them into shape and cut them to allow us to build further and extend the village. It is also necessary to clear the woods to create pasture so as to allow our people to be fed well throughout the year. Already we have eaten enough of the shellfish and are longing for meat.

I am learning quickly and am developing into a skilled carpenter; it is a skill that will always be useful, even to a warrior. My products remain quite crude but increasingly useful, and I have a mentor in one of the craftsmen who came with us from Dyflinn.

It is clear to all of us that Ingamund has done well in finding us this new home, and it is widely noticed that his negotiating skills have achieved much more for us than Ragnald's ferocious aggression and strength. Despite that Ragnald remains the undisputed leader as no one has yet the courage to dispute his kingship. It will be interesting for us all to observe how the power and influence moves between Ragnald and Ingamund in the future. I want to ensure that Ragnald restores his status and influence within this community, as my fortune depends on his opinion of me. I am already energetically pointing out to my neighbours that it was Ragnald that directed Ingamund to seek out new possibilities, so that he gets a share of the credit.

Nevertheless it is Ingamund who is often being acknowledged as the better leader among the gossip of this community and the Wirral is seen as his land. Ragnald is considered just a guest in his place. We will, however, see who emerges as the most powerful king in the long run, and my allegiance remains firmly with Ragnald.

Aud is much more closely attuned to all of the gossip among the women and she tells me that the views of the community are now split evenly as to who the better leader is. Ingamund is seen as the effective diplomat and has the greater respect among the women but Ragnald is seen as the greater warrior and is favoured by more of the men. Therefore in this society Ragnald is quite secure, women have no vote and little real influence except through their husbands.

Now that the first houses are built and we have shelter, food and a degree of safety, we can think about developing more trade opportunities. It will be very much more difficult here to trade in slaves, the subject of our traditional business, as we have lost the Irskric hinterland that supplied us with such rich resources. It is not possible to raid our hosts, the Angles to our south and east, or the Danir who live in Danelaw to our north, without provoking crippling retaliation. This just leaves the Britons, who are now west of us, but even they are becoming more difficult to surprise, they are well-armed and have become very wary. We must either look for different goods to trade in or look further afield.

I have decided that I will specialise my skills, not in the timber that I was cutting in the last few weeks, but in making iron goods. This fulfils a long held wish to work in iron and I see a great commercial opportunity in this trade. There are only the three others among those Ragnald persuaded to stay with us on Dalkey Island who can provide this need for iron goods in our village. Aud is delighted with my interest in this new form of trade as it will not take me away from home, and I can play the role of the perfect husband and father, always at home and ready to take on home duties. She encourages me to spend as much time as I need to acquire the skills of this trade. We are in complete harmony of thought on the issue.

I know something of this craft from earlier times in Dyflinn when I studied it from interest rather than any expectation that it would be truly of use to me. How I wish now that I had taken far greater interest, while I could have learnt under the true specialists we had there. The smoke, flames and bright red metal have always fascinated me. There are few artisans here who have this skill so if I can remember or invent ways of working then I should do well. Those artisans seem to be reluctant to teach me, seeking to keep their trade secrets to themselves, but I have some influence with Ragnald now and they will be persuaded to help me. There is a great demand for iron goods here, especially to replace farming implements, as the old ones have been left behind. There is more than enough work for all of us iron workers.

If I can truly master this art then I might eventually be able to start to make swords. They are always in demand and therefore very valuable and command a very high price, but they are also the most difficult and time consuming article to make. They must not be brittle as that would make them break in the height of battle, exposing their bearer to great danger.

Only the best iron workers will make swords, as it needs the best metal, forged in the largest fires at the greatest temperature. There is also a great amount of skill and technique in making them, and only a few have this knowledge. It requires the making of two iron bars which are then bent and intertwined while still red hot, forged again in the searing heat of the fire and then hammered long and hard to form them into one blade before being tempered and quenched. Finally the edge is hardened, polished and ground into a finely edged blade.

A few iron workers also make iron helmets which protect the head of the wearer in battle. There are very few of these helmets and most warriors wear a leather helmet which produces only a little benefit. If the head is struck full on, a blade can cut straight through them. Only those of very high status wear metal helmets, and I only know of one such helmet, which is worn by Ragnald himself.

Our king is very keen to have as much production of weapons as it is possible to organise. The provision of these new arms will prove a great asset to his men's ability to fight and raid, eventually to provide weapons for his new army which he needs to fulfil his destiny to take vengeance on the Irskrs and retake Dyflinn. He encourages me to ensure the training and development of new iron workers, not only myself, and I have his authority behind me to ensure the reluctant artisans share their knowledge and skills.

It has become much more important for me to have a stable trade to support my family, as there will be no plunder for a while. Not only do I have Aud but also our two mothers to protect and provide for. Aud has become quite sickly these last few weeks and my mother is therefore predicting that she is with child. This would be a wonderful thing for all of us, a great thing to symbolise renewal and the rebuilding of our shattered lives. I truly hope and pray that it will come true, though I am also concerned for Aud. Childbirth is always a dangerous event for the mother.

We all seem so very happy here after the trauma and turmoil of our exit from Dyflinn and the subsequent wanderings. It is delightful to have our own place in the house and a small piece of land which we have cleared and are already using to raise geese. We already have ambitions to add pigs, sheep and perhaps cattle later as my mother Edda has the very valuable gift and craft of tending and healing sick animals.

Aud is very much interested and involved in the farm even though she is getting larger. She is enjoying being the centre of attention, not just from me, but of the two mothers. Her bump represents so many hopes and aspirations for us all, and our family suddenly has a future as well as a painful past.

Aud has always been a happy girl, with a radiant smile, but now she has really bloomed into a mature woman, a pillar of our community. Wherever she goes you can hear laughter and see people smiling, she is delighted at the imminent arrival of her first child and it always shows in her attitude. Whenever I meet her then, whatever my previous moods, I instantly feel happy. It's just the magical effect she has on me, her special gift, as she is one of nature's blessed people. Her radiant youth and glowing good health are at their very peak and she is wonderful to see. Even better, she seems to feel the same about me and we are having the very happiest period of our lives. Whenever we look back on this period of our lives we can remember only the laughter and the happiness, as though there was always sunshine and warmth all day long every day. It is Spring in every sense, the beginning of a new season of growth.

The cheerfulness is contagious too and my mother and mother-in-law catch it, and have finally overcome their previous grief and the melancholy mood which has hung over them for months. We can all see the prospect of a happy future here. The farm has started to progress well and we have already extended the area under pasture. We acquired some sheep to graze there, in addition to the geese we captured on the estuary early on. All of my women seem to have a natural talent for this kind of work, and obviously enjoy doing it.

My iron working has started tentatively and I gathered a great deal of wood from the forests which I made into charcoal. My first product was an iron hearth which contained the fire and above which I smelt the ore or bog iron into an iron I can work. I have also been able to make a pair of bellows from two planks of timber and some leather hides. Like the hearth it is very crude and would not be suitable to sell, but these basic tools have allowed me to start my trade. No doubt I will replace them with more sophisticated implements when I have the craft to improve them. Although I have had little teaching I have remembered a great deal, innovated new methods and the whole process is proving quite successful.

I have taken a young man named Brodir to assist me in my iron making and he is gaining in skills too. Now that we are two we can produce a lot more, taking different roles in which we specialise to make the goods quicker, he is always making the charcoal and feeding the fire while I get the heavy work of hammering the metal. It is a good way of co-operative working and he also earns a fair living from our trade.

The worst problem is getting hold of either iron or the ore to make it, and I can only do this by trading with the Angles, who seem able to get large amounts of it. In exchange we need to sell on the eggs from the geese, the geese themselves and occasionally even a lamb or two. The farm has become our main means of support and the efforts of my three women in maintaining it have been extremely successful. It took time, but is now yielding results. They have a vast pool of knowledge about animal husbandry, and I am very much in their debt. I help with some of the hard labour and in providing tools, and so we have developed a wonderful co-operative effort around the development of both the farm and the iron making.

Gradually my skills improve and I produce ploughs and harnesses to assist others in producing grain and growing vegetables. I have a little stock of silver myself now as a result of my trade, mostly Saxon coins showing the head of Edward the King of Wessex and also a few Danir coins from Jorvik. All of the farms here are thriving and our little community has quickly developed into a prosperous village, mostly based on farming, fishing and trade but with Ragnald and Ingamund involved there will always be an occasional raid to supplement our prosperity.

Ragnald is especially fond of raiding Vannin to spite his adversary Ottar, against whom he still holds a particular grudge. It is possible to raid there and the land of Gwynedd without upsetting our hosts or allies here. It is from one of those raids that I was able to add five sheep to our little menagerie, a very useful addition to our wealth.

The trading in metal goods with the Angles allows me to earn a good living but is always dependant on buying the ore from them to make new metal. So we often find ourselves venturing into the nearby Anglian city of Ceaster. It is a regular trip every month and, of course, Aud loves to accompany me on these trips.

The Angles regard Ceaster as the far edge of Mercia, the wildest and most hostile place, including our home in the Wirral. They see us as a potential threat but we are certainly thought of as civilised and sensible people in comparison with the Britons, who the Anglo-Saxons call Welsc, the foreigners. They have good reason to fear the Welsc as every one of them detests Angles and Saxons alike, even more than they hate the Norse. King Alfred, known as the Great, had brought them under control and had a pact with Gwynedd but now he is gone they are unlikely to respect that pact and are always looking for the chance to kill Angles and Saxons.

The town of Ceaster, sitting in a bend of the River Dee, is very impressive as it has many stone buildings, the first we have ever seen. They are a source of amazement to us and we admire them greatly. I know from the conversations we have with the people of Ceaster that these buildings were built by the Romans many, many centuries before any of us were born. What amazing people they must have been to build like this. The Angles do have masons but no one has those skills any more. It is still a great defensive position, better than any other I know. Even Ottar's castle with its great cliffs is not so formidable! It is not just a fort but a huge area of construction that encloses a whole town.

It is not too difficult to converse with the Angles. Although they do not speak our language there are so many of their words that I can understand. They sound very similar to Norse. Both we and the Mercian Angles have learnt something of the other's languages and a good level of communication is possible. Everyone knows enough for us to learn a little of what we see around us, and to make bargains. In fact, we find that many of the merchants here are not

Angle at all, but often Danir and Norse. There are even a few of our fellow migrants who fled Dyflinn at the same time as we did, or even earlier, who have already arrived here by travelling independently away from the main groups.

The stone buildings are the creations of the Romans, an ancient people who brought great knowledge and sophistication here long ago. Now most of their knowledge has been lost, though there are a few who can still work in stone and these artisans are being used to rebuild the ancient castles and even to build new walls. I can see that this will become a very fine city and a great fortress. If only we could have built Dyflinn like this we could have defended it and would still be in possession of it.

The city has seen regeneration in recent times and it was the response to Danir aggression that has caused it. After the Dane Halfdan came here some years ago and occupied the city for a short time the Angles have taken a great interest in rebuilding it. The rebuilding of the walls is entirely designed to keep out aggressive Vikings. They have also created a secure place where it is safe to trade and the city has therefore become a flourishing market town.

The river banks here remind me very much of Dyflinn with a large number of boats drawn up on the banks. Many are Viking boats but there are also many built by both the Irskr and the Angles. Both of those people are building their boats in imitation of our boats which were once so much better than theirs. By imitating our designs they are now enjoying the same ability to trade that we have.

Many of these boats are involved in trading between the Irskr and the Angle. This trade has increased since we left Dyflinn as the Angles have taken over a great deal of the trade which was once done between with us and the Irskr. I pause, as I think of this, to wonder what fate befell the tradespeople we set on the shore at Dalkey Island. They had to take their chances in walking back to their homes and becoming subjects of the King of Leinster. No one knows whether they are still alive or dead.

As we enter the city through a stone gate we can see that there is an armed guard and we are recognised as Norse people. They are not greatly hostile to us but there is clearly some level of distrust and so a check is made to ensure we do not bring in any weapons. As we do not have any we are permitted to pass, the Mercian Angles are suspicious but they know the value of trade as well as we do! As we pass we are aware that that the guards are looking very carefully at us. Anyone who has been here before and been accused of fraudulent or dishonest trading will be refused entry. The Angles are trying to impose honest dealings, at least on any foreigner they allow in. An Angle or Saxon who is accused of cheating a foreigner is much more likely to be allowed to continue to trade but no Norseman would be permitted that level of tolerance.

Once inside the city I seek out the market place and try to find any merchants who have iron to sell, mostly it is in the form of ore but some have bars of iron itself already smelted. I prefer that form but, of course, it is more expensive. I have to barter with the merchants to exchange my iron goods with them. I must always have a surplus to sell for some silver pennies that are so often used here as a means of exchange.

Although silver was sometimes used in Dyflinn to assist trade most deals were done by direct barter, and exchange of goods. Here it is much more common to use silver coins as a medium of exchange and it makes trading much more flexible. It is a great deal easier to buy the exact things that you want since everyone will accept the silver coins as an exchange.

Aud loves having some silver coins in her hand, knowing the power that it gives her to obtain any goods that she wants. It's a peculiar delight that takes her when she can wander from merchant to merchant viewing all of their goods before she finally decides on something to buy. It is always something quite unnecessary such as fabrics or jewellery but it gives her so much pleasure to buy these things that I cannot find it in me to stop her. We have everything we need, why should she not buy a few things we do not need but love to have?

When you look down the side streets you can watch the way that the money is made. There are smoky buildings full of fire there, in which there are artisans making the coins, often with the head of their king on them. These buildings are quite distinct in their architecture.

The buildings are very sturdily built, with very thick walls and massive doors. There are few windows and these are small, high and heavily barred. It looks like a building capable of sustaining a heavy and prolonged assault. The coin makers must have to work in near darkness. Above these buildings is the accommodation for the owners who prefer to be always able to keep an eye on how their business is being conducted.

Like most houses they are long and narrow and inside the buildings there are benches along which the workers are passing their product through several stages before it emerges at the end as money. The place is busy and noisy with the sounds of fires and especially the constant striking of hammers.

They have cast the silver into sheets and are cutting the coins out of the sheets using a punch to produces a blank disc. Boxes hold the blank discs before they are passed on to be made into money, cast with the head of their king on it along with a few words. It takes great skill to make the iron dies that they use and few blacksmiths would have the talent to make them. All over Europe Anglo-Saxon coin is known as the truest coin, the weight is considered reliable and the silver is always pure. Their king has agents who check the coins in circulation and there are heavy penalties for any coin maker who acts dishonestly.

We can see how helpful these methods of trading are, especially the use of money. Aud is very keen to take their ideas and exploit them to our advantage. Just as they have copied our boat making, we can copy their ability to make money.

On our return to our home she outlines her plan. Next time we are in Ceaster, she intends to buy silver ingots instead of iron. Then she wants me to make iron dies from which we can press the head of Ragnald onto a coin, we will then get Brodir to smelt the silver and cast silver pennies. It is a bold plan but I am not completely convinced as it takes Brodir away from the iron making tasks that I have in mind for him.

For now the bold plan is forgotten, as at last Aud has gone into labour, and we are all excited about this event. That excitement does not last long though and is replaced by a great anxiety as her labour lasts for two days. I am terrified by the screams as I fear that I might lose her as we all know that many women die in childbirth. Nothing I have endured so far could be worse than the loss of my wife.

Eventually it all turns out well, and we have our first child, a daughter, who is immediately the apple of her grandmothers' eyes. They think she is the image of her mother but to me she just looks like a small bundle of skin. Of course, the most wonderful bundle that there ever was, my beautiful little daughter.

Her mother is wonderful too, pale and exhausted but happily recovering fast from her ordeal, though very glad that it is over and swearing never to do it again. She is delighted to be suckling her infant, as though it is the most wonderful thing that ever happened to her. We have decided to call our new daughter Astrithr.

During this wonderful idyll I have heard little or nothing from Ragnald for several weeks. It is as though he does not want to see my normal life, the way I am delighting in my family and my every day occupation. He is very dismissive of these things, almost angry about them, saying they are not the life of a warrior. It is all a bit eccentric and tells me that his own home life is not going as well as he wished.

All of this time he is with Thora, who was Ivarr's queen, so his reaction makes me wonder if all is going well between them. I can imagine that being Ragnald's concubine may be stressful for any woman, and I am sure she wants to have her title as queen restored to her. It seems that both of her relationships must be based on some different grounds than mine with Aud. We have no other reason to be together than we love each other and only need to be together to make each other intensely happy.

I am sure Ragnald's reaction shows that he envies us and wants to have a life like this for himself and is perhaps rather jealous since he knows it is not in his nature to be calm enough to lead such a life. He would always make an inappropriate remark or an angry one which would destroy a normal relationship. I am sure he is a very unhappy man but he is also very ambitious and that makes him a dangerous man, so I will continue to take care in all my dealings with him, and support his ambitions.

Of course, it is not long before Ragnald calls on me with a new task. In a way it is not a great surprise but I had hoped to be left alone for a longer period so as to enjoy my new trade, my new daughter, my new happiness, but perhaps that is simply not the warrior's way! It is certainly not Ragnald's way.

He invites me to meet a group of traders who have come here from Danelaw, which is not so far away. They are living just north of us across the river Mersam, and although they are Danir they speak a similar language to ours, though they do not speak it as well as we do, and it is sometimes difficult to hear them through their strange accent. They also have some strange words and many funny expressions.

It is a natural and helpful development to build a good relationship with them. It offers us great prospect of trade and also military co-operation. In terms of kinship it is a much more obvious relationship than with the Angles who are different from us. Yet ironically we have developed far greater co-operation with the Angles so far.

In this meeting the Danir are very friendly, calling us fellow Scandinavians and seeking to build the same good relationship that we want. Although it has not always been like this with the Danir; they pick and choose when we are friends or opponents, but this time it suits all of us to remember our similarities and forget our differences. They have goods to sell and look to exchange some articles from us; they seem to have access to goods that have come from very distant lands. We used to have these same expensive goods to sell when we had boats travelling regularly to Scandinavia but those routes have been closed to us since we left our home. All of our boats and efforts are now fully engaged in surviving.

More importantly they have stories to tell us, stories of great Viking successes. They tell us that the Danir kingdom is now well established in England after a period of great wars and the Angles and Saxons have recognised Danelaw with the King of Jorvik as its ruler. It is a very large and prosperous land with expansive farmlands with many of the Danir Jarls having been given land to hold as a reward for their support of the wars, making them very rich and powerful. That word "powerful" has an instant effect on Ragnald, making him sit up and listen intently. It is what he has always been looking for, and knows that he needs powerful allies who might allow him to recapture Dyflinn. We do not yet have sufficient resources to do that alone, and might always need help.

Regaining Dyflinn and gaining vengeance has become the unspoken goal, the object of Ragnald's dreams and aspirations. It hangs over us all of the time, always guiding our plans but is little spoken of. All of us are sworn to this objective as well, though there are many who would now prefer to forget it and settle down to peace here. It remains an obsession with our king. I can sympathise with the idea of settling here, even though I still feel something of that longing to return myself. Our king will certainly not change his aim though and I know it is my duty to fellow him. A duty I could not escape, even if I chose to.

I often wonder where our duty comes from. Is it always our duty to follow our Jarls in this world? Or does duty lie somewhere else, with our family perhaps? Or with a higher force, determined by Thor or Odin or Vollun or Freyja? Maybe it is better not to ask, since it is certain that the Jarls have enough power to ensure that we see our duty as following them, or else we and our families will suffer the consequences.

These visits from the Danish traders become very regular, and we soon get news from Jorvik. Their kings, it seems there are three joint rulers, have now heard of our arrival and know of Ragnald, his courage and his fighting ability. One of the kings is Halfdan, Thora's cousin. Maybe they have also heard the tales of his great treasure as that might also add to his status. Ragnald is invited to meet him and our new Danir friends are able to help him by advising how to find the easiest route to Jorvik. It is first by sea, going out of our river and then to the north. There another great river empties into sea and we can row far inland up this estuary, so sailing a lot of the distance towards Jorvik.

Ragnald has decided that we will be going soon, maybe even tomorrow, and so is planning whom and what he needs to take with him. He will take a small, handpicked group of advisers, which will certainly include me, just one drakken boat and a small crew of thirty men.

Now I have to tell Aud this news, and I cannot hope for it being welcomed by her. I hate to have to tell her and see how unhappy it makes her. We are sure to have tears and perhaps some anger too. This is the worst part of being Ragnald's closest confidante and adviser, often being required to be away from my family. She is certain to be disappointed but she is a sensible woman and she trusts me. After the tears she will realise that it is a necessary part of my duties. My role as Ragnald's adviser has been good for us; it has raised our social position and may yet bring us great wealth. If I continue to support his ambitions and he achieves the power and wealth that he is looking for I can expect to be rewarded.

The price we are paying now is to be apart at times, but she has the consolation of the constant company of her mother and mine, who are delighted to help her with little Astrithr. They both love their new roles as grandmothers, and are very good at it.

It seems likely that our peaceful, happy time here may be at an end, or, at the very least, it will be significantly interrupted.

As a consolation for Aud I have submitted to her plan to make money. The first step was to reinforce our house with thicker walls and heavier doors, just as we saw the moneyers do in Ceaster. I have made the iron casts and dies, as best I can, that will allow Brodir to cast the silver coins as Aud has planned. They are not as well made as the Anglian or Saxon dies but now the Lochlain of the Wirral have their first silver coins, though I suspect that few seeing them will recognise the head on them as the image of Ragnald. I have to confess that my dies are not very skilfully made as I did not have sufficient time to refine my skill at engraving them.

For a time at least it will earn Aud and Brodir a good living while I am away. The community will all benefit especially in gaining status as a developed society but we will benefit the most by becoming wealthier. The coins have a face value which is greater than the metal that goes into them.

My clever wife has, quite literally, found a way of making money for us.

Chapter Five

JORVÍK

The day we are due to leave for Jorvik comes too soon, and it is heartbreaking to have to say my good byes as the day breaks to a tearful Aud and the gurgling Astrithr at her breast, plus the two mothers. It is not a happy moment, and there is so much weeping that I feel something of a relief to get away as the boat hits the water and we start to row away from the shore. All those exhausting emotions are left behind on the shore, they are waving goodbye to me, and I wave back. The men just get their heads down and concentrate on the tasks before them, which is wise; there is a great deal to do.

This time the silver hoard has stayed behind with Thora, so Ragnald must feel he has somewhere safe for it to rest now that he is leaving again on this adventure. I have no idea where it is or whether it has a guardian beyond Thora. Let us hope that his faith is well-founded and his trust will not be betrayed. I am happier to not know about the location of the treasure, as that knowledge carries great danger with it.

We are leaving on the high tide so it is easier to find the deep water in which to move the boat easily without any danger of grounding. It is necessary to row as we cannot sail with the wind in our faces and we are organised into two crews to row alternatively. As we move downstream the flow starts to empty the water out of the estuary and we get a substantial push out of the river into the open sea beyond. Now we are turning the wind is on our beam and we can raise the sail and use the wind to assist our passage rather than row. That makes life much easier for the warriors as once again the heavy woollen sail fills and stretches, taking the strain and giving the rowers an easy time. We are soon passing the entrance to the River Mersam and get another strong push as that tidal stream moves us away from the shore. We expect to complete the first part of our journey, the sea crossing, today. Now we are well out to sea which is perhaps a blessing since we know this shore has many sand banks and swirling currents.

Soon we are passing a low lying foreland and making the slow passage to the north east into the new river, they call it the Ripam. Here we are heading east with the wind at our backs, so we can raise the sail for a time. We are in a vast, wide estuary with low land on either side, but we can see more distant hills and these are said to be where we will eventually travel.

The wind behind is us now, filling the sail, and the tide will soon start to flow with us too, so we will make good progress as long as we stay in the middle of the river away from sand banks. At low tide this is easy as we can see them all towering above us as we move up the river. As the river narrows the sand gives way to mud banks and now the tide is certainly pushing us and the water is rising. This is the best way to travel, the wind and tide doing all the work and taking the strain off the oarsmen.

We are soon passing into the river itself, away from the estuary and alongside marshes and eventually the green flood plains. Above us on the north bank we can see a sandy ridge with a village on the top, another collection of timber longhouses, so here we pull our boat onto the bank and make our way up to meet our Danir comrades, hoping for a friendly welcome.

We actually get quite a surly greeting from the red-headed inhabitants of the town, but at least it's not openly hostile or aggressive. We can buy enough food for a meal with some mead to drink as well to refresh us. Ragnald pays grudgingly for our provisions with a few of his precious silver coins. We are in a place which was called the Priests Tun when the Angles were here, and the Danir have not changed its name, though they say it as Prestune.

They have, however, replaced or rebuilt most of the buildings in the village since arriving.

Although small the village has a wonderful position, high and therefore dry on a sandy, well-drained ridge, overlooking the river and well above the level of any flood. The river is close by and deep enough for boats to come here at most states of the tide, and so is very easily accessible to the sea although several hours hard rowing away from it. It has a wide hinterland with a wooded plain to the north and broad marshes to the south which are full of wild fowl. The flood plain itself is excellent farming land and the black earth that covers it is fertile and constantly renewed by silt from the winter floods.

Ragnald immediately thinks this is a better place for us to live than the current settlement. In any case that community is known as Ingamund's group. I think he must want to establish a place that is distinctly his own. I am not as happy with this idea as the people have already moved twice and are enjoying their new life on the Wirral. I have a different view of life than Ragnald as I enjoy the opportunities for trade with the Angles whereas he simply views them as a military threat. This issue will have to wait though as our immediate priority is to make our journey to meet the Northumbrian kings.

As soon as we can buy enough food to provide for our journey we are back on our longboat and rowing with the tide, further up the river towards its highest navigable point which is only another hour up the river. Here we find that point marked by a small number of longboats already drawn up on the river bank. As the river shallows here, and is above the reach of the highest tide, there is a ford across the river. The shallow water allows people to walk across albeit up to their waists in water, but prevents boats from going any further. Here our boat grounds and we must haul it onto the bank, and leave it with just a small guard.

The road out of the town goes east and along the valley towards Jorvik. It's a poor road with many cart tracks and little surface other than the rutted mud. Nevertheless it shows us the way to get to our destination and so we set off on foot knowing that it is likely to be a long walk of several days.

By nightfall we are still moving along the river valley but have found ourselves on a far better road, covered with paving stones, and it is much easier to walk. We are told that it is left there from those days long ago when the Romans were here. They may be all long dead now but we are thankful to them as they are still helping us make much better progress.

It is a delight to walk in the sunshine among these low, lush green hills, alongside the winding river. It reminds me very much of the Dyflinnarskiri, our home, which is still not so very far away, but is denied to us. This is also a very scenic land, with valleys with rich farm lands. The Danes are clearly very happy to have settled here.

It's a further two long days of hard, fast walking, over the hills, through the valleys and finally towards a wide fertile plain where we finally see the city of Jorvik appear before us in the distance as evening falls. It is especially obvious from the large amount of smoke rising from many fires in many houses.

Next morning, as we grow closer, it turns from just a smoky blur into a large array of wooden buildings. In among it we can see larger and more impressive stone buildings, unlike any we have seen before.

As we draw really close we can smell it too; a pungent mixture of wood smoke and rotting waste. It is a large town, a very large town, far bigger than any we have ever seen before, much larger than either Dyflinn or even Ceaster. The town has a defensive palisade around it, and a number of gates. I am sure that they serve a good function in reassuring the citizens of their safety but, as we know from our own bitter experience, wooden palisades are of limited value.

We find the west gate and enter the city without any one taking any interest in us at all. It is certainly easier to enter this city than to get into Ceaster, there are few guards and they all seem very sure that they are not going to be attacked. Or maybe we look just like the average citizen here whereas we are seen as foreigners in Ceaster.

The city has a strange shape; it is divided into regular blocks along broad, straight and lengthy streets. The houses are packed very closely together, with each seeming to have the same size of plot, and built along regular lines, as though someone in authority has designed the layout of the streets.

In that respect it is quite different from our settlements that grow up quite randomly wherever the builder chooses to put the buildings. I wonder if that is also a part of the legacy that this place owes to the Romans who were once here.

The town is so large that it is not possible to count the number of houses or, as we get into the town itself, to guess the number of boats that are pulled up on the river banks. We have tried to do so as it how we normally judge the size of a settlement but, in the end, I can just tell you that it is a very large number.

We are impressed by Jorvik, not just because of the size, but the complexity of commercial life that goes with it. It has many trades and so many shops selling goods from all around the Viking world. There are glass makers, metal workers, weavers and spinners, as well as jewellery makers working in bone, antler, amber and jet. The jet is the rarest of all and is distinguished by its pure black colour. It only comes from an area on the coast of this region.

There are even more exotic goods from further away, such as silks, which reach us here via Scandinavia but have come from very distant lands in the East. Naturally these are only for Jarls and kings. They are so very expensive that they are beyond the reach of any ordinary men.

Just as we have seen in Ceaster the old Roman fortress is still here and there are masons working to restore its walls. Stone buildings are very rare; I have never seen them anywhere before except Ceaster and just a few ruins left from earlier times near Prestune. There were certainly none in the Dyflinnarskiri. The kings of Jorvik have made their palace in the great arched entrance that was left by the Romans. Unusually it is built, or rather rebuilt, in stone. So the Danir have found some masons who still have the skill to work in stone.

Jorvik is one of the richest towns in the whole of Europe, greater than any of the big towns of Mercia: Oxford, Glaewcester or London, maybe even bigger than Winchester. The whole of the Roman city is still very obvious and many of its buildings are still standing although 500 years have passed since they left. Along the river there is a massive stone wharf with eight great towers, and beyond it the great hall of Constantine still covered with a roof and in use as a hall.

The Danish area is most developed south of the Roman fort around the Foss. This area is the most densely inhabited and you can tell by the smells. It is damp and dirty with all the rubbish that human settlement creates, but it is also humming with life and activity. The craftsmen are all at work here, so many things being created to foster trade and create wealth. Carpenters, jewellery makers, leather and metal workers all thrive.

Wide bellied knarr boats that are designed to carry large quantities of goods lie on the Foss, loading and unloading to take goods to Scandinavia and beyond. Others are ready, carrying goods by cart over the hills and down the Ribble to be sent on to Ireland.

Jorvik also has a great variety of food available to it, fish from the rivers and the sea, meats from the cattle and pigs of the plain, sheep from the hills and many forms of grain and vegetables from the farms all around the city. In season there will be many fruits on sale here too. In addition, there are many things available to drink too. Not just the mead and beer we have found elsewhere but even wine that they have imported from Germany. We are unlikely to taste any of that, as Ragnald will not pay the price they are asking for it.

Under the Angles this was a great centre for the Christian faith and many of the Anglian monks are still here, tolerated by the new kings who have been baptised themselves, and now working hard to convert the people to Christianity. Many of the Danir have taken up the new belief, though many of us still hang onto the traditional view of the gods. It will take a great deal to make me believe in this new faith; it is all very mysterious to me and I am frightened of offending Woden. He and Thor have looked over us extremely well in our adventures so far.

It is a large and very complex city, full of wonders and connections with many strange and faraway places; it is truly worthy of being the capital of the Viking world. Although I have travelled a great deal it is only here that I can truly appreciate the wonderful variety of things that fill the world.

The people too are complex and interesting. Naturally they are mostly Danir and Norse but there are so many other people here too. Of course, there are Angles here and a few Saxons too but some Jutes, Franks and Germans as well. Occasionally there are Picts, trading items from the far north.

Although we seemed to be recognised at the gate as people who look right for this city we have a strange reception when we start to speak to people. They all have a strange dull throaty accent to our ears and they claim that we are talking in a strange language too. Although it is fairly obvious that they understand most of what we say, they seem to think our pronunciation is quite funny. It verges on bad manners and several of the Danir suffer from boxed ears when they laugh at Ragnald. None of them retaliate and none do it more than once, but it leaves a dreadfully tense atmosphere.

I have to urge Ragnald to leave urgently on several occasions when are in danger of confronting a growing number of hostile Danes. Ragnald may be the largest man involved but he cannot confront a whole mob on his own.

The vast numbers of people living in such a small space has its problems, and the stench of rotting waste which we detected even when well away from the city is vastly more unpleasant now we are inside it. The citizens have a very poor idea of any need to clean the streets and the waste from their toilets and the peelings from their foods are piled high in the street. No doubt in the hope that the wind and rain will clear them away into the river.

Ragnald has noticed the smell and the accompanying waste and is much less impressed by the complicated and wonderful things of

Jorvic than I am, and he seems permanently very bad-tempered. Perhaps he is just anxious to meet the kings. It seems there is a very confused situation with three Jarls of royal blood all believing that they should be king and so all are currently accepting an uneasy truce which allows them to work together. Halfdan, Eowulf and Ivarr have all agreed to be joint rulers so as to prevent bloodshed between them and to allow them to use their common strength to keep the common enemy, the Anglo-Saxons, at bay.

It's not a situation that Ragnald readily understands as he could not work in such a way; he is not a natural co-operator, more a natural competitor. Nevertheless he understands that he must meet with at least one of them and gets an invitation to meet Halfdan the Younger in the Palace within the Roman arch. Ragnald is very greatly assisted in this by his connection with Thora, his current concubine and Ivarr the Younger's former queen. She is also Halfdan's cousin and has therefore some influence with him.

Halfdan listens patiently to Ragnald's plea for assistance and for "co-operation" between our warriors and their "Great Army". It seems that Ragnald understands enough about the idea of co-operation to exploit it for as much advantage as he can get out of it. He is initially very pleased with the response too, as Halfdan agrees to make a large force of warriors available to him, if Ragnald can match their number from his own force. This should give him a combined force of around 150 boats. If they can spring a surprise attack on the Irskrs that might be a large enough force to carry out a powerful attack and re-capture the town. It might not, however, be enough to hold the city once the foreigners have got their whole army together again. If indeed they ever could raise such a force again as that would require them to co-operate between themselves as they did when we were expelled.

Ragnald and I consider this offer, and the conditions attached to it. These conditions are important, very important: that the combined force must first rehearse and demonstrate its fighting ability with a great raid on the Picts of Fortriu in the far north of this land, and bring back a great deal of plunder and slaves. This is

83

the kind of work that Ragnald enjoys, but it is not really a direct assistance to his own cause, perhaps only in adding to his war chest. More importantly for the Danir king it reduces a powerful competitor in lands not too far away from his own land.

It does, of course, allow Ragnald an ideal opportunity to demonstrate his formidable fighting ability to the kings of Jorvik. I have my doubts as to whether this is really the kind of expedition that will help us achieve our goal and am not convinced that Halfdan will really meet his commitment to help us at all after this first adventure is completed. The whole expedition appeals to Ragnald's warrior instincts though, and so he overrules my concerns and accepts the offer and its terms.

Ragnald will now return to his own community to raise his Lochlain army and will meet up with the Danir force which Halfdan already has near at hand. These will then need to be organised into one fighting unit. Each of these two leaders will accept responsibility for arming and feeding the warriors but Ragnald will lead them in the north and into battle. Each leader will share the spoils equally providing that his force is supplied in the full numbers agreed.

The plan is to sail our forces up towards Fortriu and then join the Danir who will march north. We will join together at the head of the long fjord that leads into that land. It may be quite difficult to get the two armies together but the location of such large armies seem to send out news, the majority of people talk about them, though in that land we may have difficulty conversing with the ordinary people. Halfdan has some people who speak Brythonic and sends one of them to join with us and travel with us. Although this will not help us in Fortriu, where the natives speak Pictish, it will be useful in the country we will need to cross to get there.

It is agreed that both armies will set off in twenty days time, to meet and join together in forty days; this allows us time to return to our community and make the necessary preparations, and raise the army. I can imagine how unpopular this will be with all the warriors who have come to enjoy their time building homes, farming and being happy with their families. They will need to realise, as I have to, that such a life is not normal for a Viking warrior. It is just not our destiny to live such ordinary lives; we are a warlike people and have our destiny to fulfil and our gods and our Jarls to serve.

So we must make the long walk back the way we came, over the hills and along the valley until we reach the ford near the village of Prestune where left our single boat. The journey is wearying but otherwise uneventful. Although these roads are thought to be dangerous the law of the Danir seems to holding here and we have seen no evidence of any crime. Perhaps that is the beneficial effect of the rule of law, or perhaps we simply have a large enough group of strong, armed men to protect ourselves. It is a relief and a minor surprise to find our boat still there, apparently untouched and unharmed. Just one more day of rowing or sailing before we can get back to our own people again.

After a night's rest we push the boat out into the river and leave, assisted by the flow of the river Ripam. In fact, we sail very little on our return journey. It is almost all rowing, with just a short period when we approach our own river that we can raise the sail to take us up the river. Naturally we have calculated our departure time to allow us the best use of the tides, and it certainly eases our labour considerably again. We again divide ourselves into two crews so that one rows while the other rests. Nevertheless we are all completely exhausted when we finally get the boat pulled up onto our own beach.

Once there I am immediately back with my dear Aud, she is holding Astithr in her arms, running down the beach to meet me. It seems she has been watching the river for days hoping to see us approach. I can see that she is very lonely without me and longs to be with her husband. At first she is as inclined to scold me for leaving her as to welcome me home but soon that initial coolness melts and we are in love again. Tonight is like our second honeymoon, as though we were just married again.

All of the travellers are delighted to see their families but it is a bitter sweet feeling as we all know that we will soon be leaving again.

This time we will be going away for a long period and will face many great dangers along the way. We all know that there will be some who will never return, though none of know which of us that will be!

Our fates remain in the hands of the three Norns who determine the destiny of all in this world.

Chapter Six

JOURNEY TO THE NORTH

There is a period of frenzied activity now as we prepare to take all of the available men and boats north to Fortriu, the land of the Picts. As I expected there are many who have little enthusiasm for this expedition, having become fat and lazy in their comfortable new lives, but there are also a surprisingly large number who welcome the chance for new journeys having wearied of domestic life and who are now longing for adventures. My sympathies lie mostly with the ones who love their home life, but the others make my task easier.

It falls to me to visit each warrior, and tell him that he will be travelling north with us. With those who are reluctant I must cajole and persuade enthusiastically, even if my heart is not really in it. We all know that the persuasion is only for show and in the end they will be required to go, whether they wish to or not. They owe a duty to their king and to the gods, who will insist that they fulfil it. I know that the hidden threat is the deciding factor with many of these reluctant warriors who really wish to be simple farmers.

Why would any of us willingly put our lives at risk? The big benefits always accrue to the Jarls and kings. It seems that there are some who enjoy the risk, and see the campaigns as a great adventure. There are many others who enjoy the prospect of the booty; even though experience shows that our share often seems to be quite modest.

There is a lot of work to do, especially preparation of a great quantity of dried foods for the long journey. We must take as much as we can carry since it will be difficult to feed an army of this size off the land.

I face a difficult decision as to how many warriors to leave behind to guard our land and our families. We need all the warriors that we can muster but we are also conscious that Irskrs or the British might raid us here at any time. Although relations with the Saxons and Danir have always seemed friendly, it is not always possible to be entirely sure of them either. Every community contains greedy and dangerous men prepared to rob their neighbours, and so none of them are to be trusted.

Although the stories of our possessing silver and treasure seem to have quietened down, they might still draw in raiders at a time when our guard is seen to be down. I have little idea where Ragnald has put the great trunk containing his great silver hoard; he has certainly kept it silent and it would have appeared to have disappeared. Even I, who consider myself to be his most trusted friend and adviser, am not trusted with knowing the location of the chest. I last saw it as I carried it into the woods above his house but I know from my many visits there since that it is not to be seen now. I am sure he is wise to keep it out of sight and hope that it will be forgotten.

So the risk of losing the hoard seems relatively small. The risk of it drawing in thieves who might plunder our settlement and kill our families is much higher.

The youngest and the oldest warriors are left behind together with those who are currently injured or sick, which turns out to be a rather larger number than expected. I know some of these have illnesses that will be miraculously cured the moment the boats leave, but I accept it as they describe it, with no further questioning. Their presence will make the community safer so I diplomatically turn a blind eye.

We have around a thousand swords in the end and these men will travel in around forty boats. This fleet will still look hugely impressive when it sails and will certainly strike terror into the hearts of all who see it approaching them.

Ragnald has given Ingamund the responsibility for staying behind and organising the security of the settlement in his absence.

It seems a generous gesture in a way as it allows Ingamund to have the easier task, and also gives him considerable power and status in the community which remains here. On the other hand it also sidelines him from the attention of the army and therefore takes him out of serious reckoning as a rival to Ragnald at least in the short term. Ragnald will, however, need to succeed and return alive, with great wealth if he is to be seen as Ingamund's superior.

In the eyes of the warriors Ingamund will be seen as a second rate Jarl, only fit to sit at home with the women. He still has charge of a group of over a hundred men, mostly old and sick, to defend the village, along with a similar number of juvenile boys.

The time to leave comes sooner than I had expected, those twenty happy, busy days have come and gone in what seems like the twinkling of an eye! I am devastated to be leaving Aud and Astrithr once more but secretly I am excited by the great adventure we are about to embark on. We can become wealthy people if this goes well, but I cannot show this excitement to my wife. It is important to look as sad and as disappointed as I can over the next few days.

When we sail this time I am in the lead boat, standing beside Ragnald, and have been excused my duty as an oarsman, at least for the present. It seems I am being raised up into the higher level of Norse society and have earned my place at the side of my king. Maybe I will also become a Jarl if all goes well.

It is just a few hours rowing before we can see the mountains of Vannin appear as a smudge on the horizon, and very slowly they get nearer and appear larger. It seems like an eternity as we get closer and there seems to be a huge effort going into the rowing for just a small movement towards the island. Ragnald hopes to get there before nightfall, so we can eat and sleep in relative comfort on land. The whole of the voyage to Fortriu is well known to us and we can move in one day stages if we choose, sleeping overnight on land every evening. This will allow us to sleep properly and enjoy the passage. It also allows us to take some foods from the lands we visit and we will be constantly able to take fresh water. All of that makes the journey more comfortable, and we might also be able to take some plunder from unwitting victims as we go, and to build up our war chest.

The fleet moves steadily towards Vannin and I wonder if we are heading to our previous home on the sweeping bay. It would be a good place to stay overnight, and with its large sandy beaches it offers good shelter for our boats and plenty of space for them all. Ragnald has another idea though, he has sailed this entire island many times, and is taking us east of the island. We move steadily north along its shores until the sun sets and we find ourselves moving into another large bay, which also has broad beaches for us to ground our fleet. It offers a peaceful night's rest for most of us, but apparently not for me.

I have a small group who are given the task of guarding the site overnight. It seems that staying here has some dangers being so close to Ottar's base and Ragnald is concerned about the danger of being attacked. I am to earn my status and privileges with some difficult and unwanted tasks. Being the most trusted deputy of a king clearly often means doing the tasks he chooses not to undertake himself.

In the morning my weary guards and I are the first to break our fast with a poor meal of flat bread and pounded beans, but we are the last to get into the boats. Then we have our chance to sleep, but not the peaceful sleep we would have had on land during the hours of darkness. We sleep as we are tossed around in the bottom of the boat, desperately trying to find a few dry places. We are constantly woken again by the movement of the boat in the waves. We are all left feeling groggy, light-headed and exhausted.

It had been a long and quiet night for the main army, and they are all well-rested. Fortunately there was no sign of Ottar's men appearing. We had feared that they might have seen us and marched across from their fortress on the other side of the island, which is not more than a night's march away. Probably they left later and are on their way there right now as we leave and sail, again north and we get round the northernmost cape of the island at midday. We can now see another land to the north of us and here, we know, lives another group of Britons, probably as hostile as those who expelled us from Môn. They hold this land and a great more to the north of it. We will soon be crossing their territory but for now we can just row past it, hard rowing directly into the wind.

Seeing our position, which I also know from our previous reconnaissance of the island, I know that Ottar's fort is not far south of us now, along the westward side of the island. I wonder whether Ottar's men will have set off to look for us on the east of the island. It is very likely, as they are certain to know by now that we have been there. We have such a large fleet that we cannot easily move about unnoticed. He would definitely react to our presence since our men have been here a few times recently to steal his cattle and sheep. As I am aware of Ragnald's feeling towards Ottar I suggest to him that this might be the ideal time to pay a visit to his home base. His warriors are likely to be away, patrolling the area next to our overnight camp, still expecting to see us there. They might well have left their own base lightly protected, and we can raid and plunder it. Opportunity beckons!

It's an idea that he seizes on with glee, and so the whole fleet turns south along the island's coast, clinging close to the shore, despite the danger of rocks, to make it more difficult for us to be seen from the castle. All the boats are now rowed, even though the wind direction would have allowed us to sail if we had chosen, we are much less visible from the shore this way. It is not long before we can see the fortress on the small island but are hoping that they will not have seen us. In order to improve our chances of taking them by surprise, we beach the boats in two gravelly bays, out of view of the fortress, and climb the cliffs to approach our enemies on foot.

It works and it very nearly works completely! We get very close to the town before we are spotted. Once we are seen all hell breaks out, and the people of the town run as fast as they can for the fort, with all of us in hot pursuit, swords and axes in hand. Most of them make it to the fort in time and as we reach the edge of the fortified island we see that they have escaped. Just a few of the elderly and infirm are left behind and they are of no interest to us. They have no value as slaves.

We cannot easily reach the Danir inside their fort and we would take a great risk of losing many of our men. It is much more sensible to ransack the abandoned town and look for what plunder we can find. There are indeed rich takings to be had, since the inhabitants have been taken by complete surprise. There was little or no time for them to take any of their goods with them. Only the lightest and most easily portable goods have gone.

We find lots of weapons, some silver coins and manufactured goods including jewellery, leather goods and other textiles. There is a great deal of fresh food and good stocks of mead that naturally we always value. This time we will not consume it all on the spot though, remembering that was a small disaster for us on Môn at Maes Osfeilion. In particular I remember losing my raven haired maiden. As usual Ragnald is claiming the silver for himself but is content to allow all other goods to be distributed among the successful warriors.

To our surprise a group of six horsemen now appear, approaching and then riding into the town as though unaware of anything unusual happening. They are clearly wealthy, high status people, dressed well, and carrying banners and weapons. They are completely unaware that their town has fallen into the hands of a rival group and ride straight into our midst expecting us to part and let them through. It is obviously an unpleasant surprise to find their way forward blocked, especially as the throng then closes behind them too.

The look to fight but quickly think better of it, six men will not last long among a thousand enemies, so they have to yield. A fine rich group of captives, with lots of expensive mail and weapons to take. Best of all, the group includes King Ottar himself, and he is surprised and not at all pleased to find himself detained, a prisoner of his detested adversary Ragnald.

Ragnald on the other hand is beside himself with glee, I have never seen him so laugh so much, he is delighted and excited. I remind him that Ottar still has an army out somewhere looking for us, so it is best to take Ottar as our prisoner along with our plunder and to quietly make our escape before their return. So we are off again, barely more an hour after our arrival, having not fought any one and with no casualties on either side, but we are laden with booty and taking the despised Ottar as hostage for a great ransom.

Ottar is stripped of his weapons and mail, then dragged, bound hand and feet, into the boat. By then he has taken quite a kicking and is covered in bruises on every part of his body and bleeding profusely from gashes on his face and arms. It is a great humiliation for him and he is now fully aware of the danger he is in. The man is completely terrified, and justifiably in great fear for his life. He knows he is worth a large ransom but he also knows he is the hands of a competitor who hates him, would gladly eliminate him and is quite likely to do exactly that.

Ottar may also have some doubts about whether his own family will want to ransom him, or he may even doubt their ability to raise the money needed. It is certainly not likely to be a small sum, but he will know far more than we do about the circumstances of their wealth.

The other five men in his group are treated with much more respect but they are also required to join us on the boat, it is not an invitation. No doubt they are also in fear of their lives but Ragnald's intention towards them is to recruit them into his army and get them to participate as free men. Of course, being free men does not mean they will be given a choice in the matter. If they resist they will still be coming with us, but unarmed and with shaven heads to denote that they are slaves. Additional warriors will be far more valuable to us than slaves though where we are going. These men might be especially useful as they are genuine fighting men: full time, professional huskarls.

We have not all gone back by foot to the bay where our boats lie. Ragnald and I, along with our prisoner are going back in boats provided by our "hosts". We have deprived them of twenty of their finest drakken boats, taking ten and towing another ten behind us to be released to drift out to sea. This strengthens our fleet as we can now spread our warriors around more vessels and also makes it more difficult for the defeated Danes to pursue us. It takes a long time and a great deal of skilled labour to build a new boat, let alone replace twenty of them.

Ragnald is ecstatic with the amazingly successful raid and cannot congratulate himself enough for having had such a brilliant idea, which is sure to bring him great acclaim across the Norse world. His status will be greatly enhanced by this adventure and few will now pick an argument with such a successful warrior and raider. I have mixed feelings about his selective memory, as it is clear that I will not get the credit I deserve for the idea. On the other hand he will know, probably deep in his subconscious, that I have made a hugely valuable contribution to his success and I do expect that it will enhance his view of my abilities.

In the short term there is a decision to be made, do we continue north to meet up with our comrades from Jorvik taking our prisoner with us, or return home with him? Or even find a place from which we can contact Ottar's people and negotiate his ransom? It is not part of my plan to kill off Ottar when he represents so much value in ransom but Ragnald has some doubts about that idea. It is obvious that his hatred of Ottar runs very deep, and he might well choose to just kill Ottar and forget the ransom. He is, however, the true pragmatist and always responds to the idea of acquiring more silver. A dull light comes into his eyes whenever there is the prospect of getting more treasure for his hoard.

His eventual decision, which I am sure is the right one, is to find a place on the coast north of here to hold the fleet, ideally as much out of sight as possible. Our intention is to send an ambassador to negotiate a ransom and then to exchange Ottar for as much silver as can possibly be had. Ragnald states boldly that he will accept nothing less than ten skippunds, which is literally a king's ransom.

Ragnald would be fairly happy if the Vannin Danir were not prepared to pay a ransom so that he can slit Ottar's throat in an offering to Woden. I even think he might prefer that, though it makes little sense to me. I even feel some sympathy for the poor, terrified old man. His only real crime was greed and foolishness, there are plenty, including some quite nearby, who are equally guilty of both of those.

So we are sailing north and feeling very fortunate as even the wind is going in our favour. In the deep twilight we can just spot and enter a large estuary with sandy beaches, wide bays and rocky islands on either side and we take the entire fleet far down the river estuary and eventually, as it turns a corner and narrows, we take the boats ashore, again at the highest point that the tide can reach. The banks are narrower here and the river itself is too shallow for our boats.

There is a tiny village here but the inhabitants have wisely all fled as they saw our fleet approach. We have the place to ourselves and make use of their shelters and the fires that are still burning. It is difficult to imagine the natives of this remote place ever being able to get a large enough army to expel us, we are secure here. No one will ever find us in such a remote place.

The mood among our warriors is extremely joyous and they are allowed to celebrate their victory with a great feast made up of the fresh foods plundered from their victim's town, including a lot of meat, and all washed down with a great quantity of mead. It has been a very long day but a hugely successful one. Now it is safe to celebrate as none, other than the chosen ambassador, will need to be active in the next few days. The celebrations continue late into the night and for once there is great laughter and no fighting or brawling among the drunken warriors.

So the ambassador is chosen and sent off to negotiate, and the bad news is that I am the chosen one. It is certainly not a task I welcome as the people we are meeting are unlikely to welcome us. I am certain that it will be extremely dangerous as I remember how Ottar treated the previous messenger from Ragnald. This would not be the first time that the messengers were slaughtered in revenge if it were to happen.

On the other hand they will know that if we are harmed it will end any possibility of Ottar being released alive. It is quite possible that his family will be pleased to get the news that he is alive, they must now fear that he has been killed already since they must be aware of Ragnald's reputation and his hatred of Ottar.

We leave on high tide the next day and the ebb flow assists our return down the estuary, and the trip takes us little more than half a day to reach the family's seat on Vannin. We arrive as the sun is setting and fortunately we are received politely, if more than a little frostily. The atmosphere is very tense and so we are very much aware of the dangers we face. Ottar's family are represented by his heir, Bardr Ottarson, who is both very angry and, at the same time, very anxious to recover his father unharmed. He knows that this will only be possible if we are returned safely, and reluctantly accepts this, though it is also clear that he is burning with a desire for revenge and would happily take it out on us.

I present Ragnald's demand for silver which I increase to twelve skippunds to allow some scope for negotiation. It does not improve the mood at all as it is clearly much more than Bardr had expected to be asked to pay. It seems that Vannin has very little silver, none is mined here and they have not traded in it very much, despite this being common and increasing practice in the Viking world. It seems that the money economy has not really yet reached Vannin. They want me to take boats and animals as ransom, what a primitive people they are!

I explain that I am not really here to negotiate about the amount, as that has been determined by Ragnald, but simply to agree the detail of how to make the exchange. I can see that Bardr does not like this but, as a very young man, he has perhaps not more than sixteen years, he does not really know how to conduct the discussion. He veers from angry outbursts to whimpering pleadings, but none of that has any impact on my position. I must remain detached and unemotional; I am simply waiting for hard information and a tangible offer.

The emotion is simply unwelcome extra baggage which is delaying us but it is obviously an issue I need to deal with. I am confident that if I remain calm Bardr will come to terms with the limitations of his own position. I know my role is to remain calm and resolute, and to be patient. The shouting, whimpering and hectoring goes on for two days but I do not make any concessions or change my position.

Eventually it becomes clear that while Bardr has been going through his anguish his mother, who after all is the only adult involved, has been collecting as much silver as she can get her hands on. It amounts to seven skippunds, a great deal less than I have been told to collect.

Fortunately I get the opportunity to talk to Bardr's mother informally that evening and explain the limitations in my negotiating position. In turn I have to accept her limitations in gathering silver and ask whether there is any other item of value that can be added to their offer in order to secure her husband's freedom. She is silent and it is clear that this is now her time to accept something which she is finding difficult to take. I leave her to think over the position overnight.

In the morning she has also come to terms with her problem and increases the offer of seven skippunds to nine. It seems that additional silver which did not exist yesterday has since come to light, or perhaps they have found a way of borrowing it. Now I do truly believe that they have emptied their coffers of all their silver. I am inclined to accept and take on the tough task of persuading Ragnald to accept this amount which is a huge amount of silver to add to his current hoard. I decide to sleep on it despite my discomfort at extending my stay, I am very conscious of the danger of outstaying my welcome here.

In the morning Ottar's wife has now become the frustrated and emotional one, and she is threatening me with death in order to get us to accept the deal. It is a very intimidating atmosphere as her large band of warriors all stand behind her, each glowering at us, showing their weapons and making it clear that they are also very angry at this situation. I know that I have gone as far as I can with these discussions and promise to put their offer to Ragnald rather than accept it on his behalf.

From my own point of view it is a terrible outcome as I will now need a second trip into this cauldron of hatred. I will need to come once more into this horrible atmosphere, perhaps to ask for yet more silver, and to risk the reaction that will provoke. It does have the huge immediate advantage of getting me out of this place. Last time I was here I was looking at this fort and wishing for a warlock who could turn me and my men into ravens so we could fly in. This time I want us to become the ravens so we can fly away, I feel not only uncomfortable here but also very frightened.

I can see that my opponents are equally horrified at this outcome, as it at least means their king will have his stay in the hands of Ragnald substantially extended, and the threat to his life will be intensified. I am clearly suggesting to them that my king will not be content with the current offering. They must know enough about Ragnald's character to know that he is very capable of happily resolving the deadlock by slitting Ottar's throat.

As I prepare to leave Bardr and his mother come forward with one last throw of the dice. In addition to this large amount of silver they also have a small amount of gold. It is clearly very precious to them and they only give it up very grudgingly, but they can also see that the moment has come to include all they own in order to get a successful conclusion. I accept the offer as graciously as I can on Ragnald's behalf, and I am genuinely touched by their grief and anxiety over Ottar's fate, even though I know it is my job to remain unaffected by it. He is clearly the object of some genuine affection for them; they are a very close knit family despite their contempt for everyone else, including their own subjects.

Having agreed the terms the discussion can finally come to the matter of how to make the exchange. I know they will want it to be here on this island, but they must know that cannot possibly be acceptable to me. It would allow the greatest probability of treachery as they could hide large numbers of warriors around the meeting site to release their king with the ransom unpaid, and slaughter all of us in vengeance. In fact, there is absolutely no doubt that they would do exactly that.

Ottar has already breached the Norse code of honour when he refused to meet Ragnald in single combat and I do not trust his family at all. So I propose that the exchange is done at sea, half way between the island and the land to the north at midday three days after I have left. We will both need to carry white sails on our boats so we can maximise our chances of finding each other in the open sea.

The timetable and the proposed venue gives them some indication of where our fleet are positioned but I doubt if they have sufficient information to find us, or sufficient boats left to attack us even if they did. I will, however, be taking great care to see whether we are followed when I leave, or even observed from the north point of the island. I consider going south and then north along the east of the island but rule this out as it will just take too long. I also know that the island has an awkward tidal race to avoid off the south west corner, and that would add a lot of time and distance if we are to avoid the most dangerous places.

So we go directly and we will take our chance on rejoining our group in as quick a time as possible, knowing that my comrades will already be wondering why we are away so long.

It is time to return to Ragnald and his fleet and I am very glad to go, my time here has been filled with fear. No wonder I dream of warlocks and black ravens that turn into warriors when I visit this place. It is a place of dread and fear for me. I have slept little and uneasily while I was on Vannin. Several times the terror dreams that I first had after the battle of Dyflinn have returned. They leave me jolting awake cold and sweating. Images of heavily armed enemies about to strike my head off constantly dwell in those dreadful nights.

We leave at the first light of dawn. The voyage is not so far and should take less than a day; the only difficulty is in finding the large estuary again. After some time going along the coast we finally find it. I had deliberately turned too far west, in part to misdirect any observers but also to put ourselves upwind to allow us to sail back much more easily with the strong wind behind us. Nevertheless it has taken much longer than I had expected, and for a time I had started to fear that we had missed it completely. The estuary looks very different when approached from the west than from our original approach off the open sea. Of course, we also arrived originally in the dark. Navigation is an imprecise process with a great deal of guess work and estimation in it. Many boats are lost as these are dangerous waters.

Now we are rowing wearily into the estuary, and once more the light is starting to fade. We are only six in this crew, the very minimum that could handle the boat, proof, if it was needed, that Ragnald has understood how dangerous the mission was. He has put as few men at risk as he can. We are all completely exhausted and heartily relieved and very glad to be at our journey's end. When we eventually reach the beach our comrades run out and we leave them to pull the boat out of the water, and over the high tide mark.

Ragnald is delighted with the news of the deal I have struck, as he had started to fear that something had gone amiss with the delay in our return. I am barely able to explain it all to him before I collapse into a deep sleep. It is mostly from nervous exhaustion, and for once my terror dreams leave me alone.

In the morning I find the miserable Ottar. He is still frightened; as frightened as I have been, but at least his bruises have started to fade. I am pleased to see that he has not been given any fresh beatings and I take him some food and talk to him. It looks like he has had little to eat and he has lost quite a lot of weight and the strain of his ordeal shows in his face. His skin looks grey and more heavily wrinkled than I remember.

I am happy to be able to tell him the news he wants to hear, particularly that the ransom is agreed and that he will soon be going home. I think he draws a little comfort from my being prepared to talk to him in a polite way, I am sure that has not happened for a while now. He has only been subjected to continual abuse and threats here. I can see the relief flowing across his face at the news I bring. Although his ordeal is not over yet the prospect of its end is now before him. I am not sure he believed that his family would be prepared to give up their valuable silver to get him back.

At the appointed time in the morning of the third day we set sail from our hidden estuary in just a single boat carrying a white sail, and I am again the master of this vessel. Ottar is with us, in the bottom of the boat. He was handed over to me bound and gagged, but I take the gag off immediately. There is little point in making his ordeal any worse than it must be. He thanks me and I think he feels some relief at now being in the hands of one whom he can see bears him no malice. In other circumstances we might even have been friends but not now, I just have a job to do.

Not so far behind us the main fleet are following, they intend to remain in sight of us in case of any danger. They will not be bearing any sail and they will therefore be difficult to see, despite their numbers. Nevertheless they will need to keep their distance, as they could easily scare off the Vannin Danir who will be as suspicious of our reneging on the deal as we are suspicious of them.

We move quite a long way upwind, searching for their boat bearing the ransom, our sail flapping uselessly all the time. We need to keep it raised as the signal of our position but it cannot fill properly while we are moving into the wind. All of our progress is due to rowing which gets us into a good position upwind to sail back gently and easily. So far there is no sign of our enemies but we have agreed quite an imprecise rendezvous at quite a vague time. There is no precise way of saying when it is midday, we are all trying to look at the sun through the clouds and estimating when it is at its height.

Now we turn and return slowly trying to stay well away from the position of our fleet, which are much closer to that northern shore and also trying to get upwind. There is still no sign of that white sail, and we start to wonder if they are playing with us. Perhaps they have changed their minds, or have some trick to play?

Eventually we see their white sail, which is quite distant, much closer to Vannin than we had expected, and obviously inviting us to sail closer to that island than we would choose to be. I decide to take that risk and move nearer towards them, though trying to draw them further from the land. Ottar is visibly happier now, believing that his ordeal is almost at an end.

I am much less happy, realising that we are nearing the most difficult and dangerous part of the entire mission. There is every chance that the Vannin warriors will attack us either before or, more likely, just after we have handed the hostage over. It was clear to me that the agreed ransom was clearing every silver penny out of that family and I am confident they will try something to regain it, perhaps a trick or perhaps even an open assault. Because of that I have the largest available boat which is packed with eighty of the strongest and best of our warriors. We are prepared for the worst they can throw at us, and are also very ready to slit Ottar's throat at the first sign of deception. Perhaps it is as well that this thought seems not to have occurred to him. Not yet any way!

It is not an easy thing to raft two boats together in a heaving sea, and complicated by our need to get away as quickly as possible once we have the silver. The last thing we want is to be lashed securely to a boat full of vengeance seeking Vikings once they have their hostage back. After three failed attempts we are tied onto them. I have two men with sharp knives attending the lines with orders to cut them as soon as I give the order.

They want to hand over just five bags before they get their king with the remaining four and the gold to come later. This is not acceptable to me, I need all the ransom before I hand over the prisoner but will put him where they can see him, so they can see he is ready to be exchanged and that we are in good faith. They can also see that Ottar has two of our largest men either side of him with short swords and sharp knives. Our men are ready and prepared to kill him at the first sign of any treachery.

Slowly the bags are handed over and there is said to be a skippund in each leather pouch. I have a bag of sand in one hand which I have previously checked weighed one skippund. I hold the sack of sand in one hand and the silver in the other hand. It is a crude way of weighing them, to see if they feel equal and my judgement says that the weights are about right. I do, however, also check the contents of each to ensure that they are truly filled with silver.

They hand over seven bags but then refuse to release the others until they have their king. They are afraid that we will take the ransom but still refuse to hand over Ottar, which is an understandable concern. They propose to throw the remaining bags over as the king comes the other way. There is deadlock on this matter and a long standoff, so finally I agree to this. Our large warriors throw Ottar bodily across and he lands with a crash in the bottom of their longboat, no doubt giving him a new set of bruises. We get three bags coming the other way, each aimed at one of our warriors and one is caught in the chest and is knocked off his feet, and lands with a great crash in the bilges. These bags are supposedly filled with the balance of silver and gold, but in fact, when we open them they are all filled with pebbles. There has been a deceit, as I feared, but it is only partially successful. It is not such a great surprise to me, and we still have seven genuine bags of silver.

I immediately give the order to cut the lines suspecting further tricks and we are free of them, just as the boats separate several of their warriors do attempt to jump across and attack us. Six succeed in getting into our boat, but a larger number end up swimming alongside as we set the sail and pull away running down the wind as quickly as we can. Those who fell into the water are unfortunate; they will all drown as they are wearing mail and sink directly to the sea floor. Only if they can release their mail quickly enough to swim can they survive though they may be recovered from the water and still get home this night.

The six who got into our boat are hopelessly outnumbered and are immediately at our mercy. I call on them to drop their weapons and I will spare their lives. It is a hopeless position for them and they do yield and are all soon bound, and left lying tied up in the bilges. Another small group of warriors have been recruited to join our adventure in the north.

Now the Vannin fleet that has been hiding just on the horizon put in their appearance as expected, a host of sails being raised from upwind of us, and they start to pursue us. I tack across to keep ahead of them but moving north away from their island towards where our own fleet are supposed to be. There is no sign of them. This could be serious trouble for us!

Just as I start to be seriously concerned we see our own fleet, also upwind, and raising their sails to converge with the track taken by the Vannin boats. Our fleet is a little further back but outnumbers them by around two to one, no doubt as result of our having either stolen or set loose so many of their drakken boats when we raided them. The game is up for them now, and so they turn away to get home safely, as fast as they can go. They are aware of their limitations and therefore are wisely content just to have recovered their king. They will have to accept that their seven bags of silver are gone!

I find myself meeting Ragnald and jumping across to his boat, stumbling, bruising and cutting myself in the process, in order to make my report to him. He is a very happy man opening the sacks of silver and congratulates me on the way I have handled the negotiations. It is a very rare moment of gratitude and acknowledgement from my grateful king.

He is more philosophical that I expect in respect of the three bags of pebbles that he has received instead of the additional two of silver and one of gold that were in the agreement. He is actually delighted with his seven leather bags full of silver, and even more delighted at the humiliation he has inflicted on Ottar. He seems relatively unconcerned that Ottar has lived to fight again, as he is convinced that his opponent has gone home a frightened and broken man.

Now the big issue is how to make that silver safe with our army about to resume its delayed expedition to Fortriu. If the treasure is taken north with us there is a danger that it will be seen as part of the plunder from that expedition and the Danes are then sure to claim a half share. There are also major difficulties in carrying that amount of weight around with an army and keeping it secure. It is clearly better to take this hoard back to our own community to be kept there alongside the silver that was retrieved from Dyflinn, and the additional money acquired since.

This gives Ragnald quite a diliemna, as he is now more than a week delayed in meeting the Danes. Most of the initial forty days since leaving Jorvik have already expired, and we had agreed to meet the Danes in the north in those forty days. He can hardly go back again with his entire fleet or there will be no chance of fulfilling our commitment. It makes far more sense to send a smaller group back to bury or otherwise secure the hoard, and who will then travel north to meet up with him and the Danes. This task can only be given to someone who is both completely trustworthy and loyal to our king and also capable of completing both the task and returning to make the journey north. There is only one candidate for that role, as my fortunes are now at their highest and Ragnald trusts me completely, even with his beloved silver.

So I find myself in charge of the seven leather bags filled with silver and heading south, passing well, well clear to the west of the hostile Isle of Vannin, seeing very little of it through the rain and mist, and then sweeping around to get the full benefit of a strong wind to set course directly back to our home in the wide estuary. The sight of a full sail is a joyous one when you are heading home. I love to ride the waves as we run before the wind. If only we could always be sailing with the wind at our backs! The sea is rough but the wind is favourable and so we can ride hard and fast along the waves and across the stormy waters.

Agreeing with Ragnald on how to do this had proved surprisingly difficult. I know that we will have great problems crossing the land of Britons when we eventually follow him north, and so I was very concerned by his proposal to give me just one boat and thirty men. I thought that would leave us very vulnerable in that foreign and hostile land. Even more so as I have no one who can speak their language. The sole man among us who can understand Brythonic is the Dane who came with us from Jorvik, and he will stay with Ragnald.

It seems Ragnald wants as few men with me as possible in my group since he does not like the idea of them knowing anything of the whereabouts of the treasure. He would also wish to keep as much of his army intact as possible. He sees my task as a simple one, just getting quickly home and then back to his fleet. I anticipate a difficult and perhaps dangerous search for him among the hostile natives at the head of the great fjord where he is heading.

In the end he conceded, with extreme bad grace, that three boats and a hundred men would travel with me. It is a very significant part of his force and will allow me a considerable degree of protection when we approach Fortriu. So I am grateful that he could be persuaded to take this approach.

I had set off immediately after we made the agreement and travelled as quickly as I could past Vannin and towards our home on the Dee. Soon we are back again in our own estuary, after a very rapid and thankfully uneventful journey, and are pulling the boats up onto our own beach. This time Aud is not there to greet me, as this visit will come as a complete surprise to her.

As soon as we arrive I go immediately to see Aud and my family but I have little time for greetings. There is just time for a cuddle with my wife and small daughter and I attempt the briefest of explanations as to why I am here. My family, including my mother and Aud's mother, is all assembled to hear of our adventures. There are so many questions and the short conversation I intended takes several hours until a messenger comes to summon me to see Thora. Naturally she is too grand to come to see me herself!

I must quickly get to meet Thora, Ragnald's concubine, as he has ordered me to hand all the silver over to her. He told me that she will know where to put it and how to store it; clearly it will go together with the existing hoard of treasure. It is obvious now that the main hoard is held safely somewhere nearby, probably buried in the ground very close at hand. I offer to assist Thora in hiding it, as I expect there to be some heavy digging and the silver itself is heavy, but she vigorously refuses.

No doubt she has her reasons, there is a great deal of emotion and danger starting to attach itself to this hoard, especially fear, and so the fewer people are aware of its hiding place the better. It leaves her to carry a very substantial weight of metal herself, and no doubt the very heavy work of digging a hole big enough and deep enough to contain that weight.

Thora also has other news for me to pass back to Ragnald, as he will soon be the father of her new child. Now she clearly expects him to marry her and make her the queen, if there was ever any doubt of her intentions on that issue it has certainly gone now. I am absolutely unsure of how he will react to this, but I am looking forward to telling him and finding out.

In the immediate future I have happier times ahead since I will get a few happy days with Aud and Astrithr. I would love to stay longer but cannot delay further. Naturally my wife pleads with me to stay longer and I am delighted that she wants my company so much. It is wonderful to spend the night in her arms, after the anxiety and unhappiness that has bedevilled our recent times.

It seems that she and Brodir have been very active in developing their new business as moneyers and have already replaced the crude dies that I made with much better ones that they have designed and made together. Their coins now really do seem like true currency.

It turns out to be the first of several days that we spend together, more than I had first expected to stay, because events are about to take an interesting and disturbing turn which will delay us further.

Chapter Seven

An Unwelcome Visit

My hundred warriors are on the beach and already approaching the boats in preparation to depart when we hear reports of a large troop of horse borne Angles who appear to be heading rapidly towards us from Ceaster. Fortunately they have been spotted from a hilltop while still some distance off, so we have an early warning of their approach. Without it we would have left without knowing anything of them.

Under the terms of the agreement with Ingamund and the King of Mercia, the Angles have the right to send warriors here to inspect what we, the Norse people, are doing, but they have never been here before and naturally we are puzzled and concerned by their arrival now. We have often had visitors involved in trade, but these men are numerous and well-armed, and they definitely do not look like traders. What has happened recently to arouse their interest in us? Naturally I am very worried about this development and turn around to witness and to influence this event before I and my one hundred warriors leave.

I am interested to find out more and immediately wonder whether they are here because they know that Ragnald and the main group of men are away. No doubt news from the Isle of Vannin has travelled fast too, they may therefore believe that the colony is unprotected; they might even believe that Ottar's ransom is here. I am sure that they would probably be surprised and delighted to know that both are essentially true, as they would then turn the village over searching for the treasure and torture any one that they thought might know where it is concealed.

Therefore it is my job to conceal the truth from them, persuade them that the village is well defended, that there is no treasure here and that they should return peacefully to their own territory. I need to take responsibility for this situation and it is fortunate that I became aware of it before I left.

Relations with the Angles have previously always been cordial and even good-natured. There has been a lot of trade to mutual benefit and I definitely do not want that to alter this harmonious co-existence at this moment when we are at our most vulnerable. It is imperative to build on our harmony with them, at least until we are stronger.

I order all of my men, plus all of the old and infirm men left behind here when Ragnald departed, to assemble, and to show their presence as fully armed as they possibly can be. I hope to give the impression that the colony has a much larger protective force than it really has. In calling the assembly, I have forgotten to consult Ingamund although he is the Jarl, and not me. There is little time to react, so swift and decisive action is required and I have decided and acted.

Not only do I tell the men to arm themselves and demonstrate the biggest presence that we can, we also dress many of the women and girls as men, although we have to get them to stand behind us so they are partly obscured. Perhaps they can hold a shield across themselves if they can find one, then it should appear that, even in the absence of its king, the place is well defended. We do indeed look like a substantial and formidable force but we will take great care not to be provoked into a fight. Not only because we are much less strong than we appear, but also because of the need to preserve good relationship with the Saxons. This situation calls for diplomacy and deceit rather than military action.

Now that the Angles are nearby I remember Ingamund's position and go to make my apologies to him. He is surprisingly cordial and accepting of the situation and, although I am a commoner with no royal blood, he courteously accepts me as an equal. It shows how much my standing is rising in this community.

I respectfully ask him to represent the community in dealing with the Angles, rather than myself. They know him because he negotiated our original agreement with them, they are well aware of his status and will immediately respect him without any formalities or need for introduction. He is the ideal man for this role and I willingly defer to him as the highest status leader present.

When the Angles arrive they are greeted with a large, silent crowd of around four or five hundred armed "men", with my hundred fit, heavily armed and mature warriors in full sight at the front together with the best of Ingamund's defenders, including the so called sick, who all seem to have fully recovered as soon the fleet had left. The visitors are around fifty in number and certainly look surprised, and perhaps even a little intimidated at the strength of numbers facing them.

I move forward to greet them in a friendly and polite manner and find that, as I suspected, they are lead by a Danir speaking gentleman. No doubt that ability was once more the reason for his selection for this task. I can understand a little of the Anglo-Saxon tongue and they can clearly understand much of what we say too. There has been enough understanding for a considerable amount of trade and exchanges, but there have been more than enough misunderstandings too. When that happened the outcome was usually settled by violence, and I am very anxious to avoid that now. The services of the translator are very welcome in such a potentially sensitive negotiation.

He accompanies me into Ingamund's house while the other Angles are offered hospitality in the form of food and drink by some of the older women. All the time they will be aware that are being observed watchfully and pointedly by my warriors.

The discussions are calm but rather confusing. When asked by Ingamund why the Saxon has come to see us there is a short awkward silence, before he does indeed quote the right of the Saxons to monitor our activities under the terms of Ingamund's agreement with King Ethelred. It is not at all clear what he is monitoring or why he came now, although I can see that he is certainly very curious, asking questions and observing everything he can see around him. He obviously feels no need to make any secret of this curiosity either.

Not surprisingly he asks about the whereabouts of Ragnald and is very sharply told by Ingamund that Ragnald is not the Jarl here, he Ingamund, is in charge of this settlement. Ragnald does not rule here. Although the Saxon ambassador apologises for any misunderstanding about status he still presses the question again. I tell him the Ragnald is currently away for a short time visiting old friends in Vannin. In a way it has a core of truth in it, though I wonder how much the Saxon knows of the true story of the interactions between Ottar and Ragnald. I have stretched the definition of friendship a lot further than most people understand that word. By now Ragnald is very much further away than Vannin.

It is quite possible, or even likely, that the Ottar's family will have had to borrow silver in order to raise even the part ransom that they actually paid for the release of the hostage. They may even have approached Ethelred or his wife, who often acts for him, in order to borrow enough silver. If so, then the Saxons might well know what has happened and sense an opportunity to steal the ransom from us. Maybe this visit is intended to evaluate whether the silver has actually come back here.

Eventually they come to their apparent objective here, and ask that future tributes are paid in silver, rather than in sheep and other animals as previously agreed. Ingamund reacts with fury and tells them very aggressively and convincingly that he has no silver as this is just a small farming and fishing community. In any case this new demand is a violation of the agreement. They greet this with surly silence and obviously do not believe him on the question of silver. Having seen how he conducts himself, I would believe him, he looks completely sincere.

It is evident to me now that Ingamund has truly never been aware of the silver that Ragnald collected for himself in Dyflinn, or the additional silver that Ragnald took off Ivarr at the time of his death, or even the recent ransom of Ottar. In addition, he has failed to observe any of the movements of the chest.

As I reflect on past events I recall that he has so often been absent on every occasion when the silver was in view. Even when chest was handled into and out of the boats he was perhaps away on his mission to liaise with the Angles. He definitely could not have been present when Ottar was first kidnapped and then ransomed. Maybe I was unfair in my first judgement on him; he has perhaps not been so guilty of being as completely gullible as I had first thought. His ignorance is quite useful now!

Does it also mean that there is less chatter about the silver than I had feared? That less people are aware of the silver? Is it at least not being discussed openly within our community? That would be very good news. Or is Ingamund simply just out of contact with the gossip?

It could have been quite reassuring if the Angles had not been demonstrating so very obviously that they are fully aware that we have silver. I am very concerned by their presence and am in no doubt at all that we will soon face continuous demands for large payments in silver to the Saxons. My worst fear is that they will come back once I have left and ransack our settlement while it is so lightly defended.

In the longer term this change in circumstances will clearly have a strongly negative impact on our relationship with the Angles. Ragnald is certain to prefer to fight them rather than pay them in silver, and Ingamund now seems to be taking that line too. I wonder if they realise how much future trouble is certain to come from this meeting. I guess they must believe that we are still weak and must accept any terms they choose to impose. If they believe that they will be in for a very rude shock, though perhaps not in the short term.

It is quite possible that Aud's venture in becoming a moneyer has also added to the perception of silver being in plentiful circulation here. So I will ask her to suspend that activity until the whole of Ragnald's force returns. I certainly do not want her to be the subject of attention from armed and dangerous thieves. Heavy walls might have some defensive advantage but it is much better to be just left alone.

In the short term Ingamund's ignorance is very valuable to us and it may have bought us some much needed time. This is turning out to be a very bad time for Ragnald to be conducting such a large scale expedition so far away in Fortriu. If the Angles visit had happened even a few days earlier, before I arrived with my warriors, the village would indeed have been very vulnerable. I am confident that the Angles would then have sent in a large force to search every place in our village for the silver. As it is we may have assembled a large enough display of force to convince them that they would have to fight their way in with a large number of men and take substantial casualties. There is, however, no doubt that they do have as many numbers as they might need, so it is vital to give the impression that the silver is not here.

I amuse them and myself with the pointed story of our visit to Jorvik, letting them know that Ragnald's queen is the cousin of the King of Jorvik and how Ragnald is forming a military pact with the Danir of Jorvik. It's a double-sided point as it might go down very badly with the Angles to hear that we are forging close contacts with their deadly enemy, and could create hostility towards us. It will certainly not surprise them though; we and the Danir are fellow Scandinavians after all. On the other hand it clearly makes them aware that we are not just a small vulnerable group alone in the world with no important friends. It is always a good thing in this hostile world to be seen to have powerful allies who might want to avenge any overt aggression towards us. The Danir are certainly that powerful ally and even the Mercian Saxons are fearful and very wary of them.

So the conversation is concluded with no changes agreed and the Angles leave peacefully this time. I hope and believe that their reconnaissance mission will have convinced them that we are neither defenceless nor without friends. They must now believe that it will be dangerous for them to attack us, and importantly, they will have had found absolutely nothing to encourage them to believe that any silver is here. Ingamund's angry response to their questions looked convincing, and they may well know enough about him from their previous meetings to believe that he is not a devious man and would struggle to act out a lie in a convincing way.

They had originally agreed to let Ingamund settle here in the belief that he represented just a small community, a fraction of those expelled from Dyflinn. In fact, the majority of the community that left that city are now living here after our flight from Vannin. Now that they know Ragnald and his group are here too they may have realised this has become a much larger community, which would at least make them want to increase the tribute payable.

They will have got some mixed messages about that matter too. There are few boats present on the beach at present and many people judge the size of a Norse community by the number of boats they hold. Naturally, most of the boats are currently away with Ragnald. On the other hand they will have seen a larger group of warriors than they might have expected. In fact, most of the people here will appear to be warriors since we have dressed the women and girls as warriors. They may possibly have noticed that there are few people here other than warriors, just a few older women, and that will be confusing for them.

The whole incident leaves me with a considerable concern about the safety of our settlement and I decide to leave at least half of my hundred men here to reinforce the old and sick that were left here before. That will leave me with a much smaller group, which is a grave concern if we have to fight our way through the Britons in order to rejoin Ragnald. We have no idea what will face us in that land and naturally I would be more confident if we had a larger force. I will, however, have to balance our resources against the variety of risks which we face.

I anticipate that Ragnald will be initially angry when he finds I have returned with less than half of the force he gave me but, no doubt, he will share my concerns about the safety of the settlement, and be persuaded that it was the right thing to do. I hope he will share my concerns about the women and children but, if not, he will

114

certainly be concerned about the security of his silver. That silver hoard is becoming a horrible liability and endangers our people as long as it is here. It is much too dangerous to be held in the village.

I wonder whether I should tell Thora to give it to me to remove and bury somewhere else but I know that she is most unlikely to agree. The last thing I want is a queen with a grudge against me. So I am trying to build a positive, friendly relationship with her and her children. I will, however, certainly advise Ragnald to remove it and bury it somewhere far away where only a few trustworthy people know where it is, once he returns from war. Anyone who knows its location will be carrying a very dangerous knowledge and will be in permanent danger.

I tell all of this to Aud and she sees the opportunity to suggest that I should be among those who stay here, though she really knows this is simply not possible. I must leave as soon as I can now, there are only a few days remaining of the original forty days for us to join up with the Danir army, as agreed in our visit to Jorvik. I hope and expect that Ragnald will already be there to fulfil our agreement.

She is not at all happy when asked to suspend her new business as a moneyer but reluctantly she does agree to do so. She is aware of the existence of the hoard and can see the probability that it is adding danger to our community. She can see the logic in my argument although she still feels unhappy that her great idea of creating money is to be stopped for the present. It will not be very easy to explain to the rest of the community either.

So it is necessary to say our farewells all over again, and this time it seems even more stressful to leave my family. I am worried for those left behind because of the threat that the Saxons pose, and I am especially concerned for my own little family. Aud also knows that this will be a very dangerous journey for a relatively small party of just fifty men in hostile territory, and is therefore also afraid for my safety.

My wife's instincts are sound and I am sure that she will be soon proved right; things will be very dangerous on this new adventure.

Chapter Eight

che campaign in forcriu

Once more we are sailing past the hostile territory of the island of Vannin, keeping a safe distance and making fast time in a strong southerly breeze and soon heading into the turbulent waters of the north channel, which marks the end of our sea and gives access to the open ocean.

This time the reduced group can all fit into just a single boat, albeit our largest and a very crowded boat too. We are very intent on the swiftest and most incident free voyage, avoiding any trouble. It is a concern to raise the sail, as rowing would make us less visible, but I prefer the speed and so bring our single square sail high into the breeze. It proves to be a successful tactic and we go past the island unobserved, or at least unmolested.

Despite the wind dropping we continue overnight by splitting the men into three crews so that two can sleep, as best they can in these conditions, while the other crew sails or rows the boat. Later another of the teams will take a turn, so all will get some rest.

As dawn breaks on the second day we are already heading into that vast and very wide estuary that leads to the heart of the British kingdom. The power of the Briton people who live here was partly broken long ago by the raids carried out by Olafr the White and the first Ivarr from Dyflinn, when our settlement there was at the height of its power. The people here have never completely recovered from that devastation and as a result have been dominated by the Picts since then. Naturally they still remain hostile to us and are very capable of inflicting destruction on our small depleted group if we allow them to. We must be very vigilant once we reach land but while we remain at sea we are very safe.

Since the Picts now have the dominance and the wealth there, this time we, and our Danir comrades, will raid them with a great army. At least, we will have a great army if we can ever join our forces together. Meeting up seems to be the greatest immediate challenge; our agreement was quite vague as to the exact location we would meet. There is the danger, or perhaps the likelihood, that both Viking armies will circle around looking for each other but continually pass each other.

The voyage up this long estuary is a pleasant one as the rain and clouds have stayed away today and we can sail over the tranquil waters in the breeze, but also enjoy the bright sunshine. The water all ahead of us remains calm a dark grey mass with just the occasion splash of white water. Behind us it turns into a great shining, silvery mass, with dazzling light gleaming off its surface.

We are passing a number of islands varying greatly in size, and situated to the left and right, some close by, some far off in this wide expanse of water. To the north of us there is a large island with towering, jagged mountains. At times it feels like being back in Norway, the land of our forefathers.

The waters here are filled with dolphins which delight in swimming around our boats, jumping in groups beside the boat and collecting to swim alongside in the bow waves. We can look over the prow of the boat and see them in the water just a very short distance away. They seem to know we are looking at them and sometimes turn to look back at us. It seems that they have just as much curiosity about us as we have about them. After several hours of playing around the boat they do eventually get bored with us and then they disappear just as suddenly as they first appeared.

Eventually the fjord turns to the east and, although there are other channels to the north, our guide has sailing instructions that tell us that this is the main channel into Fortriu. I hope we are taking the same route as Ragnald, as this decision is a critical one. As we have no further information to base the decision upon we follow the guide's advice. It does make sense to follow this channel as we are now aiming both east into the hinterland and perhaps just a little further north. The river narrows considerably but continues for many miles into the hinterland, deep and easily navigable, although we now have to row rather than sail. The breeze remains strong but it is not reliably in line with the river so we need to control the direction of the boat's travel and steer clear of the rocks we can see protruding through the surface close to each shore.

We can see the occasional fort high above the river on a natural rock, but on this occasion we are not interested in them and row on past them. The natives take the opportunity to show their hostility though. Jeering and chanting loudly from their forts as we pass by them.

Eventually, on the second day of travel into this long estuary we round a turn in the river, already much narrower and shallower now, and have the reassurance of seeing all of Ragnald's boats beached high on the river bank. This is the highest navigable point of the river, and it is quite a sight as there are so many boats here. Indeed our boat does start to ground here, and so my men must jump into the water and haul it ashore to lie beside the rest of the fleet. It is safe for our men to jump over the sides of the boat into the shallow water and carry the boat out of the river. There is a guard of around fifty men stationed there, which strikes me as an extraordinarily small number to guard such a vital asset in such hostile territory. The loss of these boats would be a disaster when the expedition is over and we will need them to carry us and our plunder home again.

The group of guards is lead by a tall blond man who tells me that there is a village of the Britons quite close at hand, and he is aware that they have been sending horsemen to spy on our boats and the men who guard them. I can see that he is clearly concerned that they are increasingly tempted to attack us, and is looking to me, as the high status leader, for guidance on how to handle the situation.

When Ragnald arrived with his very large force the first reaction of these natives was to flee. It was certainly very wise of them to do so, but now Ragnald has moved on they have crept back and are certainly no longer afraid of this small rearguard. In fact, the situation has reversed as the guard are now heavily outnumbered and are very apprehensive about the presence of these Britons.

My first thought is to negotiate a treaty with them, but I have no one who can speak their language, and it is most unlikely that they will have Norse speakers. Diplomacy is not an option. It seems that our only realistic option is to frighten them away by a full scale assault on their village, and so that is what we will do.

I believe that when it is necessary to attack it is best to attack suddenly, quickly and with maximum force, catching them by surprise if possible and inflicting the maximum number of casualties in the initial confusion. The boats have already been here for a week already and the main force has moved on so the Britons seem to have come to believe that they are again safe living near the boats. They seem unaware of the arrival of my small force which came in just one boat. It changes the balance a little though, as we have doubled the number of the guards from fifty to a hundred. I also bring a different kind of thinking to the situation. My blond friend is nervous of taking the initiative, especially as he is afraid of the responsibility for losing. There is little doubt that the Britons still have more warriors and outnumber us at least two to one, but initiative, courage and particularly the element of surprise can easily reverse that advantage.

I resolve to make the assault but not today, my men must have a day to recover, to rest and to eat properly. A successful assault could also leave the guard with a good supply of food to last them for a long time. My blond comrade takes a little persuading to take what he sees as a high risk option, but the prospect of food and plunder persuades him. We are resolved to go ahead with the raid.

I walk forward together with my new assistant commander to reconnoitre the British village and identify a slope down which we will attack. The small hill allows us to get very close without being seen. So in the evening, after it is fully dark, we creep up to the edge of the village. All of the available Vikings are here so we are leaving the boats completely unguarded. This time we will not form a circle the village, we think it is to our advantage to allow as many as can to escape, that way helping to even out our numeric disadvantage.

I am not Ragnald so when I launch the attack it is with a silent gesture, a wave, I want get right into the village and to be striking down some of our opponents before they know we are there. They do have a guard of four men but they only spot us at the last moment and are only just able to let out a scream before they are struck down. It is too little warning for their friends to get much benefit, but adds to the confusion and they are soon streaming out of their shelters and running away. Many of their men are struck down as they run and they take a lot of casualties. Finally a brave few, maybe twenty, gather their weapons and turn to confront us but my men have a lot of adrenalin running through their bodies and immediately charge to attack them.

It seems they are not so brave after all, as they turn and run away. No doubt they realise they are sure to die if they confront the enraged Viking warriors, who would also greatly outnumber this small group. Several of these, the most courageous Britons, do pay for their courage with their lives. We have taken the village by surprise and completely routed them. We have just a dozen men injured and only two of them seriously injured.

The rewards include enough food for several weeks but our best acquisition from the plunder is a group of horses, there are just twenty-one of them. So that will be the number of men I will take on the next stage of the journey. Anyone who cannot ride will be left behind to reinforce the guard on the boats and we have only just enough skilled horsemen among our hundred to take up the twenty mounts. I am always happier to exchange numbers for additional speed and flexibility, and I am also happy that it leaves a larger number to guard the boats. We definitely need these boats to be completely safe, they will be vital to the army when it comes to return home.

Overall, I am delighted with the outcome. The raid has been a great success, not only giving us a plentiful supply of food but also making it very unlikely that the Britons will be tempted to stray anywhere near our boats again. The major benefit is that I feel our boats are much more secure now, so it is time to move on searching for the main army. We are told that they have headed north from here, moving directly over the nearby hills, and so that is also the route we will take. It takes another day before I feel we are all in top condition, very well fed and mostly recovered from the effects of the drink we took from the Britons. We all had headaches the following day, which I suspect was something to do with that drink. Perhaps it was poisonous, but if so, we have all survived its effects.

As we ride north over the hills the weather changes and turns cooler and cloudier before, inevitably in this country, the rain starts to fall. We cannot afford to allow this to slow us down though, and we cover ourselves with leather hides taken during the recent raid. We trot steadily upwards for most of the day, pausing only for a short time to drink and take some food.

We reach the watershed and then follow the course of a stream as it tumbles down to the valley below where it merges with another stream and then yet another wider stream until they form a substantial brook. This brook flows ever downwards onto a crumpled plain which stretches a long way ahead of us.

We have not seen any of the hostile people that we know live here, and are making good progress towards the far hills when we suddenly reach a Briton village. Naturally our appearance there causes a lot of concern and there is a period of frenzied activity, before a heavily armed group of warriors comes out to confront us. I have no wish to attack them and try to start a discussion with them, but it is useless. They cannot understand any more Norse than I can understand Brythonic. Information about whether they have seen Ragnald's army would have been invaluable to us but we are certainly not going to get it from these people.

So we move past them and go rapidly on, as quickly as the horses can carry us, and before any danger of pursuit develops. I am very concerned that they may assault us as we are now just a very small group, and we must get as far away from them as we can. It is not well-timed for the horses which have already had a long trek across the mountains, but we need to keep going for some time to get well away from the danger. Eventually we stop to rest for the night besides a wide shallow river, at a point where it flows in a broad semi-circle around a small conical hill, with larger mountains surrounding the river valley.

The following morning we have to guess which way to go to have the best chance of finding Ragnald's army. From the valley floor there is a path which winds its way up the hillside, probably to a mountain pass. I do not think that is the most likely route they will have taken so I follow the river as it winds its way downhill. As the horses are very tired from the previous day's journey we resolve to move more slowly today and not so far. We must be very close to our comrades, but they are still out of sight.

The river moves from a valley to a great plain, with very fertile farm land and many villages. It passes through a vast lake where we can see other people are fishing and gathering food. We take care to avoid them all, we are few and want as peaceful a passage as it is possible to achieve.

Eventually we come across a camp in the middle of the plain, it is obviously a great army, just like Ragnald's but we recognise no one among the warriors. So we stop close by and dismount, hoping we have not been seen. I keep most of my men back and out of sight as I crawl up a small incline to view the assembled army. It is immediately clear that they are also Scandinavian men. Their dress, weapons and language immediately gives them away, but there is no one I recognise, so this cannot be Ragnald's force. Naturally it must be the Danir army that Ragnald is expected to meet up with, and it is also clear that he has not met them yet.

I judge that it is safe and necessary for us to show ourselves to them, and we all come forward riding our horses into the centre of the camp. It is a dramatic entrance and naturally viewed with some initial suspicion. We do, however, have the same language as these people and so it is easy to explain ourselves. I have already met the commander of this group in Jorvik, so it is not difficult to convince him that I am part of Ragnald's army. Ironically this is only a day or two beyond the fortieth day after our departure from Jorvik; I am late but have almost hit the agreed schedule coming up here late, while Ragnald and his army, which had such a start on us, are still missing.

The commander is initially very glad to see me as he assumes that I can take him straight to Ragnald, so the combined force can begin its raiding. He is confused and a little frustrated to learn that I do not know where Ragnald is. I also have to explain how I got detached from Ragnald, which is a little awkward, and I invent a story, telling them that I had to return to take back Ragnald's concubine after she had got pregnant. It is not uncommon for the leader to take his woman with him on an expedition, but a pregnant woman would obviously struggle in the conditions of an expedition, and need to return. So the story of returning her to our settlement is accepted without any further discussion.

He dismisses the story quickly as he has real little interest in the reasons we cannot find our comrades, and I am not sure he is even listening. He is much more serious when he suggests to me that it is my responsibility to find them. Naturally I was looking for them anyway and as I do have the horses it is quite possible for me to divide our horsemen into two groups the next day and to send them to search in different directions. I think it sensible for all the Danir to stay here where they have plentiful water and can obtain food.

On the first day I take ten men and ride north from here, with another group of ten going south, each of us takes a Brythonic translator supplied by the Danes. Now we can communicate with the Britons, always a dangerous action but potentially a very valuable source of information. I can find no trace of my king or his army and return late in the day to the Danish camp.

My other riders have returned too, and although they have not found Ragnald they have come across some of the Britons who have reported seeing a Viking army marching through their territory.

Perhaps this is Ragnald and his army but it could also be a late report of the Danir force that we are now among.

So the next day both groups of riders head eastwards, I to the north east and my comrades to the south east, in order to cover as much ground as possible. Around midday I finally find them.

First we see a small group of warriors carrying out a reconnaissance just like us, and fortunately we recognise each other. There could have a disaster if we had not and started to fight each other. They quickly take us to the main group, and there is Ragnald himself, looking healthier and quite a bit slimmer than when I last saw him, but he has a huge smile across his face and he is laughing with relief and very happy to see me; maybe a little surprised too.

We have a lot to discuss. He is very pleased to hear the news of Thora's baby and hopes that it will be a boy to become his heir and successor. He is extremely happy that I can show him the way to join the Danir of Jorvik, as he has been looking for them for many days and feared that they had not actually sent any men to join him in the north. He is very much less pleased to hear of the Angles interest in our settlement. The worst news of all, as far as he is concerned, is that I have returned with just twenty of the hundred men he gave me. I can reassure him that the loss of these men to the expedition has achieved a very necessary reinforcement of the guards left both at our own settlement, looking after our families, and also looking after our boats and both increase the overall safety of our community.

After a lengthy discussion I can give him a small taste of the drink taken from the Britons and that certainly seems to make him happier. Given a little time for thought he will accept my logic in the various uses of my one hundred men. Now I leave him, so as to ride back to the Danes, judging it better to keep them informed. I can tell them that Ragnald and his men are nearby and have already left their camp and are moving west to meet them.

They do not appear that evening but the Danir now strike their camp too and move east, the direction from which our Lochlain army is approaching them, and soon the forces do meet. Greeting each other with wild shouts and exchanging much abuse and "light hearted" banter. There is a general release of tension, as we all know that we are all safer together and now we can finally combine into a great Scandinavian army. The meeting takes place beside a great black rock, which stands prominently at the centre of the wide, flat valley of the river. We have now been following the river for some time and found each other beside this truly dramatic piece of scenery. It must be a holy place of great significance.

The leaders now get together for a meeting, and the Dane acknowledges that he has orders to defer to Ragnald as the overall leader. I hear this with a great sense of relief. The first problems have been overcome, and we are indeed going to be one united army. Viking leaders are prone to forgetting their agreements and fighting among themselves for control, but this time it will go well. We will be one strong army under one strong and very determined leader.

A plan of action is made between us. Naturally Ragnald is anxious to drive his whole army north immediately but listens when I suggest that we use the horse riders to go ahead, perhaps for two days and report on what is in front of us, perhaps to find the centres of Pict wealth so we can target our attacks. In the four days before they return to report the main army can send out groups to gather food and build up a stock for our march north. We can then re-evaluate our route and take the fight to the place we are most likely to find the greatest plunder. Once the main army is moving it is best to get it into position as quickly as possible and to attempt to take the enemy while they are least prepared.

The Danes readily agree to action this scheme, but Ragnald is more impatient and suggests that the main army moves on the morning of the fourth day, before the scouts return, going towards them and so saving a day. This may also reduce the time given to the Picts to respond to the approach of our force, although it is likely that they already know where we are and may well guess our objective is to attack their main centres. In the morning the horse riders are instructed to go forward in two independent groups and to glean as much information as they can about the land and the people of Fortriu.

On the morning of the fourth day the main army leaves in line with Ragnald's amendment to the plan, and marches north along a side valley in a state of high excitement and in anticipation of great glory and huge riches. There are reputations to be made for every man in this force.

Moving an army of nearly two thousand men is difficult and they are likely to get spread out over a considerable distance. That would make us vulnerable to the small splinter groups being attacked when they become isolated. As I am the only one left with a horse among the main army I take it on myself to move between the front movers, often slowing them down, and chiding the stragglers, urging them to speed up rejoin the main group. It proves to be a permanent role, as soon as one group rejoins the army another strays off. Holding up the faster movers is more successful, but is not popular with the impatient Ragnald who is always up at the front. Even he knows that it is worthwhile to keep the army as tightly packed as we can, but it goes against his instinct. The result is slow progress, which is frustrating for everyone.

We do, however, have some news from the returning riders. It is not good news as one group has been ambushed and most of them were killed. This is the constant danger for small groups moving around in this unfriendly land. Even those with the advantages of being mounted and able to move quickly can be caught unawares. As a result they have been turned back without reaching the Picts settlements and gathered have much less information than we had hoped.

The Picts are clearly further north than we had first expected, and it will take us at least three more days of marching to reach the point where our riders had been attacked. We can certainly expect to be harassed from that point onwards, or maybe earlier. There can be no advantage of surprise now; we will simply need to fight our way through.

The land around us is always hilly and our route constantly takes us through river valleys which twist and turn. Although generally heading north we are often taken off to the east as well by following the trend of the valleys. We keep off the hills as much as we can and follow the low ground wherever possible. There are roads of a kind there but they are very rough and muddy, and we are mostly heading uphill, a very laborious task while our warriors are being driven hard to make the best time possible. There is constant and often persistent rain, they are getting drenched through and are usually very cold as a result, despite the pelts we are all wearing. The men are getting exhausted and, although there is certainly plenty of water, there is no way to scavenge any food and supplies in this wild land and the supplies we have brought are therefore running down.

The harassing attacks on us have come, though not on the scale I feared. Inevitably they target the smallest groups who, despite my urging, still get detached to the rear. There have been several raids and the most devastating come in the middle of the night, often catching our men sleeping; sometimes even the guards were asleep. It is amazing to me that they could be so complacent in such hostile territory, but they were very weary.

The increasing regularity and mounting intensity of attacks does suggest to me that we are already in the heartland of the Picts and we have come across a number of abandoned villages as we move. They seem to have been deserted just ahead of our arrival. All have been stripped clean of any goods that might be of value to us, and there is certainly no food or drink there. It is easy to find water but the lack of food is becoming a serious problem. After struggling uphill for so long we have passed through the bitterly cold air of a high, rocky mountain pass and are now moving down hill again along the path of another stream before eventually reaching a large wide river valley. At times it forms a vast fertile plain and the Picts have established many farms here. I imagine that the farmers will have been very reluctant to abandon them in the face of our advance, but they are all abandoned by the time we reach them.

The harassment is still growing in intensity as we move north and eventually we have lost around a hundred men in total, with minimal casualties to the Picts, and so the mood is very morose and unhappy. Some of the men are grumbling and even saying it is time to go back. They must know that we will not go back without reaching our target and getting the plunder that we have come for. That is just how the cowards talk.

After four days of hard marching we come to a halt for the night and it is time for the leaders to meet up again and reconsider our plan. I can see immediately that it is not going to be possible to assess the best course of action without better information; we will need the riders to go out again. The riders are not best pleased with the idea, as they know that they are surrounded by hostile people, who are intent on killing them.

I must therefore personally lead the task of taking the reluctant horsemen forward and we gallop rapidly out early in the morning before the sun rises. We have decided that the main army will stop and await our news; it will also give them a chance to rest for a short time. As we know that we outriders are vulnerable it is agreed that after a few hours a large group of two hundred men will advance towards the direction we are expected to return. This will unsettle the Picts and give us a better chance to return. The Picts will not know which route we will take but they will have seen us leave, and certainly know that we will return to the main army, so we will be most liable to attack during that approach.

In fact, we are very easily seen on horseback any way and they seek to attack us frequently, so it is necessary to constantly change route. Within a short time though, we have been forced onto higher ground above the valley floor and from here we can readily see that they have a very large settlement in the centre of the valley just a day's march ahead of our army. This is the very information that we need, it identifies our ultimate target, so I turn and get our riders back as quickly as possible. It goes well until we are in sight of the main army when we are confronted with a large group of armed men blocking our way. There is no option but to turn away and retreat, we are so heavily outnumbered that we could not hope to fight our way through them.

So we circle around our army and try to approach from another angle, but again there is the same result and we turn away again. Now we are again being forced onto the higher ground so we can easily see our own army even though we cannot reach it. We are all frightened and feel very vulnerable, but I cannot show my fear or even any concern, and put on a show of bravado to reassure the others. Now we are in the hills we have a chance to dismount and let the horses rest, they have been ridden hard today and are all sweating heavily, steaming in the cool air.

We are only safe here for a short time; the Picts will have seen our route and so they will soon follow on foot. We do, however, have the advantage of being able to see what is happening in the valley below and see that as agreed the group of two hundred warriors are advancing from the main group. As they do we can see groups of Picts rushing to attack them, no doubt they think this is the start of the main advance on their city.

I order our men to mount up and we set off again. We will not attempt to approach the advance guard but turn towards the rear of our army and rejoin them from that direction. This works well and we do get very close before we encounter a group of five of the foreigners who stand in our way. This is very foolish of them, as we are determined not to be turned away by such a small group and readily hack them down with swords from our horses. Height above the ground always gives horsemen a natural advantage, and we use it ruthlessly.

This proves to be the only obstacle in our way and so we are able rejoin the Norse army quickly. When I find Ragnald he is surprised to find me already back as he had expected the trip to take longer, our target to be further away, and he is also surprised that I had not come back through the force that had gone out to cover us, but from the rear. It is clear that group is now involved in some very heavy fighting. I suggest that Ragnald to release his main army onto the Picts to relieve the front movers, and he does so immediately. I think he is delighted to have a reason to get involved in the fighting himself, and he is soon right at the front of the attack.

The arrival of the main army swings the battle in our favour, as the Picts cannot match our numbers. Seeing that we are winning the day they break off and pull away. Our men have taken a lot of casualties, but in doing so they have also inflicted heavy losses on the enemy too. As we are left holding the battle field we can send out a group of warriors to finish off the enemy wounded, and to bring back our own wounded to have their injuries dressed. There is a great mound of corpses left littering the battle field even though this is only a preliminary skirmish. We are all aware that there will be much worse to come. The main battle for the heart of Fortriu is about to take place.

We will take a great deal of confidence from the outcome of this first skirmish though and we have also gained a good number of weapons, and even some food. Viking morale is therefore restored and although our men are still tired and hungry they are eager for the battle to begin. We still take the night to rest, more confident that they will not dare to attack us tonight as we now have the entire army assembled in one tightly packed group.

I find little rest that night. As so often before a battle I have the return of my terrible dreams and fears and awake sweating. In my dreams I recall the friends hacked to pieces by the Irskr, alongside me in Dyflinn. These demons seem to pursue me across all places.

When we see the assembled armies in the morning, we are surprised by their numbers. Both forces are quite large for these times and seem equally matched, we represent the combined forces from Dyflinn and Jorvik, and the Picts have assembled from all over Fortriu to defend their heartland. We are amazed at how many spears they have assembled to confront us. They must have a larger population than we had thought, which means it will be a greater fight but also there will be greater booty if we triumph over them.

We take up our respective positions both on slopes the next morning, facing each other across a valley. Tempers rise as these masses of manhood flaunt their spears, axes, shields and blades at one another and fling their jibes across that narrow space. There is a great shouting of abuse, screeching and banging of shields. Both sides believe they can triumph against the other but still both hold back as though they were waiting for some signal to attack, which will never come.

Although I have been elevated in status, on this occasion I have been given few privileges, other than the right to hold my own banner, and I must line up among all the other warriors. It is the first time I have held my own banner above me in battle and it is a very proud moment. Naturally it is the black raven, always my favourite tribute to Woden. I am especially proud of the bright red feet and beak that have been painted on it. Ragnald has his usual red and gold banner bearing the boar's head.

Ragnald does not know how to judge the moment to strike, but knows that to go forward and concede the high ground might be a disadvantage. I am not beside him to give advice this time, and the clash when it comes is the result of a spontaneous movement. Once one warrior moved forward all of the others followed in charging the Picts. It is ferocious and very violent, many die on both sides in the first minutes.

Our shields assist us as we raise them and crash into the Picts, but our charge turns out to be an error as the Picts stay on the higher ground and have an advantage. Our impact is much reduced by running up the hill towards them and we can not break their shield wall, basic and uneven though it is.

Despite that in the clashes beside me the Pictish leader fled after several hours of the battle when we strike down those near him as we break through a gap in their shield wall. We are eventually forced back with significant casualties though. I am beside one of my childhood friends when he is cut down, a spear splitting his skull, and I was covered in a shower of his blood. Death was never far away from me and I was very much afraid during these moments. Our charge had drawn the main body of the Picts towards us and it allowed the Danir on their side of the field to press forward, gaining the high ground and they then outflank the Picts who eventually withdraw. We are all exhausted and covered in blood, so we do not pursue them. All of us have bruises and many have cuts and gashes too. The battle peters out into an undeclared truce. Each side withdraws to re-assess and to lick their wounds.

Both sides spend an uncomfortable night, in an uneasy but exhausted sleep, each wary that the other might strike during the hours of darkness and keeping a strong guard. Once more there is little for the weary men to eat, as we have little of our food stocks left. Neither side enjoyed much quality rest and were in equally poor condition on the following day. This night the trembling and shaking returns to me, the fear that has accompanied my nightmares since I survived the battle in which we left Dyflinn. I am left very weary and miserable after a terrible night.

Nevertheless tactics are abandoned in the morning and the real fighting began as both sides surged forward in a frantic attack on the other, neither side maintains a proper shield wall and so the rival masses fall on each other with great fervour using spears, axes and swords, and all morning long the fight rages until around midday. It is a terrifying and exhausting experience for all involved. We look our enemy directly in their face and try to strike down the nearest man. All kinds of moves are used: kicking and punching as much as stabbing and cutting. Any man who flags or loses concentration, even for a second, is immediately cut into pieces.

The battle lasts much longer than we had expected with little drop in intensity. As much as anything it is a contest in endurance as the physical effort has to be maintained over many hours.

At one point it seems that our left flank has collapsed as the Picts seem to surge forward but we manage to reinforce that side and the shield wall is reformed to push the Picts back. The threatened disaster is averted, or perhaps delayed.

It is early afternoon when Ragnald makes the critical battle winning move. Naturally it is not the sophisticated move of a strategist but the brute force of a warrior; he drops his sword and sets among the Picts with his axe, cutting down several in his first few thrusts and so inspires a great surge in the Viking attacks, breaking the Pict's line. Once they start to pull back our men pour forward and the Picts give way and retreat in chaos.

First a few move back but then the panic spreads and more turn to drop back, and then they run away, believing that the battle is lost. It is their own panic that sets in that beats them, creating the opportunity for a very long period of slaughter as we pursue the fleeing foreigners, cutting them down in vast numbers as they ran before us.

Although it is a glorious victory many, many of our comrades have been killed and many more injured, of those the majority will subsequently die of their wounds. We have a very limited ability to dress their wounds and care for them. I have a cut on my left arm which is deep but fortunately clean, so I ignore it. The blood that was running from another gash above my eye has stopped now. I am among the fortunate ones as that cut and those gashes will heal over the next week or two.

While our losses are large the Picts have suffered far more and most of their men folk have been largely eliminated. The survivors are almost entirely women and children and have disappeared into the surrounding mountains as soon as they could see the battle turning against them. Clearly this retreat has been carefully pre-planned and we will never find them in their secret hideaways, so we will take just a few slaves. Their towns and settlements are mostly abandoned and we can plunder them as we please. The first thing we seek is food and drink and this time we find it a plenty.

Once more the aftermath of the battle resembles a great party for those who are still standing. Of course, there are still many of our men, and Picts, lying in agony on the battlefield. Most of them will die, though not necessarily quickly and often in great agony. We can again send out a group of warriors to finish off the enemy wounded, slitting their throats and then taking care to search their bodies for plunder. The Picts have taken huge casualties and lost an entire generation of their men, perhaps two generations. It will be a very long time before they will be again a powerful force in this land, unless there are many others hiding in these mountains, and that seems unlikely. They must have brought most of their men into battle to confront us with all the force they could muster.

There are so many impenetrable valleys among these mountains that there will be a great number of people hidden there, mostly women and children. Only when those children are fully grown and perhaps have had their own children will this community start to recover from today's events. They are very spread out across the hills, mountains and the countryside of this high land as they are essentially farmers and the majority do not live in towns or even villages. It is a cold, wet, hostile landscape which offers a hard living and I do not envy them their lot, especially with so few men left among them to carry out the work. This will be a community of women and children for some time now.

We also need to bring back our own wounded, to give them food and water and to have their injuries dressed. There are very many dead left lying on the field, the piles of corpses are all around the battle site and already the hawks, crows and other carrion birds are circling and gathering, pecking at their bodies. Soon the wolves will join them, and threaten the survivors too if we stay here.

All that is left is for us to search the settlement thoroughly to ensure that we have found all the plunder that is there. There is a great deal of wealth in jewellery, gold and silver in the largest houses, which must be where their Jarls and king have lived. We also search the fields and woods around the town before finding a recently turned patch of earth. Underneath that we find a number of bags of silver that have been recently buried. Such items of great value are claimed by Ragnald and I assume they will be part of the booty of which half will go to the King of Jorvik, and other half into Ragnald's hoard.

The silver hoard that was left at our own settlement so far away had already worried me, as it attracted the attention of greedy and dangerous foreigners. Now many more of the Danes will also know that Ragnald holds a great store of treasure, and they all gossip wildly about such things. During our return journey I will certainly advise him to take it far away from our current settlement and hide it in a safe place out of the sight of prying eyes. It is a growing matter of great concern to me.

That is all for the future for now and we must take a little time to recover from our exhaustion and our wounds. Ragnald has also been wounded and carries a great gash across his face with a cut which must have got very close to blinding him. For some days it frightens us as it threatens to go bad as the infection can easily kill men, even large and strong men like Ragnald, but after a few days it dries up and he is safe. True to his nature he seems delighted with the horrible scar it leaves, and wears it with great pride, as though it is evidence of his great achievement as the bravest of the brave warriors who is always seen at the heart of the action. I am sure he is right; many of us will see it exactly that way.

Now we must retrace our steps across the hostile land with a smaller army than before. We have taken great losses and left so many of our comrades behind us to lie in the soil of Fortriu. The life time of a warrior is a short one in these very violent times and the Valkyrie will be guiding many of our good friends to their seats beside Woden right now. I am amazed to have survived again, after being at the heart of such terrible battles and start to believe that I must have some considerable skill for battles.

We are reminded of the death of so many of our comrades as we stay for two days, hoping some of the wounded will recover, but many more of them are still dying. We must make progress towards our return and this means carrying the surviving wounded with us. Some can walk, some can ride on the few horses that we have taken, but many need to be carried and the whole army is greatly delayed by their rate of progress. They will need to be left at some point but clearly not here in the Pict heartland, where they would not survive our departure very long. Although the Picts have few warriors left, even their women would be delighted by any opportunity to take vengeance, and the wounded and dying would be immediately slaughtered unmercifully.

We want to stop, after two days of slow progress, to establish a camp where they will be left but when we arrive on the second day we find that the terrain is too mountainous here and we must continue to carry them for another whole day. Then those survivors who cannot move easily are left with a few brave volunteer helpers, who will assist them in the midst of this foreign land. Often those volunteering do so because they are also wounded and weary themselves. Even as we have travelled a few more have died and the fate of the others is likely to be a lingering death. Only a very few will survive and even then they will be alone among the hostile foreigners.

Finally we reach the holy place beside the towering black rock in the wide valley, where we first joined up with the Danir army and settle down for a much needed respite. There is good cultivated land and it provides us with some fresh food and, best of all, the opportunity for a good night's sleep on low, level land free of stones. It is my first good night's sleep for several weeks and for a short while I am free of the constant feeling of exhaustion.

During the night the plunder is divided, although not without an argument or two. In each case Ragnald takes the role of king and in the case of dispute he decides to allot treasures, sometimes to the Danir and sometimes to himself. He seems to me to be taking care to err on the generous side. I imagine he does not want any further fighting between ourselves at this point. Especially since the original reason for the campaign was for him to demonstrate his ability to lead the combined army, with the future invasion of Dyflinn in mind. The two armies must part here and they will take their separate routes back home.

For now our great adventure is over, though I know that in Ragnald's mind it is just on hold. He expects this combined army to re-assemble soon to take on the real task of re-capturing Dyflinn. He hopes it will now be just a few weeks away. He may be unrealistic in this thought, the height of this summer is already past and no one fights major campaigns in the winter when the rivers are in flood and there are no crops and few animals to raid.

The surrounding countryside is ravaged again before there is a last night of feasting and drinking as we say goodbye to old comrades, now firmly established as trusted friends. All of our differences had been forgotten as we fought shoulder to shoulder but now our old identities are being brought out again.

The Danir will march south to Jorvik, and they must undertake another very hazardous journey, as they pass though more hostile territory in which they will encounter both Britons and Angles. It is a long hard march too, and they will need to complete it quickly to allow their enemies little time to plan and organise to attack them. They will certainly be a very attractive target if their enemies get to know how much treasure they are carrying home with them!

We will move westwards, hoping to find our boats unharmed so that we can sail back home. We have the best chance to return unhindered, as we travel by water. It will still be a long and tiring journey, but we Vikings are always happier travelling by boat. The sea is part of our heritage, and we revel in it despite it meaning that we spend every day cold, wet and being thrown around by the waves! The constant motion stays in our legs even when we go ashore and I sometimes feel more sea sick on my first day on land.

We have another day's march towards our boats but we can move quickly now across the flatter ground and more easily recognise where we are, so we eventually rediscover the site where they lie. The guard are still faithfully looking after them but have clearly become very bored with their task, and are delighted to see to us. They are relieved that we have survived and delighted to see how we have gained so much plunder, but are they also quite shocked at the level of casualties that we have taken. Not many more than half of our original force is returning and very few of us without injury of some sort. I realise how lightly I have been wounded and am suddenly terrified again by the thought of the great danger that I have passed through. My old restless nights of terrible dreams have come back again and will haunt me for some time. Each morning I wake in a heavy sweat, often shaking, and the exhaustion from a lack of good sleep lies heavily on me every day.

We are very happy when we can take the boats onto the river and by sailing we can move so much more easily and quickly than by the endless marching. It is especially better for the walking wounded, many of whom have endured a terrible ordeal on the return journey. We no longer have the number of men needed to crew all the boats and each boat will attempt to tow another one, though we all have orders to cut the towed boat free if we have difficult weather. No Viking will ever abandon a boat unless it is really necessary, and we are grateful that it is very calm as we set off, it is well worth the attempt to save the boats.

We are heartily glad to leave this cold, wet and miserable country, with its high and barren lands, but I am sure that its people will be even gladder to see us leave. We have brought them little but death and misery, and as we leave we are taking much of their wealth with us. They will not now be a threat to any one for generations to come.

In the event our voyage is remarkably straight-forward, even through the turbulent waters of the north channel at the narrow entrance to our sea. It is only one more uneventful and rather tedious day and night at sea before we return home, passing confidently past the Isle of Vannin, with all of our boats under full sail, and not caring whether they see us or not. We almost hope that they will come and challenge us as we are fully confident of dealing with them.

All of the boats that set off for this great adventure have been brought safely back home. In contrast the men are battered, scarred and far fewer in number, but the survivors are, for the moment, also both triumphant and very happy to return safely home. All of us will have a share in the plunder and will be wealthy men for a while.

There are many women in this community that are learning that they are now widows, and many children who are hearing that they will never see their father ever again. I have a tearful and very emotional reunion with Aud who can instantly see from the bruises, cuts and scars on my face and body how much danger I have been through. There is great weeping and mourning throughout the whole place. Those wives like Aud whose husbands have returned, no matter how scarred and injured, feel guilty at not being part of that grief.

The campaign has been very successful in enriching the survivors, especially Ragnald, and therefore enhancing the treasure chest which he feels is needed to invade Dyflinn but it has lost so many of the army we already had. Despite Ragnald's great jubilation at his successes, it has to be seen as a more of a setback than progress towards our real objective of recapturing Dyflinn.

Thora is horrified by the great scar that Ragnald now has on his face from a sword wound which cut his face and nearly blinded him. It scares her to see how much her husband put himself in danger and she will now always counsel him to find safer roles for himself as Ivarr always did. Perhaps Thora was the influence that kept him away from the midst of the fighting in Dyflinn. That did not work so well for Ivarr's reputation in the end, but Ragnald is a very different man in very different circumstances. No one will ever doubt his aggression and courage, and the scar on his face is a permanent proof of that. Ragnald himself loves it and wears it as a warrior's badge of honour.

For now the Irskrs remain safe in our homes, across the sea. We still do not have the strength to oust them, and I suspect that the future co-operation of the Danir remains uncertain, though Ragnald is still convinced of their support.

Chapter Nine

ᚳһᴇ ꜱɪʟᴠᴇʀ һᴏᴀʀᴅ

Now that we are home we need a proper period of peace and reflection as the war weary men need to recover. Few of us would be prepared to follow our king if he thought to propose any more expeditions right now. His standing in this community has been severely threatened by the scale of the losses he has produced by his war.

In contrast Ingamund is seen to have been wise and brought those under his care a safe and secure life. His standing in the community is now higher than Ragnald's, at least among the women. The surviving men feel far better about Ragnald's war now that their pockets are bulging with a share of the Pictish silver which we took in plunder. The widows have differing views about the silver they have received; many would have preferred to see their husbands home safe. A significant number of them seem happier with the money though!

The problem of the security of Ragnald's silver hoard is bearing heavily upon me again, and I believe that it has become an even larger problem now that we have obtained even more silver from the campaign in Fortriu to store. That wooden chest is now even fuller, there is little room remaining inside it which must be a sign that it is time to stop filling it.

Ragnald is initially inclined to be quite dismissive of the issue, believing our numbers here will deter any attacker but clearly we no longer had the number we once had and I am insistent. I have a great fear that it will draw attacks on the community. I have now found a strong ally in Thora, who has had the responsibility of the hoard in our absence. She has clearly been very frightened by the persistent Anglian interest in us and our silver.

It seems that we have had two more visits from the Angles while we were away; clearly they were not completely convinced by Ingamund on their first visit. Thora does not know what has been the subject of discussion during their subsequent visits as they were only interested in parleying with Ingamund, who they recognise as the Jarl in charge here. It is clear that they were trying to find information from him that would lead them to the money. Perhaps they eventually concluded that Ragnald had taken it with him, as they would certainly know that he was away with many of the men.

Ingamund is not much more informative either as to the purpose of their visits, but he was clearly angry with the Anglian visitors who have often come from their nearby stronghold in Ceaster. He was confused and frustrated by their persistent questioning of him, which he sees as impertinent, and did not understand why they have been so persistent in asking for future tributes to be paid in silver. He is also very angry with them, and strongly inclined to discontinue any future tribute payments at all. A potentially very dangerous move, as it will certainly provoke the Angles, but one that appeals to Ragnald, especially as he now feels more confident in his ability to confront the Angles after his victories in the north. I am not sure his confidence is well-placed!

News reaching us about the Angles suggests that they have problems of their own, since their King Ethelred is suffering from a debilitating disease, and is unlikely to recover. It seems that Mercia is now under the control of a woman, his queen, Lady Aethelflaed, and Ingamund feels that they are now much weaker as a result. It is not obvious to me that this will be true since Aethelflaed has her own reputation as a formidable monarch and a good leader. She is held in high esteem in Mercia as befits her status as Alfred the Great's daughter.

Ingamund is becoming impatient to strike at the Angles in Ceaster, to revenge what he perceives as the insults and disrespect that they have shown to him. I think he might also be jealous of the prestige and fame that Ragnald has achieved by his adventures both in Vannin and battles in Fortriu, as it seems the stories of these incidents has spread far and wide and he is seen as a very clever and capable leader, as well as a ferocious warrior.

A number of Danir warriors in search of a strong leader to lead them to wealth and glory, have come here to seek out Ragnald and pledge themselves to serve him. While the campaign has done some harm to Ragnald's standing in this community, who have taken the casualties, it has given him a formidable reputation as a strong warrior among the wider Danish and Saxon world. He is very much admired in this violent and tempestuous world where the successful warrior is thought to be the strongest and the best, regardless of how many deaths are caused by him. Everyone just wants to be on the winning side.

Now Ingamund wants to press for an opportunity to enhance his own reputation as a fighter, and is advocating an attack on the nearby Anglian stronghold at Ceaster. Since Ragnald has returned our settlement is much better defended, but ironically those Angle visitors may well be more interested in us, rather than less. It could well be that they will believe we have returned bringing large amounts of silver with us, and that is certainly true.

If the Mercians did decide to make a committed and well-organised attack they may well have the numbers to invade us though perhaps not easily, and we could not successfully resist them without substantial Danir help. I believe it is a matter of urgency to remove the hoard to a safe place far from our village and to make it well-known that we have done so. That might finally stop the Angle threat to our safety, and so I strongly advocate we take that line of action immediately.

Ragnald can be stubborn, and is certainly opinionated, but he normally sees sense when confronted with sound argument and does so this time. He has, however, become so tired of the subject that he is refusing to be involved with the burying of the hoard. As so often when he finds a task inconvenient, distasteful or irksome he will give that task to me. This time there is a poetic justice in giving me this responsibility, since I am the one who is strongly championing its removal from the village.

Naturally, despite not participating, he still has a strong view about how and where it is to be hidden, and gives me my instructions on where to bury the treasure. He wants it put on the direct route from Jorvik to Dyflinn and sees the mid-point between them as the Ripam estuary. He seems to favour that place in many ways, and expects it to be the launch point for our eventual invasion of Dyflinn, which he now views as imminent.

He states that the hoard is to be buried as far up the river as we can take it, as close as we can get to the fording point where we started our march to Jorvik. That will put it at a distinct point, near where it is likely to be needed, and it should be easily located when it is needed at this place.

It also affirms his personal wish to move that part of this community, who see him rather than Ingamund as their leader, to Prestune. It is very much his preferred site now, and I think he will make a move to relocate his group soon. I am not pleased at the idea since Aud and our family is so well settled here and I will certainly be expected to go with him.

Prestune is the most likely place where we might need to start making payments to a mercenary army, as Jorvik is the only place that we could possibly raise that army. So I agree that it makes sense to go there, and we can most easily move it to that point. Taking it overland from the Ripam would have huge dangers as it would be easily seen and recognised, and we might not have the men to provide the huge guard it would need. Even among the Danir we would be in grave danger of attack when such a large amount of wealth is involved. Our losses in the war in Fortriu have made it essential to recruit as we have no possibility to raise enough warriors alone.

Ragnald has decided that a journey to Jorvik to consult with the Northumberland kings is our next action, but even he needs some time at home, especially now his own family is about to get larger. For once he is very attentive to Thora and it is clear that he is delighted with the imminent arrival of his first son. He has already decided that the infant will be a son; perhaps as a king he can decide these things!

My family are also suitably pleased to see me, though Aud is very concerned at the scar on my arm, she knows that the army has taken huge casualties and knows that had I lost the use of my arm at the height of the battle I might not have survived. She is very frightened by the risks that I have run, despite the status and the rewards I have earned, and does not want me to undertake any further adventures. This time she really is serious and with good reason. The risks I have faced were very real, and I have really hated being involved in war, I hope that my time as a warrior might soon be coming to an end.

We have our own lives to lead and a family to raise, and these are so much more important to her than raising wealth through raiding. She wants to have more children, and for her husband to be at home to take part in their upbringing. Naturally I also want to be a good husband and father, and to provide them all with the love they need and deserve as well as a good living. Nevertheless my alliance with Ragnald has brought us wealth and status and, if we can complete the task of regaining Dyflinn, my family and I can live out our lives there in prosperity and in high esteem.

For now we are both content to stay at home and look after the farm and enjoy our family life with Astrithr, and our two mothers. My mother Edda, in particular, has needed a lot of attention recently since she has become quite ill, and although I play my part, much of this burden has fallen on Aud. We do not understand what is wrong with her but she has lost a great deal of weight and is increasingly weak, at times she has difficulty in drawing breath. During the time I have been away the condition has first developed and then worsened. We hope that she will grow out of it and be cured, but I do not know what the condition is and I fear the worst for her.

Brodir is still working my forge and for the present he is making iron goods. Now that the army is back home he can resume his role as moneyer, and Aud already has a small stock of silver ingots put aside for the purpose. She enjoys this activity and knows that it brings her some status in the community, so our standing is not just due to my actions but to our joint activities. Brodir seems to have used the time well and has produced dies for new coins of good quality. He has devoted all his time to metal working is getting to be highly skilled in his craft.

My mother's ill health is also a good reason to stay and not to undertake any journey, but I have been very insistent to Ragnald on moving the hoard and now that task has fallen to me. There is no way out of it, but it should only take three days, so the chances are good that nothing will happen to my mother while I am away. I feel that I must fulfil my duty to the settlement, and the consequences of refusing Ragnald would be disastrous for my relationship with him. The high status we enjoy within this community depends on that relationship, and perhaps after this short task I can relax at home and be the good husband I want to be and concentrate on my family, but for now I have these other duties to complete.

So on a cold, wet day, at mid-morning on the banks of the River Dee, in full sight of the whole community, we load Ragnald's entire silver hoard onto a drakken longboat, and this time tell everyone what we are doing. There is no suggestion of hiding what we are doing. We want everyone to know that the silver has left, and is being taken away to a safe place far away where no one can find it. We hope that word of this will reach the Angles and any others who might be interested. I tell every one of the crew and anyone else that asks that we are going to the island of Môn to leave it there in the care of the Britons. It might not sound very convincing to an informed person but at least it deflects the questions for the present.

I take the smallest crew that I could possibly take, as we want as small a number as possible to know where the treasure is buried. All of us will be in some danger in the future as the only ones who know for certain the location of the hoard. Many in the crew will not know which direction we are taking and I will be doing all I can to mislead them about the location. The one who will certainly remain threatened by possession of this knowledge is myself, and there is no way to avoid that. The danger that accompanies this knowledge will become part of my life until it is recovered and spent. For many reasons I hope that day will come soon.

The voyage out of the Dee is uneventful and, although it is cold it is otherwise very pleasant now the wind and rain have stopped. Even the clouds have thinned out and in front of us we can see a small patch of blue sky. The swell inside the estuary is very limited but develops into a significant roll as we reach the river mouth, the dark grey murky waters there are broken by a regular pattern of white crests indicating the position of the sand banks below the water. Although I am intending to head north I first continue west for quite a while and then track northwards out into the open sea.

I hope to deceive even these on board with me as to where we are going and especially where the treasure is to be buried. We have moved around in a gradual circular movement until eventually we are heading due north; there is just enough of the sun in sight to allow me to judge the direction. At this point we can relieve the oarsmen and raise the sail. Many of the crew will understand our direction in relation to the wind, so it is not likely to fool all of them, but I insist that we are going to Môn and most will just take my word for it, they are not trained in navigation. It would be quite possible to go there during this voyage had I chosen. They have no reason to believe that I am lying to them and in the main they are used to relying on someone else to plot the course for them.

After nearly half a day going west and then north I finally turn the boat east towards our real destination and soon we can see land appear again in front of us. The outline of the low hills in the distance is as familiar as the flat fields and marshes that we soon see nearby, and I can judge the approach to the estuary which we enter as night falls and continue to sail right into the river itself making good speed running before wind and with tide. Eventually the river starts to narrow and we must row instead, and therefore our progress slows quite a lot.

We pass the village, which I remember as Prestune, high on its sandy ridge, but I know better than to stop there today. We do not want to make ourselves known or to be seen and so we carry on up the river for while. To our right we see the derelict stone ruins of unknown buildings from an earlier age, now abandoned but very prominently seen beside the point where a large brook also enters the main channel. I have heard that these are also part of the remains from the Roman age, as we have seen in Ceaster and Jorvik, but these are no longer part of any city and just lie in overgrown ruins amid the fields besides a confluence point, where a small brook joins the main river.

Now we are in a wide valley with the flood plain reaching out to the wooded slopes on either side of us. The land is mostly forested but with occasional patches beside the river where the trees have been cleared to create a farm. We reach the fording point just as the tide starts to turn against us, the flow of the water being easily visible on the surface of the river. This time we have not gone as far up the river as we had been able to get on previous occasions when we were at the top of a spring tide. I carry out Ragnald's orders of burying the treasure at the highest navigable point, but I wonder if he is aware of the variation that the differing tide heights make to this point.

There are a few boats on the bank near here, no doubt there are other Vikings who have disembarked and marched onto Jorvik, as we once did. Surprisingly they have left their boats unguarded. We are able to sail just a little way beyond them before the boat grounds and we are glad to get that little way further to be away from any prying eyes.

Although exhausted we haul the boat up onto the bank, and beach it there for the night. We have just one more task before we can eat and sleep which is to take the large wooden chest out of the boat and place it high up on the river bank, sufficiently far up so that we can be sure it cannot move and fall into the river. Then I open the chest to see it is very sturdily built with a lead lining. This is my first and perhaps only view of the fabulous treasure we have come to hide from prying eyes.

I want to look at it as fully as I can in the small amount of time available. So I peer into a few of the leather bags for this one time before they go into the ground, probably for a long time, perhaps for a very long time. It is my only opportunity to examine the contents.

One bag contains silver coins, many of which I can see were minted in Jorvik but also there are many others from Wessex bearing the head of their King Edward the Elder. The strangest coins bear marks I cannot recognise and it must be that they come from some far kingdom where they use different letters. Other bags are filled with hack silver, old objects that have been cut up and retained only for the value of their metal. Yet others are old ornaments such as armlets. It's a huge variety of different items but a great weight of metal and its value must be massive, beyond my ability to imagine. I cannot forget how much blood has been spilt to accumulate all this metal, how many men have died to collect it. It will all be of no value if we cannot keep it safe or, worse still, if we cannot recover it when it is needed.

So we start to dig with our shovels and blades, and bury the box quite deep in the earth of the bank. Importantly I take a mental note of its position so it can be retrieved when it is needed, seeing that it is on an alignment of two large oak trees. I am sure that those trees will be there for many years to come, and they make a great means of defining the position of the chest without putting any physical mark on the ground that others might recognise and use to steal our treasure.

I tell our men it is necessary to get the chest deep underground before we sleep if we are to be safe this night. We must hurry with the task as we are surrounded by hostile people, which is possibly true, and that they only speak Brythonic, which is not true. We are actually in the centre of Danelaw but I am still trying to persuade them that we are in Môn.

The men are exhausted and dig slowly but steadily, creating a pit which the chest is put into. First we put stones around it, some of the quite heavy ones. Finally the hole is filled up with the rich black earth again, and the chest with its hoard is safely underground and out of sight. At last we can rest, and I allow everyone to sleep.

There is nothing left to guard now and in any event, they would all fall asleep any way. We all sleep the sound sleep of the exhausted, no dreams of any kind tonight, and the sun is already in the sky when we awake. I allow a little time for a bite to eat and drink but we are very soon back on the river and battling against the new incoming tidal current to row downstream. Our task is done and we can return home, and I am especially anxious to get home to my family as quickly as possible. For once I am prepared to take on the arduous task of rowing in opposition to the tide.

It is likely that we will be seen from the village, but they have little or no reason to think anything of our passage, as there are many boats moving up and down this river. Although no other boat has gone as far upstream as we did there are several that have left from the bank near the village. This is not good news for me, as it is a very unlikely scene if we were truly on the island of Môn. I ignore these boats and ensure that neither I nor anyone else comment on them. We simply get out to sea as quickly as we can, and hope that the crew do not wonder too much about where they are.

Once we are well away from the land we can raise the sail for a time, though we are often too close to the direction of the breeze to make very good progress. Eventually we have to abandon our increasingly futile attempts to sail and we just row, making a direct route towards the open sea. We maintain this course for several hours before turning south east, towards home. I make little pretence at a different route this time, I am just too impatient to get back home, and we are often close enough inshore to see the coast. Anyone looking over the side of the boat can see what our route is, and where we have come from. I am relying on these weary, exhausted men not taking much interest in where we are going. We reach the Dee at twilight, and get back to our home beach just as the last rays of the sun are cut off by the sun sinking over the horizon.

I am greeted by a very gloomy Aud with the shattering and disastrous news that Edda, my mother, has died during the only night that I was away. Naturally we are all distraught at the news, she will be greatly missed, perhaps even more by Aud than by me. I have never seen my wife looking so totally unhappy.

The timing of my mission was incredibly unfortunate, but the mission I undertook was both very important and very urgent and has made our entire village safer. Nevertheless it is naturally a deep regret that I was not with my mother as she left this world.

I have an uneasy feeling that some of Aud's unhappiness is directed at me for being away from home on this occasion. I can see that she is extremely unhappy and rather hurt by my absence. More so this time than on any other occasion, even much longer periods away from home. She seems not to have understood at all my need to make this voyage.

I hope she knows that I have always been a good husband, completely faithful to her at all times, although we all know that it is not the typical action of a warrior to be faithful to his wife in the way that I have. I also want to be a great father to little Astrithr and all our other children when they come along.

This is not the time for those thoughts though; it is a time for sadness and mourning.

Chapter Ten

RAGNALD'S HONEYMOON

Aud has once again become quite sickly these last few weeks and she and Grunhilde, her mother, are quite sure that she is with child once more. I hope so, as I long for a son and this would be a wonderful thing for all of us, a great thing to bind us together and rebuild our love for one another, just as little Astrithr's arrival did earlier. I hope and believe it will be a boy this time to become my heir in time, and pray that it will come true.

We all seem happy again here after the unrest caused by the expedition to Fortriu and the mission to bury the hoard. It is once more delightful to have my place in the house and to see how that small piece of land which we once cleared together has developed into a fine small farm. I see it as my mother Edda's legacy, and it is clear that Aud has gained all of her skills and crafts. Maybe Aud has even surpassed her. Together they added sheep, cattle and pigs to the geese we first raised and now have two fields which in turn grow grain and vegetables; parsnips, onions, leeks, peas and cabbages, using all the slurry from the beasts to renew the fertility of the land. During the summer months we are very well fed though it is still difficult to retain enough food in good condition to sustain us through the winter. At times we have to revert to our failsafe of shellfish; the beach is a larder which just never runs out.

Aud is again enjoying being the centre of attention, not just from me, but from her mother as well. It is a good time to stay at home and enjoy the company of my gentle, charming women. Little Astrithr is getting larger and has started to walk a little, though we need to pay great attention to her. Without supervision she will wander off and is always in danger of falling or just wandering into things and going to places she is better avoiding. Soon we expect she will start saying her first words. Everything she does is a great delight to us all.

Aud was always a happy girl, with a radiant smile, but for a while she has seemed to be burdened with cares and worries. Now the strain appears to have been lifted again and she has blossomed, though I know she misses my mother who had become a great friend to her. I remember vividly how intensely happy she was at the imminent arrival of her first child, and she is hardly less delighted with the second.

I have also taken up my iron working again, leaving young Brodir to work in silver, and despite the long period that I have been away the skills have not left me. My stock of charcoal has been quickly replenished and the hearth is alive with its red glow once more. The old suppliers of ore are still there among the Angles nearby and, although they more often ask for payment in silver now, they always eventually accept other goods in payment. Often I can supply them with freshly cut timber as I am still enlarging our fields by cutting down the woods that surround them. Some of the timber has gone into charcoal, but there is always a great deal left over to sell or trade.

Aud is very content to see me going back to this trade and often tells me how much she loves to see me working like this and how she hopes that I will stay at it forever now, giving up my role at the side of Ragnald so that I can stay with her and our children. It is a lovely idea but I know that I have gone too far in my relationship with and commitment to Ragnald for him to ever permit me to move back into a domestic role. What's more we are friends and comrades now. I also have the deadly knowledge of the location of the silver hoard; perhaps I am the only one who can find the alignment of the two oak trees that defines the position of the site. In some ways Ragnald is dependent on me, but I am equally dependant on him.

My life is certainly intertwined with the plan to regain Dyflinn for the Lochlain and when the time comes I will have no choice but to play my part, it is my destiny. For now though, the time has not come and Ragnald is also playing happy families. He has finally succumbed to Thora's plea: they are to be formally married, and she will be declared his queen. It will be a happy day for them and all of the community will celebrate with them, drinking and feasting all day long.

Naturally the wedding ceremony itself takes place on Friday, the day that is sacred to Freyja, the goddess of love and fertility. The ritual itself is quite short but includes an exchange of rings between the happy couple and Ragnald has entrusted a sword to Thora to be given to their first son. He does not expect her to hold it for very long, as she is very obviously pregnant now. She looks very happy and proud wearing her bridal crown.

There are a few visitors who have travelled here for the wedding, especially among Thora's relations in Jorvik. It is around three or four days travel from there so they have made a very special effort to get here. Naturally Thora is delighted to see them. Ragnald has family here among the community but has lost contact with the rest of his family who are probably now spread around the Irish Sea or even further beyond. The fall of Dyflinn having spread our people far and wide. There are gifts too, often jewels for both the groom and his new bride, the most lavish which we can afford, some of it silver and much decorated with amber and glass. The gifts brought from Jorvik do not seem quite so lavish but they are valued too.

At sunset on the wedding day we all gather together in Ragnald's longhouse. The usual evening meal is enlarged this night because it is a wedding feast night. A horse had been sacrificed to the old gods and the meat is spitted and roasted, and there is also roast lamb, salted fish and pork with plenty of fresh bread. For dessert we eat fresh fruit and a little honey on buttered bread.

As on so many other days the Viking women's time is spent mainly on cooking. We have a fire placed in the middle of each of the one-room houses, with kettles and cauldrons hanging above for cooking. Although there is a hole in the roof, the houses are always unpleasantly smoky, and there is a risk of fire. The floor is strewn with fresh straw today specially for the wedding feast.

The entire feast is served on wooden plates and eaten from a pointed knife, many of which have been fashioned on my forge; it is my most typical product. The spoons are made from wood, horn or animal bone and carved with delicate patterns of interlaced knot work and decorated with the heads and bodies of fantastic and unlikely looking mythical beasts and demons with scales and fierce teeth.

All of the food is to be eaten along with some beer or strong mead which is drunk from horns, similarly decorated with those knots and strange animals and sometimes with silver tips and rims for the richest people. We Vikings always love to drink alcohol and it is not uncommon to see drunken Vikings lying around the village on a feast day. Enough honey has been gathered during the summer for a month of mead drinking following the wedding, so this month of celebration is called the honeymoon. Some people, but mostly women and children, prefer to drink milk.

Although the worst of the drunkenness occurs on the night of the wedding there are a number who carry it on into the following days. There is extra food for every one as well while the celebrations continue for most of the week. We have a long week of eating and drinking which befits the importance of the occasion, and demonstrates both the wealth and generosity of the host.

Thora's extended family return to Jorvik after just three days of celebration, having been especially well treated. They have received the very best hospitality that Ragnald could afford, even including the construction of a new longhouse to accommodate them. That building will also be very useful for the community once the celebrations are over but it shows how much effort Ragnald has gone to in order to honour his guests. Our king is very disappointed though that Halfdan has not come here himself, and his absence is the centre of some attention and comment. It feels something like a snub.

154

I know that Ragnald is very conscious of the importance to him of having powerful friends in Jorvik and he is certainly anxious to be in contact with them again soon. I am sure he will soon want to raise a new army to attack the Irskrs, and recover Dyflinn at the earliest opportunity but the expedition into Fortriu not only reduced his army, but also those of Halfdan, who might therefore be reluctant to engage in another adventure. It depends on how he values the plunder against the likely attrition of his military capability. A close alliance with Halfdan will be vital to Ragnald's future plans, even if it does not produce a quick result. For now that is tomorrow's business and we will concentrate on our own affairs in our own little world.

Ragnald is concentrating on his family for a time and is unlikely to undertake a new initiative until his new child is born. This suits me extremely well as I also have a new child to be born in the near future. It engages us both for a few months, during which we enjoy being a part of a thriving and growing community.

This is high summer and the best summer for many years, not just warm but hot, very hot. We have had several weeks of hot dry weather the like of which no one can remember. The hay is ripening fast and has to be gathered in now. Our crops are growing well but they need to be watered a great deal and the streams are nearly all dry. It is back breaking work to constantly carry the water to the fields and all the more exhausting in the heat of the bright sun.

After the work is done though, it is delightful to spend the afternoons swimming in the estuary. No shortage of water there, and it's unusually warm for a while, when the tide brings it in over the hot sands which have been exposed to the hot sun all day. Aud and I get the chance to lie together in the shade of the trees after our evening, looking over the river to the hills on the other bank and looking towards the distant mountains. It is a glorious way to spend time in a glorious place. Nowhere is more beautiful on the days when we get summers like this.

Ragnald's adventures and notably his successes in Vannin and in Fortriu have become legends in the Viking world, especially among the Danir, and he is widely admired among warriors. A few travellers seek him out to express their admiration, and it is easy to see that he loves this kind of attention. There are also a number of warrior groups who make their way here, intending to be part of any future adventures that Ragnald undertakes, since they hope for a share in the spoils. A number of the Danir hearing the success of this group have come to seek land to settle here among us, and these mercenaries are made welcome. Larger numbers of warriors suits Ragnald's ambitions; they make him stronger as the ruler with a larger army. They are among the first of many recruits for his increasing force. For the present they provide extra labour for the farms but these are not peaceful men, and will not be content with that sort of work for very long.

Many of the widows are happy to see this influx of new men, as there was a shortage of men after the Fortriu campaign. The community has adopted the air of a meeting place for marriageable men and women. Lots of carousing and flirting is common place, and many new relationships have started recently. There are likely to be a few more weddings to take place over these months, followed rapidly by new births, which will surely be a very good thing for the renewal of our community.

The dull sadness that hung over this community after our return from Fortriu has passed and been replaced by a sense of renewal. The passion of new love has infiltrated the entire group. Even Aud seems receptive to me again, after her anger towards me when I was absent as my mother died.

For the present Ragnald seems content to spend his time in domestic bliss with his wife and await the birth of his new child. It suits me extremely well as I am also enjoying my time with Aud. These hot summer days are happy times for Thora and him too, and the extended honeymoon stretches over several months.

I spend much of this period improving my iron working skills, sometimes working alone but I prefer to work with the other artisans. It is not clear that they enjoy this, as many are secretive about their expertise and guard it jealously. My standing and reputation in this group as Ragnald's counsel is, however, well established. Everyone knows that I am a close confidante of the king and few would choose to cross me, no sensible person ever does, and I learn everything I need to know even if I sometimes need to insist on being told.

Soon I have sufficient knowledge to be working completely independently and make a good living. I could live indefinitely with this new period of family bliss, and naturally Aud makes it very clear that she expects me to stay at home with her now.

Iron is used to make all manner of items from nails to swords, with every one being very valuable. A fine sword would take a week or so to make by a specialist weapon smith. I do not really have that skill but I can make a number of cooking utensils and pans. The most common tool I make is probably the knife, which has an enormous number of uses just for eating, or as a specific tool just for carving wood, but it still has to be made well whatever its purpose.

In Dyflinn all of our iron came from bog iron, which was found in small pellets in the bog and bought from the Irskrs who harvested it, but here I have to buy ore from the Anglian merchants to smelt the iron myself. This was once the only way, but now it is possible to buy the iron already smelted by them into ingots. Although more expensive this saves a great deal of very messy and time consuming work and gets the products made much more quickly. Wherever I can I also take broken or discarded iron objects and reforge them to make them into new items.

The iron working keeps me extremely fit as it is heavy work, I have to hammer every item out into the necessary shape on a rock which I use as my anvil. This is exhausting but very satisfying work. Unlike many of my fellow iron workers I do my work outdoors and this saves me from breathing in the smoke, as I hate that. Of course, it also means there are often times I cannot work in the rain, which is perhaps one of the reasons they call me a part time iron worker.

Despite their taunts I know that I am progressing well in my abilities though and, to prove it, I am making myself a new sword which is among the most difficult items to make. It must be very strong so it involves working two separate bars to intertwine each other and then reworked in the flame, heated until at least red hot and hammered until they blend into one blade. The edge then needs to be strengthened, honed and ground to a fine edge. The big danger is that if the work is not done well, then the blade might be brittle and break at the time of battle. That is what all warriors fear as it might leave them defenceless, at the moment of greatest peril. It needs to be worked at a very high heat to burn out the carbon, which would increase its fragility unless burnt off.

It is my first attempt, but it looks perfect and I have decorated the hilt with silver and it has an amber pommel. I am very proud of it and will carry it with me everywhere I go as my personal weapon. I will be delighted to go into battle with such a fine weapon. It is the mark of a high status warrior as befits my increased standing in this community.

All of the iron working is very dirty work and I am very often covered in soot from the fire. I am sometimes ashamed to come home in such a filthy state and do not want Aud to see me like that, so I often run into the cool water of the river to wash it off. None of the other iron workers are as concerned about the affects of the soot, and Aud says it is not important to her, but I am still concerned about her opinion of me. I feel our relationship is not as warm as it once was, and wish to impress her in every way I can.

Around the village, or maybe I should call it a town now, there is a growing feeling of people being unsettled, impatient and undisciplined. It is principally the effect of the new incomers, mostly Danir, and particularly those who came to join Ragnald as warriors. They were expecting to be involved in raids and are impatient to start fighting, so at present they are inclined to fight among themselves. It is likely that they would attack the Angles in Ceaster if Ragnald would lead them. There is a lot of rowdy behaviour and drunkenness among them; understandably many of our women do not feel safe.

Increasingly it seems they are gathering around the elderly Ingamund, seeing in him a leader who thinks as they do, as he is certainly unhappy with the Angles and their treatment of us. They can see that he is spoiling for a fight as much as they are, and so believe that he offers them the better prospect of a chance to take plunder. It is a curious reversal of Ingamund's previous image as the leader most likely to lead us to a happy and settled life, in contrast to Ragnald the warlord.

Ragnald is our real king but he has, unwisely I now feel, left the management of our contract with the Saxons with Ingamund. It has some logic and justice as Ingamund made the original agreement. The Saxons have continued to ask for payment in silver and Ingamund continues to refuse and remains angered by this.

By now even he knows that Ragnald has, and always has had, great amounts of silver but he sees no reason why this should involve the Angles. He certainly knows that the king will allocate none of the silver towards paying off the Angles. He is much more prepared to go to war with them, and thus get rid of any requirement to pay tribute. The growing numbers of men gathering around him has increased his confidence, although we are only just back to our number before the war in Fortriu. We need time to rest and recover. Our reputation as fighters is, however, massively enhanced as is our own belief in our military capability.

Ragnald is not yet ready to go to war as his own family is not yet complete, it is expected that Thora will give birth in just a few days time. Since Ingamund and the Danir are so impatient to fight Ragnald agrees that they can attack the Angles in Ceaster. It seems a very foolish idea to me and I strongly advise him against it. For once he fails to accept my guidance, preferring to back Ingamund's opinion. I think he has been worn down by the constant harassment from both the Jarl, and the impatient newcomers.

If they succeed then Ragnald will find that Ingamund emerges as a rival king, with a strong force around him. If he fails then he may well draw down the wrath of the Angles on us. That latter possibility has, however, been much reduced by the long illness of their King

Ethelred and, although his wife Lady Aethelflaed has emerged as a capable deputy, the Anglian kingdom of Mercia is certainly weakened by indecision. Ceaster is the town which interests Aethelflaed the least; she has much greater problems hanging onto her territories in the east which are constantly threatened by the kings of Northumberland from their base in Jorvik.

There are also stories that Aethelflaed's brother Edward the Elder, King of Wessex, has his eyes on taking their land along the southern border of Mercia. In these circumstances the Mercian Angles may well have lost interest in us. Perhaps Ingamund has chosen his time well, but I have no wish to be involved in this adventure, and know that, for once, Ragnald will not require me to participate.

So he calls his trusted advisers together for a debate on the situation. Naturally we are gathered to discuss just one issue: Ingamund's plan for action, he intends to take the group of Danir warriors to attack Ceaster. I think this the height of foolishness, not only is he attacking a strong adversary but he is going straight to their strongest point. It is likely to bring trouble to us, even if he succeeds in overcoming them.

It is certainly an end to our harmonious relations with the Angles but that has some advantages, it ends the demand for tributes with its increasingly troublesome requests for payment in silver. There will be no more payments, the truce is gone. It also aligns us firmly with the great enemy of the Angles, the Viking kingdom of Danelaw, with which we are carefully developing our alliances. They are our only hope of the reinforcements we will need in our ultimate plan to attack the Irskrs.

Having heard Ingamund's intentions I draw Ragnald aside to plan our strategy, and when he returns to address Ingamund he acts on my advice on dividing the warriors into two groups. The surviving Lochlain warriors who came with us from Dyflinn and took part in the subsequent adventures in Môn, Vannin and Fortriu are Ragnald's men and will stay here with him.

The king allows Ingamund to take the Danir incomers, the mercenaries who have been gathering here since our return from

Fortriu. They are spoiling for a fight and are likely to become a problem to us, a threat to our own people. It is necessary to find them a real enemy to attack. This may quench their appetite for blood and might even slate their thirst for plunder for a short time. Once the harvest has been fully gathered then the attack on Ceaster can take place but only once the crop is safely on our barns.

Ingamund knows he has been given an ill-disciplined, unruly group but one who are likely to fight ferociously, maybe even recklessly. He believes that it gives him his chance for glory, and accepts the arrangement gladly. Maybe he is right about this project, but I think it more likely that it will end in disaster and end his chances of ever challenging Ragnald. Either way his fate is put into his own hands.

The harvest is now gathered with new energy and urgency by our Danish guests. They have been informed of Ragnald's conditions for the raid and are anxious to get on with their new adventure. It takes a few weeks during which the hot weather ends and the more normal grey overcast conditions signal the approach of autumn. Twice Ingamund declares the harvest to be completed only to be given more agricultural duties by Ragnald. It is not just about taking in this year's crop but also storing it securely and about preparing the land for the coming winter. Finally Ragnald declares himself satisfied, the crop has been declared officially gathered.

Ingamund leaves two days later and without any ceremony he marches directly on Ceaster, catching the Angles in the midst of harvesting and therefore completely by surprise and off guard. They are in the final stages of gathering the crop. He terrifies their people for many miles around the town, and causes them to flee in panic into the stone walls of the old Roman city. They leave many of their goods behind them and Ingamund's men already have some of the plunder they sought but not in sufficient quantity for these men who sense greater opportunity. A wise man might have left it at that but Ingamund is more ambitious and goes on to lay siege to the city.

At first it seems he has been able to succeed immediately and march his warriors straight into the city, catching the Angles with the gates still open. Soon, however, it becomes apparent that this is a trick by the citizens of Ceaster, who close the gates after a relatively small number of the Danes were inside, which then allowed them all to be easily captured and killed. This is a cunning move and a considerable early blow to Ingamund's expedition, but it seems he continues to attack the city despite this.

We hear no more about the expedition, other than these initial reports, for a considerable time. It seems obvious that the siege is now under way and although the Angles are frustrating Ingamund he is persisting in his assault. It is not a normal thing for Vikings to maintain sieges for a prolonged time, and is especially surprising for such an ill-disciplined rabble as Ingamund has at his disposal.

Now Ragnald's attention is turned away from those events as Thora gives birth to their son. He is ecstatically happy and it is touching to see how gently he handles the tiny child. He and his wife look so happy together. It is impossible looking at them now all together in this family scene to remember that he is the terrible warrior that he is. A man who has gloried in so much bloodshed and death is now celebrating one tiny new life. They have called their new son Egil, and we are all sure that in time he will become as a great warrior his father.

Not long afterwards a number of the Danir start to return, first a few then soon afterwards a steady stream of bedraggled warriors. They mostly carry some wounds and often these are of an unusual type, burns and multiple wasp stings. The story emerges that Ingamund has become impatient with the siege and so he stormed the walls of the city with crudely made hurdles or ladders. Not surprisingly the Angles were able to cast most of the ladders aside and finally flung boiling water and some carefully gathered wasp nests down onto the attackers, delivering the final indignity. At this rebuff the group broke up in chaos and most have returned here though a substantial number have been cut down by the pursuing Angles while fleeing.

There is no sign of Ingamund himself now, though no one has heard any word of his death. Either he has indeed been killed, or more likely, he has not returned here through the shame of his failure. He may well wander off into Danelaw now to find a quiet place to settle among the Danir. We do not expect to see him again; he is too proud a man to return to face the shame after such a failure.

It is a sad and shambolic end to his involvement in our community where he had been regarded as a great elder but it leaves Ragnald as the unchallenged leader of the Lochlain and their new found recruits. He knows now that he cannot remain inactive now and retain the Danir mercenaries. These men must be kept active and involved, or they will become dangerous.

Our next project is therefore imminent, and it is time to recover our silver hoard, raise our great army and to liberate Dyflinn from the Irskrs. The next step is to call on our old friends and allies in Jorvik, as gaining their assistance is the only way we can realistically imagine recapturing our city and fulfilling our destiny. We are very dependent on their support, and it is time for a return visit to Jorvik and a conversation to renew our alliance with Halfdan.

The adventure at Ceaster is over. It kept our Danish mercenaries occupied for a while, dealt with the question of Ingamund's future and has ended our truce with the Angles. We can never live in harmony with them in the future, but the payment of tribute has ended too.

The side show is over and it is now time for the main event, the recapture of Dyflinn.

Chapter Eleven

RETURN TO JORVIK

Once again the longboats leave before the first light of the day, to take advantage of the tidal stream as the water flows out of the Dee and carries us swiftly towards the open sea. The heavy woollen sails are pulled out and prepared while we are still in the estuary.

I leave with a very heavy heart as Aud has delivered our new son; we have called him Thorfinn, just three days ago. It is a very bad time for a new father to be leaving his family, and Aud was quite openly angry with me, which I have never seen before. I am not sure what she expects of me; she knows that I have little control over events: Ragnald is the king and has been impatient to leave for over a week now. I have only been able to persuade him to delay a while because of my pressing domestic issues, but his patience is now completely spent and he insists that we must get on with our business.

Although I am on the boat with him all my thoughts are left behind on the shore with my wife, daughter and new son. For once our friendship has been put under strain. Why could not Ragnald understand this when he has also been though this experience so recently? At least Aud still has her mother Grunhilde with her to care for her, though the old lady is not as sprightly as she once was. We are both concerned for her health too, we can both remember all too clearly and painfully the rapid decline of my mother in her last days.

As so often before we are moving along the river and eventually we feel the kick of the grey turbulent water of the sea with its white caps. That familiar motion, rising and falling, has become a part of my life. We will take the most direct route into the Ripam, skirting between the sand banks despite the dangers of stranding the boat on a falling tide, and up that long narrow estuary, taking care to stay in the centre so as to avoid the sand banks that are just below the surface all around us, unseen at mid-tide. This boat is perfectly designed for such shallow waters and so we are able to make good progress.

It is a long hard row up the estuary, mostly against the tide though eventually we are in slack water at the low tide. Now the great sand banks tower above us and we must pick our way carefully up the narrow sandy channel made by the fresh water of the river. Fortunately it is a bright dry day and we can enjoy the passage. It is heavy work rowing all the way but we have a full crew to undertake the work.

Ragnald has brought a great number of the Danir mercenaries with him, mostly because he is cautious of leaving them behind in our community. It was easy to persuade them to move as they are mostly single men, here as mercenaries and with no wish to put down roots. He has decided that they will be located here on the Ripam and will build a new settlement here, extending the existing Danir settlement at Prestune. This reflects his long expressed view that the Ripam is a better base than the Dee, with far better access to Jorvik.

The disastrous raid on Ceaster has helped him in this objective too, the Wirral settlement will be in much greater danger of attack from the Mercian Angles now, perhaps as retaliation from the attack on their town, or simply because we have failed to make the tribute payments. So moving out of their reach suddenly makes a lot more sense!

We stop besides the village, to take some refreshments and much of this new army will stay here indefinitely and undertake the task of building new longhouses to house themselves. The whole group stops here and the work of finding timber and clearing land for new houses is organised and begins. It is a very good thing to keep these men fully occupied. The next issue to be tackled is the preparation of farming land to grow crops to feed them.

The work having begun Ragnald and I move beyond Prestune and towards the ford point, which is also the highest navigable point of the river beyond Prestune. This time the tide is much lower and we need to carry the boat for the final stretch. I am left carefully looking for those two oak trees. It is a relief when we reach the place and find the two trees, indicating the site of the buried hoard. Ragnald is briefly interested in hearing about the location of the hoard but is content with a brief description, never a man for great detail, and we leave it there.

There is no point in digging up the hoard now with all the attendant risk, just to have the task of carrying its weight to Jorvik, which is a den of thieves anyway. It will be much better to recover it when we get our army to this point, ready to embark for the invasion.

He tells me that he has little need to remember the exact site as that is my job. If I was not able to find it when he needs it, he would devote the treasure as a sacrifice to Thor, and bury my flayed body beside it as an additional gift to the god.

Once again we travel the familiar route to Jorvik, up the valley and over the lush green hills for three days before we see Jorvik in the middle distance across the plain. The town looks even larger and more prosperous now than we remember it just a year or so earlier. The smoke and the stench seem to have grown as well.

It is easy to find lodgings and we eat very well here, though the cost is a few more ounces of Ragnald's silver which, as always, he gives up with great reluctance. This time he pays with the silver coins made by Brodir under Aud's guidance. They bear Ragnald's own image, which he is very proud of. The innkeeper insults Ragnald by nicking the coins with a knife to test them to ensure that they are made from pure silver and not just a coating on the outside. There are often fake coins made which are of impure metal which is often harder and can also be detected by the point of a knife. Despite Ragnald's bad temper over the issue the innkeeper has good reason to check that the unfamiliar coins are truly pure silver. Eventually, though with extreme bad grace, he does accept them. Only just in time to save himself from being throttled by Ragnald.

Next morning we seek out the house of the rulers of this great kingdom of Northumberland, which now stretches from the borders of Fortriu down to the southern edge of East Anglia in the south. Our conversation in the taverns allows us to hear of the way Danelaw has strengthened its grip on this country. The East Angles, though nominally independent, are very much under the dominance of the Danir, as is most of eastern Mercia, though Wessex remains as the great seat of Saxon strength. They in turn have taken control of Cent and of southern Mercia. The Welsc remain in control of the west so the country has divided into three great power blocs, which eye each other relentlessly looking for weakness. Each is endlessly plotting to take power, wealth and land from the other.

Ragnald has sent a messenger to Thora's cousin Halfdan who is one of the three kings who jointly rule Danelaw from this their capital city. The others are Eowils and Ivarr, but it seems they expect Halfdan to represent them, and we have never met the other two.

Once at the palace, which is built in the remains of an old Roman fort, we are left to await an audience with Halfdan. We are made to hand in our weapons before entering the palace and Ragnald does not like that, though it is normal protocol in such a place. He has little option but to agree though as he needs to get to see the kings of Northumberland. All of our plans depend on their co-operation.

The hall in which we are seated is hung with impressive tapestries in brilliant colours, reds, blues and greens, the like of which we have not seen before. They are obviously expensive goods imported from faraway places and depict foreign people who are dressed in elegant clothes quite unlike those of our own people. This place is designed to show the wealth, power and extensive influence of the Northumberland kings. We are offered drinks, including wine imported from far off foreign lands, which Ragnald drinks with relish. We all impressed with these luxuries and enjoy the wine, an unusual treat.

In an hour we are escorted into see the king. Unfortunately our conversation with Halfdan does not go as well as we hope; he is clearly not as impressed by Ragnald's campaign in Fortriu as Ragnald himself was. The loss of so many men obviously weighed heavily with him, despite the rich haul of silver. No doubt it has limited his ability to undertake other military adventures in the south. Perhaps this is the reason why he did not take the time to attend Ragnald's wedding, when he married Halfdan's cousin, as an expression of his displeasure.

Ragnald tells Halfdan to honour his pledge to assist in the invasion of Dyflinn, made before we made the venture into Pictland. That expedition was principally to protect Jorvik's northern border from the Picts, and succeeded in doing that as they are massively depleted now. It also demonstrated how a combined army could perform under Ragnald's control. Now we expect him to support us in our objective, which is to move the Irskrs out of our city of Dyflinn. Halfdan has other ideas for this army though.

It seems the priority for him now is to counter the threat from King Edward of Wessex, who is the son of the Danirs' former great foe, Alfred, now deceased. It seems his power lives on with his son, as their towns remain fortified and his army constantly ready for action. Halfdan proposes the formation of a combined army, along the lines of our army that went into Fortriu, to raid deep into Anglo-Saxon territory. Although Mercia is weak it looks like Wessex which was once on the verge of yielding to the Danir, has successfully reinvented itself. Maybe an expedition, once successful in Mercia, might venture even into Wessex itself, to attack the core of their strength. We have already done that with the Picts, and therefore we might establish Viking dominance of the whole of the island of Alba.

The Anglo-Saxon territories will be better defended though, having large populations, but they are also very rich. Any army venturing into Angle or Saxon land will be quite certain to make itself wealthy from the plunder, if it succeeded. There would, of course, be significant risk that it would not survive the assault but that possibility is rarely part of Ragnald's reasoning. He always expects to triumph, and up to now, he always has.

The proposal is, however, not what Ragnald wants to hear now. He is currently focussed on retrieving his own kingdom in Dyflinn and feels that he is being asked to start all over again, having already earned support for his own mission. It is very much the same deal as he was previously offered with the Picts, except that now the Danes have proved themselves unreliable allies who do not keep their word. He has the use of Danir warriors but only to fight their wars and the price is that he has to share the plunder with them.

Ragnald is also very uncomfortable with the proposed expedition into Mercia, he knows the Saxons are both more numerous and better armed and organised than the Picts. They are a formidable, numerous and ingenious foe, as Ingamund found at Ceaster, and victory over them can never be taken for granted. The deal will obviously appeal to Halfdan; he is only risking the lives of his men in a battle that he will certainly have to fight at some time regardless of Ragnald's involvement. He will himself probably stay safe in his capital in Jorvik, well away from the dangers of battle.

We are being asked to risk our own lives in another adventure which is not relevant to our own strategic aim in return for just some plunder and the possibility that some day Halfdan might keep his pledge to assist us. It is certainly a poor deal but there are no other allies who might even possibly aid our cause. We retire to ponder our position overnight, collecting our weapons as we leave the palace. It is an uncomfortable dilemma.

Having pondered on it I feel that I should advise Ragnald not to accept the mission, or at least not until Dyflinn has been recovered. He might make Halfdan a counter proposal to take on Edward and the other Saxons, but only after he has had the help of a Danish army to recover his own kingdom. That way Halfdan would have to trust that Ragnald will not go back on his commitment rather than Ragnald needing to worry about Halfdan keeping his word. The Dane has already gone back on his word following our war with the Picts and so he cannot be trusted any further. He is also making

169

it clear to Ragnald that Halfdan regards him as an inferior, a subservient party who should accept Halfdan's demands.

Any disagreement is, however, a huge blow to our hopes for the recovery of our homeland. We have always believed that we need the co-operation and support of these Danir people, our distant kinfolk, so now we have to find another way to raise an army.

Perhaps it is time to rethink our entire strategy as we now have to consider what new courses of action are open to us. It is time to think the unthinkable and find a genuinely imaginative new course of action. It must be something that we have not previously thought of, or something we have not imagined possible before. After a while pondering other possibilities we can see a small number of other opportunities which we can consider.

We might try to raise an army of Danir mercenaries, either by putting the word out here in Jorvik, or by waiting in our own town for disillusioned Danish warriors to come to us. Having developed the new site at Prestune, inside Danelaw, and within relatively easy reach of Jorvik this has a stronger possibility to succeed. Of course, this has already happened to some extent without our actively promoting it. Although Ingamund's ill-fated sally towards Ceaster might indicate reduced confidence in the quality of these men we know they are true fighting men. Ingamund's inability to plan a proper attack was the largest problem.

Perhaps we might find less likely partners such as the King of Gwynedd or even Ottar of Vannin, but past relationships with these parties does not suggest we could easily negotiate an alliance with them. If we are considering these parties then maybe we might even form a pact with the Angles against the Danes. Had that been suggested before Ceaster it might have seemed very plausible, but that relationship has been permanently soured by Ingamund and it is simply not possible now.

Perhaps our best chance would be to search the borders of our sea in order to find our brother Lochlain groups, especially Sihtric and Guthfrith, Ragnald's cousins, who would probably share our desire to make Dyflinn Norse again. They too were party to the oath committing them to regain our city at the Althing on Dalkey all that time ago, immediately after we lost our home. We can start by seeking out all the gossip in the taverns of Jorvik. Any information that exists on their whereabouts is most likely to have reached this city.

So we spend a few nights drinking in the taverns of this city, the capital of Danelaw and centre of the whole British Scandinavian world. All the knowledge of this world is drawn to this town and the taverns here are the places where the most open and unguarded conversations take place. We are not only seeking information but also looking for men who want to fight. All of the men we meet are told that they can join Ragnald's army and that new raids will be taking place soon with the prospect of great plunder. There are a lot of people interested in such a proposition, and they all seem to know others that might also want to join our project.

The conclusions we reach are that it might well be possible to find those other refugees from Dyflinn and the possibility of negotiating a reunified army to take back our home is very worth considering. The tavern gossip says they are thought to be on the coast north of Vannin, close to where we held Ottar before ransoming him. This all seems like a very encouraging for our alternative strategy.

Before we can make a decision on whether this might be the best course of action we hear some important news. It is of the death of Ottar, King of Vannin. This changes things as it opens up a new additional possibility that we can take over his stronghold and his army, making Vannin our home and the base for our fleet. This seems to be very attractive to Ragnald, perhaps not just because of the strength of the base and its proximity to Dyflinn. Although Ottar, the target of so much bitterness, has now been removed from the picture, he stills seems to harbour a grudge against Ottar's family. Maybe he feels they still owe him the three bags of silver and gold missing from the agreed ransom.

We opt for a plan which involves creating a new alliance with the missing Jarls of Dyflinn against Bardr the new king of Vannin. The objective will be to take over his island fortress, and make a new much stronger base not just for our community but those of Sihtric and Guthfrith too. We might then be able to join together, along with the Danish mercenaries we have attracted and the additions we might still attract, to attack the Irskrs and achieve our true purpose in regaining our lost city.

Our king, having decided on his new course of action, is anxious to implement it immediately and has completely forgotten his promise to give an answer next day to Halfdan. Having reminded him of that obligation I get the difficult and unwelcome job of conveying Ragnald's refusal to the Dane.

Naturally it is not at all well received by Halfdan, and there is clearly a distinct cooling of the relationship between our king and the kings of Jorvik. Ragnald's absence is particularly badly received by Halfdan, who feels it is an insult. His perception of the relationship is that Ragnald is a minor king who is subservient to the Northumbrian crown. That is clearly not how Ragnald sees things, although he is conscious of having endured countless humiliations at the hands of these monarchs. It is part of the reason he is now prepared to turn his back on the relationship.

Halfdan has not anticipated this refusal and is suddenly feeling his own position weakened. He is revealing that his concerns about the Anglo-Saxons are actually much stronger than he has previously suggested. I can see that he is very worried that they are about to attack Danelaw in an attempt to subjugate the Viking people. So it seems Ragnald's services were more important to him than he was previously prepared to reveal. I think he has tried to play a clever game of bluff in his negotiations believing that Ragnald had no other options, so it is a shock and a keen blow to him to find Ragnald is now walking away from his proposal.

He suggests another meeting with Ragnald where I believe he will try to offer some improved terms, but it is now too little, and certainly too late. Circumstances have changed; Ragnald now has other ideas and is impatient to implement them. Halfdan, despite his wealth and power, is no longer of any great interest to him. It is a very dangerous position that Ragnald has taken. Provoking the Danes could easily back fire, but he seems blissfully unaware of that.

He has not a moment's doubt that the new plan will work and is fully engaged with carrying it out immediately.

So when I pass on Halfdan's proposal for new talks Ragnald appears not even to hear it, he is so pre-occupied with leaving as soon as he can. We are not leaving alone as several hundred Danir warriors have already answered the call for mercenaries and are coming with us. The group now marching back across the hills resembles the army that Ragnald wanted to get by negotiating with Halfdan. It seems that despite the failure of our talks we have much of what we wanted from them, with nothing given in return.

On reaching the Ripam we have insufficient boats to carry the throng back home, but no need to do so either. It is clearly much better to settle them here on the Ripam and further develop the site at Prestune. We have had no shortage of boats on the Dee, and now we have the men to fill them. It will not be long before we sail to attack Vannin. In the meantime our new Danir army is gathering within our new settlement.

Ragnald and I spend the night away from the camp in an inn within the old village of Prestune with its older and better quality buildings, as seems appropriate to status of the leaders. It is well that we did as we are sought out there by the local Jarl, Agmundr, known as Agmundr the Hold, as he holds the land in this region. It is a considerable and very rich area with many farms, and so he is a man of great influence.

He points out that we are building on his land without his permission, provoking an awkward moment before he says that he is honoured to meet Ragnald, whom he knows to be a great king and mighty warrior and seeks to form a friendship with us. Another sign, if any more were needed, that Ragnald has gained a huge reputation as an inspired leader and a successful warlord. Agmundr is given a token sum of silver not to press any claim over the land Ragnald is building on. It is better to build friendships with our neighbours rather than provoke any further enmity with the Danes.

Agmundr also has the same concerns about the Mercian Angles along his southern borders as Halfdan had expressed to us. He fears

173

them, especially as they may soon be reinforced by the Saxons of Wessex. The Mercians have already become bolder recently and scavenged across the Danir lands closest to their own northern boundary. These are Agmundr's lands and he is both angered by the raids and frightened by the prospect of them growing in the future.

Ragnald's standing and reputation in the Danelaw have grown to an enormous extent. Even a powerful man like Agmundr respects him and perhaps even fears him. That fear is reinforced by the way that Ragnald has gathered an army on the Ripam, at the centre of Agmundr's territory, removing much of his authority. He is certainly very anxious to establish friendly relations, and there are all kinds of ways in which co-operation between us will be of mutual benefit.

I quickly get to like this Jarl as he has a pleasant social manner, and seems very open and honest and is therefore someone I feel I can work with. We hope that we might also attract his support in the future when we need allies. He is a potential ally that we will do well to remember and he is also going to be a neighbour, living close to our developing home.

Ragnald finds time to linger in the tavern and it is soon clear why. He has become fascinated by one of the youngest and prettiest girls waiting at table there, a slim girl with long black hair and an attractive manner. She is always laughing and chatting with the soldiers who clearly appreciate her charms. She seems attracted to Ragnald too. Although he is certainly a few years older than her he must appear to be very athletic, dynamic and maybe even a handsome man. He is larger than most men but still lean and muscular. His scars may be seen as disfiguring but they add to his brutish and masculine manner. He looks every inch a warrior, and exudes confidence and high status. All of the warriors defer to him and call him "Lord".

During the evening they have become constant companions, she is continually staying to talk with him, seemingly entranced by his powerful personality and no doubt his reputation as well. The two are openly flirting with each other, and she sits on his knee, and there is an increasing amount of touching and petting. They do look very happy together, and there is certainly a lot of laughter and giggling. Later that evening they disappear together and I am sure that they became lovers that evening.

It seems that, having married his concubine and made her his queen, Ragnald sees the need for a new concubine. He has found one very quickly.

This is unwelcome news to me as it inevitably means that Ragnald will stay here longer; a delay at a time when I am anxious to be with my family, and we also have a newly developed strategy to implement. The new strategy that Ragnald was so anxious to implement immediately just a short time ago. I am sure it will suit Ragnald very well to have a second home here, as it fits with his view of Prestune as a better fit with his strategies. Even though that strategy has now changed the link to Jorvic is still as necessary.

Indeed it does entail delay as Ragnald dallies here a whole week and has to be persuaded quite vigorously to eventually move on to our real home where our families live. I use my time here purposefully supervising the further construction of the houses which are accommodating an ever increasing Viking army. The land we clear of trees to build the houses is developed as fields to sow crops.

New volunteers continue to reach us and quite rapidly, as the word of our offering here continues to spread. We are not paying these men; however, they seem content to accept the prospect of sharing in the plunder when we move. So it is increasingly urgent to persuade Ragnald to put our strategy into action soon.

The following morning social matters are finally put aside and we are at last moving onto one of the longboats, and put out to sea to take the quickest possible route back home. This will allow me to pursue the next stages of our new plan. It is a breezy day but we know this trip, its peculiarities and dangers and are well on the way into our own river estuary by the time the midday sun is above us.

When we arrive back at our own town on the Dee Ragnald wants me to organise a Lochlain group which will seek out Sihtric and Guthfrith. They are as central to our strategy of building up our enlarged community in Vannin, as well as the Danish mercenaries.

I have a little time overnight with Aud but I do have the chance to explain everything that has happened. She is rather shocked to hear that Ragnald has built himself a new home with a new concubine, and is suitably indignant on Thora's behalf, even though she is not a close friend. I feel that I need to tell Aud everything, no need to keep any secrets between us. She is very interested to hear it all, and I think she is wishing that she too could take part in these adventures rather than always to be tied to the home by her need to be a mother.

I can see that she has a keen mind and great ideas; indeed I intend to use some of her ideas. In different circumstances she might be a very useful adviser and guide to take with me. She is, however, very limited by her responsibility to raise our two small children.

In the morning I again need to leave, this time I am tasked by Ragnald with finding Sihtric and Guthfrith, and then negotiating their co-operation with an attack on Bardr to gain us the use of the fortress on Vannin for our coming invasion of Dyflinn.

Ragnald will himself soon return to Prestune, he apparently is telling everyone that he has further tasks to complete there. No doubt he is needed to undertake further supervision of his Danish army and the new town they have constructed.

I am sure he will enjoy himself in Prestune, now his favourite place.

Chapter Twelve

ᚦHE RAVEᚾS AᚾD
ᚦHE EAGLE

It is good to be on the sea, the wind in our faces, and I am in command at last. My mission is to search for the lost Lochlain groups under Guthric and Sihtric. The time there is no Ragnald looking over my shoulder and no other leader to consult. All of the decisions are mine, and I am relishing the responsibility.

After a long day's sail along the old familiar route past the hostile island of Vannin we find ourselves able to shelter for the night on the mainland shore to the north of that island. It has been a very full day and night too, we have covered a lot of distance.

I have eight boats and am therefore able to organise us into teams of two boats to explore all the inlets along the coast, one large bay each day, starting at the far western end of this stretch of the coast. We make a point of meeting up every night and exchanging our thoughts on how the search is going. It is not going to be easy to find our Lochlain comrades in this great space. This is a complex and winding coastline with many bays, each with multiple rivers and inlets, not only are there some very large rivers but there are also a huge number of small brooks and streams. Their settlement could be in any of these waters, and it is likely to be well hidden for defensive reasons. Or our information from the taverns of Jorvik may simply be wrong and they are not here at all.

I decide to ensure that there are never more than two boats together close into the shore, as I do not want to give the impression that we are a large aggressive force. This is a diplomatic project; we are not here to raid or plunder and must ensure the maximum possibility of negotiation and reconciliation. When we last saw these Jarls on Dalkey Island there was a strong feeling of ill blood between them and Ragnald. Now we need to reverse that feeling through careful diplomacy and form common cause with them against the common enemies; first Bardr Ottarsson and then the Irskrs.

Slowly each pair of boats looks into each river, as far as a boat can reach before grounding. We find quite a number of settlements, which involves a number of close encounters with the Britons who are the native people of this land. They are never pleased to see us, as they instantly recognise us as their old enemies.

They have little need to fear a force which consists only of two boats however, so there are some very awkward encounters where we are threatened. Keeping afloat is normally a means of keeping safe though, no matter how aggressive they are. None can match us for boat handling and they will not put themselves at risk by trying. Keeping afloat is not always easy though in shallow rivers with a restricted ability to manoeuvre.

It takes a lot of searching and a uses up a lot of time, almost a week, before we do finally find our kinfolk. The pairing of boats has meant we could search four bays with their rivers each day and that makes us very efficient. We have covered a lot of ground along a huge stretch of this wild coast.

Ironically they are near to the large estuary which we used to conceal our fleet at the time we were holding Ottar captive here. We were so close to them for all that time without realising that they were there. They are living in a settlement up another similar but slightly smaller river, just an hour or two further east. It is a narrower estuary and a little more difficult to navigate, being shallower and two of our boats are grounded on a sand bank for a while until our other boats tow them off, and the rising tide also helps raise them off the sand.

Fortunately the community we have found are pleased to see us, at least once they are reassured that we are coming in peace and looking to gain their co-operation. Naturally they have also heard a great deal about Ragnald's exploits and are somewhat awestruck by his adventures and achievements. The tales that have reached them make him sound like a very powerful and resourceful leader, apparently very different from the surly and quarrelsome teenage Jarl that they remember from our youth in Dyflinn. Even in such a remote, hidden community such as this his deeds are known, his fame has spread and he is widely admired. No one has heard anything of me in these tales though.

Sihtric and Guthfrith are clearly frustrated by the lack of opportunities that have come their way, having had a much smaller group of warriors at their disposal and having chosen to hide away in such an isolated place. It was their choice to come here and it definitely makes them safe from any large scale raids, just an occasional nocturnal intrusion from one of the boldest Britons, but they have little opportunity for the raiding and waging war which seems to be second nature to a Scandinavian.

They have harassed Bardr in a small way and their Briton neighbours in an even smaller way as those people have so little to take. Although they have succeeded in living well from peaceful pursuits, they have had little opportunity for either seeking plunder or even much trading. Consequently they feel that they are missing out and not living out their destiny as a part of our warrior race.

I sit down with them to hear their account of their journey from Dalkey Island after the battle of Dyflinn. As we already knew they had sailed north and the first place they came to was a small island off the coast of the kingdom of Brega. They settled there overnight and for a few days and were exploring its possibilities as a long term settlement. It was less than half a day sailing back to Dyflinn and so offered the prospect of resettling the town at some point. That thought must also have occurred to the King of Brega too, since he soon brought his warriors there to attack our kinsfolk and drive them off.

They then moved across the sea to Vannin, and so they attempted to settle there, in a very similar way to that which we ourselves attempted to. The outcome was also the same as ours, since they found themselves faced with demands from Ottar for very high payments of tribute to be made in silver. As this group had no silver the demand was impossible for them to meet, and they were heavily outnumbered by Ottar's men. The only sensible option was to move away, and they continued on until they reached this coast, which they found largely unoccupied except for the occasional small groups of Britons. In the main they have avoided contact with the Britons, who have also kept away from the Vikings.

They have cut down the forest, built longhouses, developed extensive farm lands and exploited the abundance of fish around this coast, just as we did. They are generally well fed, but also frustrated and feeling very isolated, having suffered from limited access to other Scandinavian people. They have been able to make a small amount of trade by boat with Danelaw, which has allowed them to hear of Ragnald and his adventures. They view those adventures with some envy; no doubt they can see the glory of his successes without understanding the great sacrifices that have also been made to achieve them.

They already have been living exactly the tranquil, peaceful agricultural life that Aud aspires to. No threats and almost perfect safety, an excellent place to bring up children. Yet they are not happy, they find it incomplete and unsatisfying. Maybe this place is simply too remote and it needs greater opportunities for trade and social connections.

As a result they welcome our arrival and the prospect it brings of trade and exchange with another Lochlain community and through us, the wider world. They seem particularly happy at the idea of ousting Ottar's successor from his seat on Vannin, he is unpopular with this group too, but as they know the strength of his fortress there, they have some considerable scepticism about the practicality of an attack on it. That castle is widely known as an exceptionally strong defensive position, and it deserves its formidable reputation.

This is wonderful progress and we are all happy to be reunited, the majority of the surviving Lochlain of old Dyflinn will soon be brought back together again in one powerful force, united under Ragnald's kingship. This is a pre-condition of co-operation which they gladly accept now. That issue that split our community at the Althing on Dalkey Island is now put into the past. They fully accept that Ragnald's subsequent achievements have now proved his kingship. This will be great news to take back to my master when I retrace my steps. For now we are very content to take part in a great feast, to eat their salmon, venison and beef and to drink large amounts of their mead and beer. They are well supplied with these delicious foods and there will be a few days of this good life before we consider going home again.

They have agreed to join a combined action against the Danes of Vannin, which I propose to schedule for around seven day's time. We will assemble off the coast of Vannin, near the impregnable fortress. I will signal to them the moment when their involvement should begin by sending a boat from our fleet to summon them.

Therefore before we leave this river I want to make sure that those sailing all of our boats are capable of finding their way back to this place, and we also build a great cairn on the headland at the mouth of this estuary. It now marks the entrance to our comrades' home. Though the numbers of this community are smaller than ours, they are a significant addition to our strength and their number might well be sufficient to sway the balance of power in our favour, especially as we do already outnumber Bardr's men.

It is time to leave our newly found comrades and return across the sea to our own community. When we reach the Dee and rejoin our people, I find Ragnald has returned from Prestune for a few days to await my return and consult his leaders ahead of the attack on Vannin. I report to my king on what I have achieved. Ragnald is delighted with my news, and particularly the proposal to attack Bardr in six days time. As always he is anxious for action and wants to carry the attack to Vannin as soon as possible.

Naturally Aud is less happy to hear that I am leaving again so soon, but this time even she is more philosophical as we both believe that Vannin might become our last base from where we might attack the Irskrs and finally regain our land. The approach of the final battle might well spell the end of our wandering and perhaps a rich, settled role of high status and wealth for me as a reward for my service to Ragnald. Although she has been happy here in the Wirral, she is also as anxious as I am to return to our green valley and live out the original childhood dream of our little farmstead in the Dyflinnarskiri. She can see that the final steps are being put together, and now the final victory is already in sight.

This is my first chance to get to know my new son, little Thorfinn, still a tiny bundle so helpless and entirely dependent on his mother. He could not have put his trust in any one better; she is entirely dedicated to his welfare. Each day she breast feeds him and cleans him and keeps him close to her, the two are quite inseparable. I think she seems even more pleased with him than with little Astrithr, who remains the apple of my eye.

My infant daughter is able to talk with me now and play games, so we spend many hours struggling and playing, with me bouncing her and throwing her around. Her mother is not impressed with such rough play, and is convinced that I am going to drop her and hurt her. So eventually we respond to Aud's chiding and play quietly together with a rattle. After all, although it may be a little less exciting, it seems to make sense to keep my precious little daughter safe.

Life has many simple pleasures but surely none are as great as walking hand in hand across the sands with your little daughter on a sunny day. The water of the Dee estuary is nearby and the hills across the river look green and fresh in the bright light. My wife is walking beside me, holding my other hand, and she has our son in her arms. The whole family are together for the first time. No man can be happier than when experiencing his family like this.

I have loved this short opportunity to get to know Astrithr and play with her and have found it delightful. I can see that being a father can become a very rewarding experience. My little children offer me such pleasure in everything I do. I will need to leave very soon, but I know now the wonderful rewards of being a father, the greatest of all incentives that I am being offered to get home safe and soon.

Other events will not stand still no matter how much we want more time to nurture and play with our families. The army is already assembled and we will sail tomorrow. I still want to make one more change before we leave, to have every boat carry a sail with a large black raven painted on it. I want this to be the symbol under which we will fight to gain the castle where I once dreamed that it could only be gained by the warriors becoming ravens and flying in. It is also the symbol of Woden and his power, and so Ragnald has accepted it as our emblem, not just my personal banner.

It's very tempting now to avoid my responsibility towards Ragnald and the army and just run away to avoid going with the fleet that sets off tomorrow and staying with my young family. I am so much enjoying my time with them; I am delighted with my tiny daughter who has just reached the age where she can really relate to me, talk to me and I suddenly feel so close to her. I know it is not possible for me to stay, my presence and participation is interwoven into the plan, which needs my presence and our king would never forgive me if I disappeared now. The die is cast, and for now I cannot break it.

As the sun dawns I bid the farewell to my young family once more, with an especially heavy heart now, and a sinking feeling of approaching doom. I must ensure that nothing happens to me, I know that I have already survived more battles than most men and the odds against my survival must be shortening each time. My time will surely come if I continue to roll the dice, but I feel confident that this is not my time yet, I believe I will get to see my family again and have the chance to move them into the safe area inside the impressive castle on Vannin.

The leaders are summoned to a meeting with Ragnald in his longhouse. I find I am expected to put a plan to Ragnald, he always expects me to explain how we will conduct the battles now, as though the planning of battles has become my job through some

183

unspoken process. Naturally I expect it and have already thought through our tactics.

I explain that the objective of my battle strategy will be to draw Bardr into a battle away from the fort; since he is just too well defended while he stays in there. I will seek to fight him on the open sea and for that purpose I propose to divide our fleet. We will use the full fleet which numbers eighty longships, and all the boats are brim full of men this time, we could have used more boats if they had been available. The Danir mercenaries that have joined us have ensured a larger, stronger force than we have ever had before. This time we must succeed and take the fort, if only by the weight of our numbers.

Ragnald will stay out of sight in a bay south of the fort with the main fleet, and I will sail a small number of boats well away from the land, passing the castle out of sight and then returning to it from the north, a group of just twelve boats that will look vulnerable and might tempt Bardr into pursuing them. We think he can raise around thirty boats, enough to take our twelve reasonably easily if he will engage with us. He is very likely to react if he believes that he does so from a position of strength. Once the Vannin Danir are pursuing us we will move past their castle to join up with Ragnald's main fleet, and then we will then have eighty boats in all. The pursuing boats will then find themselves suddenly heavily outnumbered but too far from home to retreat safely, and with the wind carrying them towards our battle fleet. The battle will then take place on the sea with hand-to-hand fighting as the boats join together but with the odds heavily stacked in our favour by our greater numbers.

My comrades all feel it is a brilliant plan but there are several ways in which it might fail. The first flaw might be that Bardr may be cleverer than I expect and not pursue the twelve boats. Bardr may appreciate that his great strength is his position inside the castle and simply stay there, but I think this unlikely. He is just not that intelligent and the temptation of taking a small group of boats will be too much for him. When it comes to a trial of strength between his greed and his brains his greed is certain to be the stronger.

There is no immediate downside to us if he stays in his castle, I will certainly be safe then, but it just becomes a non-event and we will not have achieved our goal and we will be back at the beginning, needing a new plan to entice him out. It is likely to be a lengthy siege which is never a favoured tactic among Vikings. We like our battles short, bloody and decisive.

Alternatively he may simply turn back once Ragnald's main fleet appears and this is quite possible, even probable if he sees it early enough. We must therefore allow his boats to get close to us, we are the bait and we must be a tempting bait. We have to trust in our timing and also that of Ragnald, he has to be exactly where we have agreed that he should be, to react when he needs to react. The timing and location are so critical that I want to go with him until I can see him beach his boats; I need to know precisely where he will be.

More problematic still, but much less critical, is timing the arrival of our Lochlain comrades from the north. It is more difficult to co-ordinate, but has fewer personal dangers for me. If they come too soon they will find the castle heavily defended which will be painful and possibly fatal for them. If they come too late we will already probably be there and they will play no part in the battle, a waste of resources but not disastrous as we have sufficient numbers without them. Our timing has been calculated to make the latter more likely, unless the fighting is prolonged. That can only occur if Bardr has more ships and more men than we expect, or that they are better fighters than our men. That would make them extraordinarily good warriors!

I send the boat immediately to summon Sihtric and Guthfrith, with instructions to sail straight into the small harbour beside the fortress. If the timing of their arrival is right, they might arrive to find it either undefended or very lightly defended. They should then be able to walk straight into the open gates of the castle and then hold it for us. The boat sent to summon them will leave a full day before the other boats.

I do not give any serious thought to the possibility of Bardr's defeating our fleet, numbers always count in a battle and the Danir mercenaries who are with us, though ill-disciplined, are all well-equipped and savage fighters. I know we will prevail if we can get Bardr away from the fort and committed to a sea battle.

At the last minute I decide to reduce the number of boats in my group to just six, now we will certainly appear vulnerable and the bait is therefore far more tempting, but if Bardr and his men can catch us we will be genuinely vulnerable. In fact, very few of us would be likely to survive long enough for Ragnald to rescue us.

Not surprisingly Ragnald is very enthusiastic about the plan, he see that it has every likelihood of success and there is no significant personal risk to himself. I have noticed that he always likes to fight within the middle of his large group of personal guards now. Despite his reputation for reckless courage he has changed since the battle for Fortriu, from the old Ragnald who was always issuing challenges to single combat. He now keeps away from the centre of the battle, and likes to have the odds stacked heavily in his favour. No doubt he will survive many future battles, surrounded by his huskarls, even though he may often be seen at the centre of the fighting he will be well protected. I suppose he is either becoming wiser as he grows older, or he is now listening to Thora's ideas to preserve him and keep him in greater safety.

In contrast, I seem to be increasingly likely to be at risk, right at the forefront of every action. Of course, I am taking the greater leadership role now; since I am still trying to get Ragnald to make me a Jarl but there must be time to reconsider my strategy in the future. For the first time it occurs to me that a family man with two small dependent children should not be taking such extreme risks.

There are already two fleets. One is leaving the Dee which I command, and another leaving the Ripam on the same tides which Ragnald will command, and together we will combine into a mighty fighting force which would frighten any one. Ottar and his family made a big mistake when they created an enemy out of Ragnald and his Lochlain community and Bardr is about to suffer the devastating retribution. This is a far bigger army than is required to crush any likely resistance in Vannin.

I am fortunate enough to get an extra day at home while Ragnald leaves for the Ripam as he will lead the army he has gathered there. I can wait here since I lead the group leaving from the Wirral.

We leave late on the following afternoon and the first evening at sea is uneventful. It continues through the night and in the morning we arrive off the beach of the same bay where we once sought to build our colony. From a distance it looks like our old neighbours have maintained the lands we cleared and I imagine they must have profited greatly from our efforts and will be thriving. I hope so and I wish them well. They were good people, for a while our neighbours and our friends, and they may soon be so again.

It is the dawn of the second day of our new adventure, and as the light develops I can see the Ripam fleet appear ahead of us, a great mass of sail on the surface of the water. They are passing through very turbulent waters off the south west of Vannin. A small uninhabited island juts out across the tidal flow and this produces an area of disturbed, turbulent water over which we must now pass.

I must now split the Dee fleet, the main group heading east to join Ragnald's boats inside the bay. I will stay with the small group of six boats which has set off to go west, rowing strongly far out to sea where they will be less likely to be seen. The main fleet have a shorter journey and stay well south of Bardr's fort, landing on the beach of a cove, to await our return passage which is designed to bring him and his boats out to chase us in a few hours time.

It takes more than two hours to row a sufficiently great distance to position ourselves well out to sea and to the north west of the fortress. We will be able to set sail as we approach the stronghold with the wind behind us, and it will be at the point where we raise the sails that we will become clearly visible to the defenders. Judging that position will be vital. Too soon and they will be onto us before we reach Ragnald, too late and we may be past and they may simply not follow us.

As we continue onwards, again rowing hard, we appear at first to have the entire ocean to ourselves, no other boats are visible, but we do have the company of a large friendly grey dolphin that comes out of the harbour to meet us. We take it as an omen of good fortune, maybe even Thor himself in disguise has come to look at us and wish us good fortune.

My men have already been rowing for hours now and are exhausted, so although we are just a little further away that I had ideally intended I raise the sails a bit early to give them respite. They will give us more speed anyway and should carry us past the enemy's harbour before he has enough time to react; I swell with pride as the six black ravens of Woden billow in the breeze above us, creating a bit of black magic as they carry us towards the castle.

The plan works, and it works well, too well, and certainly too soon. The boats from Vannin are coming out to attack us earlier than I had anticipated. They must have seen us much earlier than I had anticipated and I wonder if they had been watching the large dolphin when it came to greet us. That dolphin may yet prove to be less friendly than he had seemed. Thor is the most fickle of gods and he may have turned against us for failing to make sufficient sacrifices to him. Now he may be present in the form of that dolphin not to wish us well but to watch and to laugh at our deaths. The gods are very temperamental and have little respect for mortals and may turn against you at the slightest perceived slight.

Or maybe the Norns have another fate planned for us! We must have the courage to face this danger and, if necessary, to meet our death with our swords in our hands so the Valkyrie will recognise us as worthy of a place in the feasting hall of Valhalla.

We need to turn a little further to windward so as to avoid coming too close to our pursuers, but following this direction also slows our movement through the water slightly. The danger of them catching us before we reach Ragnald and his fleet is now clearly far greater than I had predicted, and we are getting much too close for comfort. Everyone in the six boats is fully aware of how close we are to Bardr's much larger and very threatening fleet, he has sent out all of his thirty boats, and I can feel the anxiety and even smell the fear in the air.

I am sure that he will remember my role in his father's ransom and that will probably mean a long slow and immensely painful death for me if I am taken alive. Perhaps they might even inflict the ritual death of the blood eagle on me, where the victim's back is cut open, and the lungs pulled out and spread across his back while he is still alive. A very slow, terrifying and very painful death is the inevitable result. Ottar's men were certainly known to inflict the blood eagle on their enemies in the past.

I hope that Ragnald has his men observing what is happening so he will react more quickly and come to save us. No sign of that yet though, and the threat is still very close, I can see the warriors on the chasing boats leaning over their shields to peer at us. They look to be very enthusiastic for the fight. No doubt they expect it to be fought on terms that greatly advantage them. I find it difficult to stay on my feet as the boat plunges around in the sea, and cannot speak. My fear is too intense. The knot in my stomach has tightened so much that I am in physical pain. I must stay calm and in control as every decision taken here is life enhancing or life threatening.

The wind direction has veered and is helping us as it is now nearly behind us and the chasers are still having to row into both the wind and the swell to get nearer to us. The gap is starting to open slightly as we are moving away from them but we must turn again to stay further off the undulating and rocky coast, this manoeuvre takes us further from our enemy but again we lose the best use of the breeze and slow down. This piece of sailing is also starting to feel dangerous, too close to the rocks and in a strong swell and with a fluky wind that keeps changing. All of our warriors are standing, silently and nervously staring over the shield rack on the side of the boat to observe the progress of our enemy behind us.

They can see that we are now heading for a narrow gap between the main island and the small islet, an area of sea that we know is just about navigable but very shallow and covered in rocks. We can see it in the middle distance; still some way off but quite distinct. Our pursuers will certainly also know this area very well and they must be confident that we will need to slow considerably to get through that strait. Taking it at speed under full sail is a very hazardous action. I hope it will make them content to wait until we reach it as I know that Ragnald's fleet is waiting for them just out of sight and will strike at them long before we get there.

The ideal speed for our strategy is one that leaves us just ahead of our enemy, close enough to make them always believe they can catch us, and we appear to have achieved that perfectly. Unfortunately it is not reassuring for us in these few ships and still very frightening now, as the chasers can now also turn to raise their sails and gain speed, following an identical track through the water behind us. They are not far behind us and the gap is no longer widening. They are even close enough to try to throw a few spears at us though these are still falling well short of our boats.

We have already succeeded in our task now, as we are near the headland which hides the cove where our own great fleet are hidden. They should appear very soon now. In fact, they should be appearing now! Where are they? Where are they? Where are they? Don't they know our lives are at stake if their timing is wrong?

My task should be complete, as we have drawn Bardr's army into the jaws of the trap, but still there is no sign of our main fleet to close those jaws. I am still in danger, though we are beyond the point where we should have been rescued. I can almost hear and feel the rough beating wings of the blood eagle as though it is following me in hot pursuit; my black raven is still flapping hard and so just managing to carry me beyond its reach.

We draw level with the cove and can see right into it, it has all of our boats and they are still on the beach! None of them have been launched; we are getting very close to the narrow strait where we will have to slow down to navigate it safely. The plan will succeed in defeating Bardr but has failed us, as we must surely be caught now. I am going to die just at the moment of my greatest triumph. This must be the terrible price of blind loyalty to Ragnald when it means taking his position in the most dangerous place. He has let me down at the most vital moment!

As we draw past the cove we can finally see all of our boats being launched from the beach, each boat heaving with fully armed men. It should terrify the Vannin men immediately behind us, but it seems they have not noticed as they are still concentrating all their attention on us. They are very confident now of taking us, and apparently unaware of their own doom, the huge fleet which is now starting to take up position behind them and follow them, closing the jaws of the trap.

It looks to me like Ragnald may have deliberately delayed the launch to make certain that all of Bardr's fleet are caught in the trap, none of them could see his fleet before they entered into an area they cannot get out of, and he has succeeded completely. They are all caught, and can have no possible means of escape.

None of them will be able to escape unless they can also scrape through the narrow strait without hitting any of the rocks and they will need to pass by my small group to do that. The outcome of the main battle is almost decided already as Ragnald's fleet is closing the trap. Bardr, his boats and his men are completely trapped in the angle between the islet and he mainland. The only question left unresolved is whether they will kill my men and I before they are all killed themselves. It's a question I have a great deal of interest in.

I decide that I will continue to run before the wind right into the strait and take my best chance with the rocks. If I can make it, we will shoot straight through under full sail and therefore at full speed. We are very, very fortunate to arrive on the high tide which gives us far more depth of water and the channel is therefore also a little wider, though still perilously narrow. I am in the first of our six boats to arrive, leading the others and indeed we do shoot through under full sail, seeing the rocks pass close by us on both sides but missing us.

At its narrowest point the strait is only two or three boat's width, so we are through very quickly and then relatively safe in the open water beyond. I heave a great sigh of relief, as it seems I will survive another battle after all.

Of the remainder of my boats, all are following me through and the next one also survives but the next three all arrive together and attempt to go through side by side. There is simply not sufficient space for this. There is a terrible dull thud and a splintering of timber as the boat nearest to the main land comes to a sudden stop, tilting forward with a jolt and spilling many of its men into the water. It has obviously hit a submerged rock at full speed and is fatally damaged. The wrecked boat slews sideways across the channel and further restricts the width of the channel but the other two are also through.

We can see a few men on the surface attempting to swim, but it seems that most have sunk into the sea, carried down by the weight of their mail and their arms. A few more appear on the surface a minute later, having apparently discarded their arms, and are swimming towards the nearby shore. Others are picked up by a preceding longboat which has now stopped to rescue them. This boat is then rammed by another boat following behind, still desperate to evade the chasing Vannin boats, which are themselves desperate to evade Ragnald's huge navy. It is a chaotic mess but both these boats are still afloat, under control and eventually they are able to continue through to the open sea beyond the strait.

Now the first of the Vannin fleet arrives at the strait and catches the rearmost of our boats bringing about a clash of spears and swords between the men on the opposing sides. A few leap from one boat to the other which is brave but foolish, as they take their chances with either the waves or their enemy. Few of those jumping will survive as the boats separate.

Bardr's fleet are now all jostling with each other to attempt the passage through the narrow strait and are forcing their comrades on the outside onto the rocks on both sides. The channel is simply too narrow for all those boats at the same time. It was dangerous enough for a single boat to cross in calm unhurried conditions. Now they are trying in complete desperation to get thirty boats through. Their anxiety and fear drives them to try to crowd through, no doubt they now know that they face death at the hands of Ragnald if they turn, so they may as well try their hand at running the gauntlet in response to nature's challenge.

Although several of their boats are grounding and being wrecked, a few do get through before the strait becomes completely blocked with the wreckage. The boats at the back of the wreckage are joined by Ragnald's fleet and our warriors flow onto these boats bringing about a true battle, but a very one-sided one as the Vannin pirates are quickly overwhelmed by our numbers, exactly as we had always planned.

As a few of their leading boats have succeeded in getting through the strait unscathed and my group, just four remaining boats now, turn to face them. We confront them but we make no move towards them. The implication of this action is clearly understood by them. We will not challenge them if they do not challenge us. We are therefore content to allow them to escape, not seeing any need for greater bloodshed, particularly our own, and clearly they quickly understand the sense of this. They have eight boats which are now able to escape and these set sail, running before the wind and disappearing fast off to the east. Where they are going we do not know, maybe they do not know either, but they will clearly land somewhere in the north of Danelaw. I guess they already know of a place where they will find some friends prepared to protect them.

It is time for us to return to our main fleet on the other side of the strait, where the battle is now over. It takes us quite a time to get there since the strait itself is effectively closed and we must row through the heavily disturbed tidal waters as we pass right around the small islet.

Half of the Vannin fleet has been captured, along with around half of the crews. The rest of their boats are either in the small escaping group or were wrecked in the strait. Many of these men were very wise, and were prepared to give up the fight and agreed to yield immediately if their lives were spared, which Ragnald readily agreed to. It makes complete sense to him as they are fellow Scandinavians and he sees them as more new recruits to his army. The battle is now over and we have a complete victory. There is no sign of Bardr, although we search high and low to find him! It may be that he died in the fight or drowned among the wrecked boats or perhaps he was among those eight boats that escaped earlier. That last possibility would be a blemish on an otherwise total success.

We are now completely free to sail our entire fleet right into the safest part of the harbour in the river estuary which is close by the castle and from there we march unopposed into the impregnable castle. Bardr's mother and his queen have witnessed the battle from the battlements and, realising that all was lost, have already fled on horseback across the island, along with the rest of their family. They are undoubtedly still somewhere on the east side of the island and so we could pursue them and probably capture them if we are quick, but we are content for them to escape. They have little value for ransom now, as we are already taking everything they own. We have no need to fear their revenge any more, as we now have the kind of overwhelming strength that everyone will respect and very few will ever challenge.

Ragnald had a ferocious reputation across Danelaw before this action and he will seem absolutely invincible now. He has taken the impregnable fortress with minimal casualties and added, not just a fine new base, but also substantially increased the size of his own forces in doing so.

Ragnald issues orders that the town must not be burnt down, and our men are made to respect the women and children they find here. They are Viking people like us and we plan to have them integrated, together with most of their men, into our community. We manage to protect the lives of the inhabitants but cannot and will not save their property; a lot of plunder is taken, especially by the Danir mercenaries who now make up the bulk of our army. This is extremely ironic as these are their fellow Danish people that they are robbing and plundering.

As is so often the case after a victory the men take to feasting and wild drinking, and it is a good thing that all of the women and children of this community were taken away into the castle for their own protection before it started. Warriors often become argumentative and dangerous when they reach a drunken state, and no one is safe then. The victors knock each other around a great deal in drunken brawls and merriment, and there are many bruised and bleeding men before the morning comes, but just a few fatalities.

I love the company of the Danes, they are the best of men to fight with, to drink with and sing with but I prefer to stay clear of these mass drunken sessions, with their bawdy songs, drunken games and deadly drunken fights. The battles are dangerous, but the celebrations of the warriors when they have tasted blood are far worse! I feel no urge to celebrate today; I simply feel relief at having survived. I have had the most horrific and terrifying experience today and I know that I am extremely fortunate to have got through this ordeal. What's more it is not over. The coming night will bring my horrors back to torment me again, my dreams will force me to go through it all again several times, probably every night for many weeks.

Just as we complete the occupation of the castle and its town we can see the fleet of Sihtric and Guthfrith who are finally arriving into the port. The timing was not too far out, only a few hours, but they have still missed the entire battle. It must all have looked so easy to them. They are still important as they are here now to join the new community, and belong to the enlarged army which will be drawn from this community and which should now be the force that will be capable of recapturing Dyflinn. Ragnald and I are both ecstatic as our long-held dream is about to come true at last.

So many years have passed since I had first looked over this castle from the nearby hill and dreamed that a warlock would carry us as black ravens into this great fortress and then turn us back into men after we had flown into it. I feared that warlock, especially if he took the side opposed to us. Now I have created the black ravens, by painting them on the sails of our boats and we are standing here as men in the impregnable castle that could not be taken, having taken it with our boats.

I feel like the warlock is right here, right now. I have become the warlock.

Chapter Thirteen

STRUGGLES WITH THE ANGLO-SAXONS

We are now based in our formidable fortress in Vannin and ready for the attack on Dyflinn, which is less than a day's sail away. We have the ideal location to descend on them unseen from the sea, and they will have absolutely no idea of the mighty force that has gathered here to sweep them away. Most of the surviving Lochlain community expelled from Dyflinn all those years ago are reunited here, and are together with a large contingent of Danir, both from Bardr's Vannin group and the mercenaries who have joined us over the past few months. We have created a position of great strength, and morale is sky high.

It is unlikely that the Irskrs have the slightest awareness of our presence here, or of our intentions. They are not going to be ready for the assault that is coming. Our revenge and our return to our home cannot be long delayed now. There is nothing to stop us.

There is however, time available to reflect a little on the next steps before we move, and it is wise to plan properly. Do we want our families to join us here immediately? Or is it better to leave them where they are and then just move them once, directly back to the Dyflinnarskiri? Do we need new reinforcements or do we have enough men? Will we have enough strength not just to take Dyflinn but to hold onto it afterwards?

For once even the ever active and impatient Ragnald pauses uncharacteristically to think things through. For some reason he decides that he needs to return to Prestune to build his strength even more, and that is the ideal place to do it. Normally I would be surprised that he chooses to go there at such a vital time, but I know that he has reasons of his own to visit that place. Although we can almost certainly take Dyflinn now, that venture can obviously wait until Ragnald has satisfied his other needs.

When we do attack we are likely to take Dyflinn unopposed, as long as we take the town by surprise. We will, however, soon come under attack again by a unified army of the kings of Leinster and Brega, who will probably come together again as they did earlier. That will take them some time but it is certain to happen. So we can take the town more easily than we can retain it and that ongoing defence is the critical aspect. We will need to station an army of men there for some time, and we will need to keep them occupied and to feed them.

We know well that it is easier to recruit a mercenary army than to keep them in place. The answer will be to set the Danir loose on the Irskric countryside, ravaging their villages and towns before their kings can bring their army together. That will also hinder the efforts of their kings to assemble their army. As they may find plunder difficult to gather it will be necessary to pay them to go in the first few months.

For that purpose Ragnald will want me to recover the buried silver, so that will be my next task. The money is needed now to feed and pay the existing army and especially to make further recruits. After that we will look to move our families to Vannin as a preliminary step to following the army back to Dyflinn. The plan is in place to achieve the objective that we set ourselves on Dalkey Island all those years ago.

Before we can act though, fate takes a different turn and gives us more issues to consider. We have a visitor from Danelaw, and it is our new friend Agmundr the Hold, who is here to request our urgent help. His lands are now being ravaged by a Mercian army who have now pressed into west Northumberland out of Mercia, having crossed the Mersam. They are pressing him hard and he is therefore in great need of help and reinforcement.

Initially Ragnald has little sympathy; he sees Agmundr is making the same request to him that Halfdan made a few weeks ago. Halfdan the King of Jorvik refused to honour his duty to help us then, as his battle with the Anglo-Saxons took priority. Why should Ragnald help the Danir now, when they did not help him? Let Agmundr go to Halfdan for that help.

I think things over and after contemplation I see things differently. So often Ragnald's ideas are limited by what he sees right in front of him. If he steps aside to view the wider context he might see that there are bigger prizes to be won. This could be Ragnald's opportunity to become king over both Jorvik and Dyflinn, and dominate the entire Scandinavian world. He now has the biggest Viking army, certainly as large as that of the Kings of Northumberland in Jorvik. He has attracted so many of their bravest and fiercest warriors already and his record of unbroken success is continuing to gain him new recruits. That is why the Danir are now turning to him rather than their own kings.

Halfdan, Eowils and Ivarr, the three Kings of Northumberland in Jorvik, are losing their battle with the Anglo-Saxons and so are likely to be deposed by their own people soon. That is one of the reasons so many of their men have come here to join Ragnald. It is not just evidence of Ragnald's strength but of their weakness, as their own army is now much reduced and under severe pressure from both the Wessex Saxons and Mercian Angles.

So Agmundr has come to ask assistance from us rather than from his own kings, knowing why their men are coming over to us in such great numbers. Although just a few weeks ago we saw our only prospect as begging assistance from the Kings of Jorvik but now our alternative strategy has succeeded so well that we are now stronger than they are. I think it is time of great opportunity; Ragnald can drive home his advantage, and take the crown of Northumberland for himself as well as take back Dyflinn.

We must, however, take care that there is a kingdom of Northumberland to rule. The Anglo-Saxons are a real and imminent threat to that kingdom and must be dealt with urgently. Their aggressive move into Danelaw makes dealing with that threat more urgent than the reconquest of Dyflinn.

If we take Northumberland from its Danish kings we can return to that Dyflinn project shortly with all of the resources of Jorvik behind us, and make its long term success even more certain. If we take Dyflinn first it will constantly drain resources out of our effort as it will then always need to be protected.

The emerging plan is therefore to divide our forces again just as we did with Ingamund, one force under Ragnald to take Jorvik and another, under Agmundr this time, to fight off the Anglo-Saxons. This is a plan we must keep covert, only Ragnald and I will know its total content.

Those most likely to stay staunchly loyal to Ragnald are the Lochlain, from the Wirral and also Gulthfrith and Sithric from the north, and so they will form the core of the force that will take Jorvik with Ragnald.

The Danir, both from Vannin and the mercenary army, might sympathise with the Kings of Jorvic in a fight against them, so they will be placed under Agmundr to fight the Anglo-Saxons. They will surely see him as one of their own, a natural leader for them in an assault on the Saxons. They will also instinctively feel that war against the Saxons is both natural and right for them, as battles between Danir and Saxon have dominated this land for several generations. It will also offer them great prospects of huge plunder, something that will appeal greatly to these greedy unruly men, and will take the pressure to provide them with rewards off us for a while.

If I say so myself it is a truly brilliant plan, incidentally one which once again allows Ragnald the chance to keep away from the most intense fighting. The city of Jorvik will already have been stripped of its troops to defend Danelaw against the Anglo-Saxons. He is very likely to take it unopposed.

There is a danger is that Agmundr will not succeed against the

Saxons, who will then continue to be a threat. Mercia may be weaker now, but it is increasingly clear that Wessex is a strong kingdom lead by a determined King. Edward the Elder is the true son to his father Alfred and has inherited his fighting abilities, his leadership skills and his understanding of strategy. Agmundr would look inexperienced and lightweight in comparison, so it is good that he is going to confront Mercia rather than Wessex.

Perhaps a greater danger though is that Agmundr will succeed and return at the head of an enlarged and confident force to turn Ragnald out of Jorvik. Ragnald decides that he will counter that prospect by offering to strengthen the planning capability of the Danish force attacking the Saxons by lending my services to Agmundr.

I will be his adviser and right-hand man during the campaign and that is a great endorsement of my capability as a military strategist. Agmundr and I are already friends, and so it is natural and easy for us both to agree to co-operate. It is very acceptable to me to have Agmundr as the leader; I have no ambition to compete with him as I am a commoner and have no noble blood. I only want my fair reward from this dangerous venture.

Besides I know now that I can influence things as much from the position of adviser and ensure that an element of the force will be loyal to me and therefore to Ragnald should the campaign end in a face off at Jorvik. The risks are very high, but it is not being offered as a choice. Ragnald promises to make me the Jarl with control over Dyflinn if I succeed. It is the great prize that I have always coveted. The time for my glory is about to come.

On the other hand it makes nonsense of my promise to Aud and my own resolution to stay out of danger and spend more time with my family, but it is clear that this one last great project can secure immense power and riches for both my king and myself. I can then obtain all of the rewards I deserve, including the right to retire to Dyflinn with my family in great luxury and with the power of a Jarl. I will not even need to work iron any more, unless I choose to.

It is clearly an appropriate reward for all my efforts on his behalf. As king of both Northumberland and Dyflinn such titles would be easily in Ragnald's gift. I am sure that he will also grant me enough land in the Dyflinarskiri to keep my family rich for generations to come. Even if he did not I would be in a position to just take it. It is a prize which is well worth one last big gamble.

The two fleets are allocated boats; around eighty boats will be available to each group now, including those that Agmundr can supply. It is a very large number which reflects our growing power and numbers. We have increased our resources considerably and our ability to raise two armies is a clear indicator of the way we have prospered.

Agmundr and I sail first for the Ripam, where he will raise his army to join mine and we will then move south together under his command. Ragnald will then follow a week later to make his move on Jorvik, although Agmundr is not made aware of this second part of our strategy. It is far better that he does not know at this point. Once Ragnald is safely established as the King of Jorvik it is certain that Agmundr be sufficiently pragmatic to accept him, but right now he might have confused loyalties having sworn to serve the triumvirate of Halfdan, Eowils and Ivarr. Once they are out of the way there will be no reason for such confusion, and Ragnald will be sure to put the trio securely in a place where they will never cause him any trouble in the future.

The approach along this estuary is very familiar now, but for once we will not proceed past the village of Prestune to the fording point where my silver is buried, nor will we continue to the old Roman road that leads to Jorvik. Agmundr takes just three days to gather his force which is quite an achievement in such a short time; it shows that he already has them in a high state of preparedness. This is the largest army I have ever seen, even larger than that which we put together to fight the Picts. It is certain to be needed as the foe we are now to encounter is more numerous, better armed, more cunning and in every way stronger than the Picts.

I am careful to keep close to Agmundr at all times, taking my place among the Jarls and confident now that I belong among them.

I may never be a king but surely I deserve that status of a Jarl already, and I know now that Ragnald will give me the title, and the wealth that goes with it once the war against the Anglo-Saxons is finally won.

I am surprised and unhappy to see Bardr Ottarson appear among Agmundr's associates, having thought that he had disappeared for ever after the battle of Vannin. I had hoped that he was dead. Naturally I complain angrily to Agmundr about his presence here. He has no right to be communicating with the Hold as though he was also an adviser. The complaint is brushed aside by Agmundr as though it is inconsequential; I am told that Bardr has no importance in this group, as he has contributed just a handful of men.

I do not like this development and consider that Agmundr is not giving me the respect to which I am entitled. Of course, it is true that Bardr is a minor player now, and I must hold real power in having Ragnald's ear. So why is Bardr here at all? It makes me very uneasy. I will be certain to tell Ragnald of this incident and its implied insult and ensure that Agmundr is at least punished for giving Bardr a place of honour as Ragnald's enemy. It also casts doubt on his trustworthiness as an ally, and this is a very unexpected and unwelcome cloud over our alliance with him.

Once the army is completely assembled we form the plan for this venture. The Mercians are likely to know about our presence here and will already know that we are preparing to move south. They will therefore have fortified the crossings over the River Mersam, as indeed Agmundr has on the northern side, making it more difficult to go that way, perhaps costing many lives. Even when we have forded that river they will be prepared for our arrival. We have a large army that could make progress but it is likely to get very well spread out across the countryside. A few horse borne raiders could harass the small groups of our rearguard if they get behind. It is also going to be difficult to find enough food to keep them alive and many of us may be hungry.

I believe the plains of north Mercia will by now have been stripped of any plunder for us, at least in the foodstuffs which will be our first and most urgent need. I predict that this route will have been made difficult for us. It is better to use our great strength which is our mobility, especially by sea, and as we have many boats now that strength is even greater.

My proposal is therefore to sail the entire army around the west coast, around the land of the Welsc and to enter into Mercia from the south. They will not be expecting us to arrive that way and we will therefore be much better able to live off the land, and make good progress, probably unopposed for some time. During that time we will be well fed and be able to gather plenty of food and plunder for the journey north.

Agmundr nods and smiles as he listens and immediately agrees it is a good plan, to start in the south and to fight our way back north again. Our intention is to ravage the Mercian lands as punishment for the way they have ravaged Danish land. This way they will learn of our military power and will not be tempted to attack us again. The plan is agreed and we load the whole army into the boats that brought us here from Vannin, plus the additional warriors that the Danir of Agmundrness have available to them.

Our boats are numerous and very full with men as we leave the Ripam. This is a very well prepared and equipped army and it is undertaking a well planned expedition but we are up against a formidable enemy. The campaign will be on a much larger scale than our venture into Fortriu, and the rewards must be huge too, in line with that scale.

Ironically, as we sail out to sea, we are passing close to my home on the Dee where Aud, Astrithr and little Thorfinn will be happily playing at this very moment. On this occasion there is no chance of diverting to see them, although my heart bleeds with anguish. I so much want to spend my time with them. This is man's business, however, and too serious to be interrupted by any other concerns. I hope to see them again soon and raise them up with me in my new status as I take my new position as the Jarl Amleth.

The journey will take us around three or four days and has a considerable number of hazards, especially high seas, tidal races and many savage rocks en route. Navigation is reasonably simple though as we only need to keep the coast in sight, initially to the south and then to the east after we pass the island of Môn. After that we pass along the west coast before turning into the Seafern Sea.

I find myself passing once more through very familiar waters as we leave the Ripam, and out into the open sea. In the distance, to the north, I can see the mountains of Vannin as they come into sight and move across the horizon as we move west. In the distant south I can see the Orme, which means the serpent, a hill which wriggles out of the land and into the sea.

Although it is late summer the rain falls continually and we are all soaking wet and cold. There is a strong wind against us and so the men must row for long periods, through a big swell, which often covers us in spray. It is hard labour in poor conditions. One or two are sea sick and their misery is compounded by being ridiculed as weaklings by the companions. This is a tough group of men with no tolerance of any weakness.

Then, as the hours pass and we go into night, we move towards Môn. As it is now dark we need to keep it well away, and keep it well to the south. We have no need to revisit those treacherous tidal races and to pass the craggy rocks that surround them. We know all too well how big their teeth are and how they can rip a boat apart. We have seen it happen before now.

Although I can see little in the dark it is enough to bring back the memories of the days immediately after we left Dyflinn. Everything that happened then is burnt onto my memory, as though that was the most important phase of my life. It was certainly the time at which my emotions were raised to burning point.

I can make out the cliffs of the cove where we first took shelter and then stayed until threatened by the King of Gwynedd. We have already passed the coast where we raided the village. The image of the black-haired maiden screaming in anguish passes over my mind again, as it has so often done before. Her fear and terror affected me like no one else's has ever done, before or since, though I have seen a lot of fear and terror.

Although we cannot see it we are now passing close to Dyflinn, our home and ultimate objective. It is just over the horizon, out of sight, but as always it is in the forefront of my thoughts. It will not be long now before we can return there with colossal strength to deliver vengeance and regain control of our homes.

During the night most of us sleep but the crew is divided into three groups so that one is always awake, steering the boat, watching the progress through the wind and the swell and always looking for hazards.

The weather was initially kind to us as we left Môn but then there was again persistent rain as there has been for almost the entire two days we have been at sea. We are passing the land of the Welsc, another old adversary, but an enemy which we can afford to avoid for a while. The priority now is to reduce the power of the Anglo-Saxons, our most immediate threat.

On the third day we get the nicest of conditions, sunshine and a strong west breeze. We find ourselves confronted with a very rocky stretch of sea with many small islands. This is the far west of the Welsc lands and a very dangerous place for boats. The tide flows unevenly here too and we find ourselves forced into passing close to shore to find the deepest water.

The water which was a dark grey green colour for much of the way is more often churned into white froth here. Standing waves are everywhere, raging and twisting the boats, and it is rumoured that dragons live in these waters. We know that we have to fight hard against the currents to keep our boats under control, and regret not having made more sacrifices to Thor. The men, who are already exhausted from the limited sleep that they have had, now have to row hard to keep us in the safe channels and off the rocks.

We get past it with only one incident where a boat is rolled over in the turbulent tide and all the men drowned. No one comes to the surface after the boat rolls, and they must have been taken by the dragons. We are pleased to get away from this evil place and we can then turn towards the east, into the calm waters of the Seafern Sea and towards the distant shores of Wessex and Mercia.

Another day uneventfully passes as we move along the north coast passing many large headlands. This must be Thor's blessing on the fighting men. They are almost all exhausted and lying around the boat sleeping. Just a few of us are awake keeping the boat safe and on course, though that is easy now in these pleasant, benign conditions. Our men will need to arrive rested and in good condition as they will be in hostile land from the minute we arrive.

We can see that the Welsc Britons have a lot of rich land here, unlike the mountainous territory of their north. It is worth remembering this, as there will be more times in the future when we will want to find riches to rob. We know the Saxons have often made raids and they have even left settlements here. Eventually we find ourselves entering a very long fjord of the Seafern between two stretches of low land. It is so wide here that we cannot see the southern shore.

The westerly winds fill our sails here and we are swiftly carried deep into the Seafern in only a day's sailing, until the low hills come into sight on the southern bank. This is our first sight of Wessex, the land of our strongest enemy. We need to pause here for a while to await the incoming tide which can carry us quickly and much further inland with deeper water; the tides are very large and fast flowing here and the water is very shallow at low tide.

The estuary is still wide and deep enough to make navigation easy as long as we can find and stay in the channel, and it remains so for many miles into the hinterland. Eventually the channel narrows so it is now clearly a tidal river rather than the open sea, and it twists and turns as we reach further inland. Now we are definitely in southern Mercia rather than Wessex. All we need to do now is to decide how far inland to travel before we start our campaign against the Angles.

We must be a terrifying sight for any Mercians that see us. A huge fleet of boats, each clearly signalling its war like intentions with our high sails, mostly with the broad red vertical stripes that are usually associated with war ships. Brightly painted shields are displayed on shield racks along the sides of the boats. Perhaps most terrifying of all will be the sight of our men. Mostly they are muscular, long-haired, heavily bearded and wild-eyed: brutal men who are thirsty for killing and greedy for loot.

We will need to take to the land soon and eventually the river decides it for us as we reach a point where all the boats ground. Although we feel we might be able to go further if we await the next tide, we are passing by good land filled with wealthy farms and we know it is time to start our plundering. Our men leap into the water to lift the boats onto the beach to unload their equipment. We have arrived and Mercia is about to know the wrath of the Vikings.

A good number of men have to be left here with the boats reducing our numbers. They are not here to guard the boats this time but to take them back to either Vannin or the Ripam. There is no point in leaving them here, we will not return to this place. Our intention is to march north, eventually returning over land to the Mersam and then back home into Danelaw. The Angles will possibly confront us somewhere, but we can have done them great damage by then and we will certainly have taken a lot of plunder.

There is no Ragnald here to take all of the silver and so for once I can gain my own fair share. I believe it is time that I gained some proper rewards for all my efforts and the huge risks that have been taken with my life. This is my time, the time to enrich myself before taking a well-earned retirement to a farm in the Dyflinskari.

After camping overnight we set out to burn all the nearby villages and every farm we encounter, taking away any livestock or grain to feed our army. The destruction of the farms is as important to us as taking plunder, since we need to demonstrate the destructive power of our army. It is important to impose ourselves on the Anglo-Saxons so that in the future they will pay tributes to persuade us to stay away from their lands.

This is rich farm land as the valley of the Seafern is extremely wide, fertile and prosperous, so we find easy and fat pickings here and no organised opposition. There is plentiful food, even to maintain such a huge horde as our army. It was a great plan to come this way, and we have clearly surprised the Mercians completely. Agmundr should be pleased with my brilliant strategy!

We already know that King Edward of Wessex is away from here assembling a fleet of ships somewhere in the far south. We should get no interference from him and may be able to complete a devastating raid on the Mercian land, burning it and laying it waste as we go, and gaining great riches for ourselves. The Christian churches give particularly good rewards as they are often filled with gold and silver objects which their worshippers have placed here to buy their eternal salvation. I wonder if their god will still honour his debt to them now that the treasures are in our hands. They say he is a caring god.

If we are very fortunate we might escape completely unchallenged by any Angle or Saxon army and perhaps with few or even no casualties. That might just be wishful thinking, as it is far more likely that we will be challenged at some point. The Mercians surely must make more attempt than this to defend their land and property.

The Wessex Saxons under Alfred built great forts or buhrs to resist the Danes. Wessex is covered in the buhrs but south Mercia has fewer and is therefore more vulnerable. They have concentrated their efforts in building in the north where they see that the threat from the Danes is much closer.

Nevertheless they have already taken a great deal of their wealth into those buhrs that they have here, especially at Gleawcestre. We get there on the second day, and find it well-defended and full of anxious and frightened Angles. That town would be a very rich prize but will take a lot of time to take. That might allow an Anglo-Saxon army to attack us from the rear, so we decide to simply bypass it and continue north. Our strategy is to strike hard and fast, then to keep moving. So much easier and safer, and we already have a massive amount of plunder.

For now there is no organised opposition and our campaign is going very well, we are delighted by our success. Each village falls in turn, with no effective resistance from any one. Just occasionally a group of brave and foolish men who choose to die in a futile defence of their land when cornered. They never last for long.

When I come across Agmundr he has fulsome praise for my strategy, and so I can also congratulate him on his handling of the army and its operations. It is a very good humoured exchange between us, full of mutual admiration and good will. We are discussing how to proceed now, but there will be little change. We just continue north, looting and plundering as we go.

Our success has depended on our ability to move quickly, and so we now continue to move rapidly, no need to delay. Everywhere we go the Angles flee in droves before us and leave us much of their wealth to plunder. We do not know this country well but it is obvious that the river Seafern goes a long way north towards our homelands. So if we follow its course it will take us most of the way home.

Our successful progress continues for several days, so successful that we are getting heavily burdened with plunder, almost too much to carry. Now we are also starting to take many slaves to carry the goods, as well capturing as oxen and horses to pull carts and all of these are filled with goods which are our rewards for this success.

Now we are even starting to leave some goods behind us, especially cattle, as we already have as many as we can sensibly herd northwards. We already have a substantial herd and the slaves are having difficulty in handling them. In turn we are stretched trying to control the slaves who continually try to escape. Most days we have to kill a dozen or so to keep control of the others. There is no difficulty in replacing them with new ones as we continually capture more land and take more captives.

The plan to harry the entire land of Mercia is succeeding better than we could ever have expected. Although they have avoided great casualties by fleeing before us we have taken great numbers as slaves and a huge amount of their wealth.

On the sixth day we are surprised to find ourselves meeting up with another Danish army which is lead by my former acquaintance King Halfdan, and his fellow King of Northumberland, Ivarr, who

I have never met before. They have heard of our initial success and brought a smaller army from Jorvik, which now combines into an even great force. They have sailed down the Trente, a long river from the east and journeyed right into the centre of Mercia. Clearly they are anxious to share in our success and will certainly intend to claim the credit for all of it.

Their first action is to stop the progress of our army to allow them to assess our strength and to allow them to take control from Agmundr and myself. This is contrary to our strategy and I think it is foolish to stop at this point. It makes me confident that the Angles will now try to join the battle with us. I have mixed feelings about the presence of the Jorvik kings for reasons of my own.

By being here they will avoid Ragnald's assault on their city. Although that makes Ragnald's success even more likely it also means that they will survive to cause future problems. Even more threateningly it leaves me in the hands of a potentially very hostile group of deposed Danir kings. I will become a hostage or the victim of their revenge. It might even be better for me if this army does need to face the Anglo-Saxon army. If they do not I will need to make an escape sometime late in the campaign, preferably taking my large group of Danir mercenaries with me if I can persuade them to come.

The addition of two kings has disrupted our command structure and Halfdan has now assumed control. He does not want any advice from either Agmundr or I, believing in his own ability to command. In effect we have been dismissed from our commands. Although we know the bulk of the men here and are aware of their strengths and limitations far better than he does he has dismissed our opinions as being of no importance. I have little or no knowledge of his ability as a war leader, but the initial signs are not promising. This does not seem too important though. In a campaign were no one opposes us any one can lead a great army. He is just here at the last minute, in order to claim the credit and steal the glory.

Instead of the mobile army of savage raiders able to manoeuvre easily and flexibly that we started with, we have become a vast lumbering train spread out over many miles and easily seen and tracked. In Fortriu I was always anxious to keep the army as compact as possible and even then we lost men to harassing Picts. Here the Viking host and the massive baggage we have acquired in the form of plunder has made that a hopeless task. Halfdan and Ivarr seem oblivious of any need to try.

This must allow the Anglo-Saxon army to find us if they choose to, but it is still not clear that they will want to engage us in a set piece battle. We are a huge formidable, well-armed albeit now badly organised force. Many of us are true warriors, trained and equipped for battle.

The combined army stays a few days to rest and to allow the change of leadership. I guess that Halfdan is thinking through his route, but I do not know what the delay is as I am not included in the discussions any more. He appears not to believe in the need for speed over the ground which was the major element of our original strategy. Clearly he thinks that the Anglo-Saxons do not have any ability to oppose him and, as we have not had any reports of any Anglo-Saxon army, he may prove correct. On the other hand he seems not to be scouting the ground around him very energetically so we might not know, even if an enemy army was nearby.

He might well change our route in order to move further east. Agmundr and I were committed to returning over the Mersam into the south west corner of Danelaw as that is near our homes, but Halfdan may well want to travel to ensure the plunder moves towards his own base in Jorvik. That would involve crossing hills rather than the easy passage through the plains that we had intended.

If he does that then he might, although he cannot know this, eventually find himself opposed by Ragnald's army, regardless of what the Saxons do. If so, I will need to take my men to join Ragnald against him. In preparation for this I spend my time among my own men, rather than among the Jarls where I am obviously less welcome now. I need to ensure that I keep in touch with them and maintain their loyalty. We need to retain a separate identity from Agmundr's army. One day we may need to fight against them.

Halfdan still has no knowledge of Ragnald's actions, but I expect that by now Jorvik may be taken, and then that news will reach Halfdan quite soon. When it does I will immediately be in great danger, but I cannot leave this Danish army now while we are in such hostile territory.

Over the next day things do move at last, and we soon find ourselves encountering continual harassing raids by groups of Saxons. This may be a sign that indicates they do have an organised army nearby and clearly they now know where we are. Halfdan's decision to stop and rest always looked dangerous to me and I fear it may have played into the hands of the Anglo-Saxons.

After a long march we reach a narrow gorge, through which the Seafern River plunges over a series of weirs, and here we suffer a great shock which changes everything dramatically.

The narrow valley is filled by a vast host of Saxons in front of us, not just a normal group but a huge and well-organised army. This is a great surprise to us, and not a nice one. It had not been part of my strategy under Agmundr to face a determined foe but to move quickly and thus avoid the need for pitched battle. I have no idea what Halfdan's strategy was, and I suspect that he has little idea either.

If necessary we will give a good account of ourselves but in recent fights the Saxons have been the more effective in a pitched battle. Having seen so much of their land ravaged, and so many men, women and children killed or enslaved they will be spoiling for a fight, desperate for revenge.

The prospect of the battle ahead is therefore a very threatening one. This new situation has changed our campaign from unlimited and unopposed success into a very serious and evenly contested war. It is time for a change in plan and a new route and so we turn away from the river and now move away from the Saxons, travelling east. We hope to outrun the Saxons and escape. We know that they will have the same problems in moving an army as we do, but at least we are already prepared and motivated to move quickly. They may be more effective in a pitched battle but we are probably better in a chase.

It is an exhausting process though and after just a day it is clear that we have not succeeded in shaking them off. It obviously calls for a new move but I have no influence on the decision making any more. It is up to Halfdan to devise our strategy now! I hope he does it well; my life and that of all these others depend on it. I find it very worrying.

The Anglo-Saxon army has pursued us vigorously and is able to continuously harass our rearguard. We are suffering substantial losses and Halfdan decides it is better to turn and fight them. I would not have done this and would have continued to fall back rather than confront them. I believe it is probably an error; certainly it plays to the Anglo-Saxons' preferred strategy.

This way Halfdan may believe that we at least get the chance to assemble our men and have our choice of battlefield. In practice, the latter turns out to be of little advantage since this is flat land; there are no high slopes to give us an advantage. Halfdan has chosen a place which we now name Woden's Field for the conflict, dedicating it to that god in the hope that he will inspire us and guide us. We make it our own by raising our pennants, I can show the black raven of Woden on my pennant, flying above my men. It may become the place where many of us will go to meet Woden as I cannot see what advantage we can gain from fighting here, it looks like a mistake to me. If I am right then it will cost many, many Scandinavian lives.

The moment has come when two great armies will clash head to head. It is going to be a far larger battle than we have fought before, either against the Picts or anyone else.

Both sides have drawn up their armies to confront each other, very close together with just a brook between us, and both must present a fearsome sight to the other. Flags and banners are waved on both sides, colourful symbols of faiths and families. Ravens, stags, skulls and boar's heads are displayed on our side, and many crosses, saints and bishops on the other. I can see my own black raven, Agmundr's red battle axe and Halfdan's grey wolf. There are so many different colourful tunics and so many men in mail, all with axes or swords in their hands.

The shouting and banging of shields creates an enormous noise as each side threatens and tries to intimidate the other. Each army is issuing threats and invoking their god or gods to defeat the god or gods of the other side. The sights and sounds of the impending battle are a great drama, and if we were not all so terrified then no doubt it would be a great thing to witness.

Although we did not choose to make this battle we are brave warriors and very determined that we will give a good account of ourselves. Our men are confident, strong and well-fed, and we all know that this is the defining moment of our lives. We must win this fight or we will certainly be killed far from home in the middle of a foreign and hostile land. It will be impossibly dangerous to take flight as part of a defeated army.

We are all frightened but we are also grimly determined. We gain huge energy from this desperation too; the adrenalin is flowing in our veins. We show all the ferocity and aggression that is always expected from Vikings. We are shouting and screaming insults and threats at the combined Angles and Saxons, who respond in the same way.

Once the two armies have assembled opposite each other the plan is to strike early and strike hard, hitting out at the main body of the Saxons. This time there is no Ragnald to inspire us, and there is no sign of Agmundr or the Danir kings either.

I finally see Agmundr alongside Bardr Ottarson on the far left flank. It looks like they have left me to lead the very centre of the main attack, looking for a less dangerous position for themselves. I can see now that Bardr has been quietly plotting with Agmundr against me all the time and this is what Agmundr has agreed to do, place me at the very heart of the fighting where I am most likely to be killed. In doing so he has gained himself a place on the flanks with a better chance of survival.

The Danir obviously look after each other and are happy to do so at the expense of a Lochlain, even though it is a betrayal of their alliance with Ragnald. Halfdan and Eowils seem to be in on the plot too, as they have gathered themselves on the far right flank. I am alone in leading the centre.

They believe Ragnald will never hear of this betrayal as they must expect that I will not survive the battle. This is not the time to ponder such things, however, as there is no time to waste now responding to their treachery and duplicity. My best response is to ensure that I do survive. The battle against the Saxons must be won first. They will be held to account for this, as I know that by now Ragnald will be in possession of Jorvik. By choosing to lead their army here, into the centre of Mercia they have removed their last chance of defending their own city and lost their crowns.

I am angry, very angry and although I will initially take out this anger on the Saxons, it will also be turned on the treacherous Agmundr and Bardr after that battle. I will wait until they are drunk and sleepy in the after battle celebrations and then strike them both down in the middle of the night. I will take my revenge in cold blood in the middle of the night.

I might not have chosen to be the great leader of warriors but that is what I must now be. I have never thought of myself as Ragnald but I have seen him in action from close quarters so many times and I know what must be done and how to do it. It must be done with the greatest courage, conviction and vigour. This is the greatest moment of my life, the climax of my career as a warrior.

I give a great shout, imitating those I have heard from Ragnald my king, and we form a solid shield wall and all throw ourselves together down the gentle slope, charging into the Saxon masses and clashing greatly with their shield wall and attempting to force our way through it. This tactic catches them by surprise. Normally the shield walls advance slowly, deliberately and reluctantly. It is the place of death and nowhere is as terrible, as terrifying. Not even the fiercest of warriors relish their place in the shield wall, and so most move cautiously into battle.

The first attempt forces them back but fails to break their wall and as they recover and hold firm they begin to push back. I have men at my back pressing me forward to resist the force of the Saxons, and I need their help though I feel I will be crushed in the middle of the mêlée. The two armies are right against each other now and hacking and flailing at each other around and under the shields. We are face to face with those who want to kill us, so close that we can smell the putrid ale on their breath. It is a terrible mess, a carnage in which no one is gaining the advantage, but swords and axes are flailing and many, many men are dying. It is a bloody stalemate in which we must continue to fight with frenzy and succeed or die.

The Saxons are trying to break our shield wall by throwing their battleaxes onto the tops of our shields; either coming down onto them to splinter the wood or hooking them over our shields so they can pull them down. Those that are pulled down are followed by our men behind us throwing spears into the Saxon ranks and they are returning those spears, throwing them into our ranks. I had wanted to assemble archers for this task but Halfdan had rejected my suggestion contemptuously. The Danes consider archery as a coward's tactic, but now they are dying in their hundreds for the sake of their foolish courage when they made that decision. The screams and gurgles of dying men ring all around me, but I can hardly hear them as my brain is totally focussed on trying to stay alive myself.

Both sides are stabbing and slashing frenziedly with their swords, around, above and below the shields. Those with short swords have the advantage in this close quarter work. There is no more room to swing a battle axe or a two-handed sword. Many men are falling on both sides, often with wounds to their ankles or legs. There are many dying and wounded but neither side has gained any real advantage.

Suddenly we become aware that there are Saxons behind us too, many of us have to turn, attempting to form a new shield wall to resist them but we are now in a desperate position, completely surrounded and trapped. We must now fight our way out, but we have not succeeded in reforming the shield wall around us. It is simply man against man in broken and chaotic fighting. I can see the wild staring eyes of the Saxon warriors, every bit as frightened and as excited as we are, all knowing that we now must triumph or die.

The Saxons are pouring through the gaps like demons and the bloodlust is upon them, they are cutting down many of our men, who are visibly shrinking before their onslaught. The Saxons have become hugely confident and our men look broken and defeated.

I find myself in the very heart of the fight facing a very tall blond Saxon, who is well-armed and beautifully clothed in cloth of many colours. He is obviously a man of some standing, wealth and almost certainly of noble birth. It seems he has recognised me as a leader too, as an opponent of high status, and has thus sought me out to attack. I admit that I feel fear but I also feel pride and defiance, I am a strong, capable warrior and can believe in my fighting abilities. I have survived so many raids and battles and I know that I can fight well, and I will do so now. Only one of us will survive here, it is a battle to the death. I expect to be that survivor; I need to be the victor.

There are very few preliminaries and such conflicts are sometimes short and bloody. Occasionally they might be long and exhausting, a great test of stamina, but they are always tests of physical and mental strength. It is survival of the strongest, the fittest and the most savage. For the first time I pray to the one handed god, Tyr, to support me in this single conflict. He has never been my protector before as I never intended to become involved in a single combat, and I have never made sacrifices to him.

I strike out hard at the Saxon lord, my blade going past his shield and clashing with his blade with a loud ringing, the vibrations travelling into my hand and arm. Then we strike out at each other again and the sound this time is quite different as we hit, more a short dull "clunk". I look down at my blade to see it has sheared off at the hilt, a straight break across the whole shaft. The blade clatters past my ear and is now lying on the floor and all I have in my hand is the handle. It is the worst horror that I can imagine in these circumstances!

I stare at it, first with shock and terror, but then with a numbing feeling of doom! Here I am in the midst of a battle to the death and am relying on this sword to save my life, but here it is useless and in pieces. The sword I made myself in my own forge and decorated,

217

but the silver and amber on the handle I am still holding are of little value to me now. My pride and joy is broken! The glorious symbol of all my successes and achievements.

I still have the sword handle in my hand, and hope that is enough for the Valkyrie to take me to the feasting hall in Valhalla.

I am clearly in mortal danger and look up towards my opponent, just in time to see his triumphant grin and the sword in his hand, which is already swinging downwards in an arc towards my head.

MAP

X Fortriu

Vannin X

Jorvik●

● Prestune

IRISH SEA

DANELAW

Dyflinn X

Môn X

Wirral

X Ceaster

GWYNNEDD

X Wodens Field

MERCIA

Gleawcestre
●

SEAFERN SEA

● Major towns

X Battle sites

WESSEX

home in the
Oyflinnarskiri

I can see the bleak, dark hills from here, looking across the green valley of the Dyflinnarskiri. The colours and shapes on the slopes are picked out clearly in the bright sunshine.

Even they, so bleak and drab on a wet autumn or winter's day, are a beautiful and very familiar sight on a warm summer's day. This scene speaks to me of so many happy days from my idyllic childhood that I spent here with the sweetheart of my youth. The great and only love of my life, whom I then married and had our two lovely children with. If only we could have been together here and now, how happy and content we would be now that we have the chance to live in peace in our own land. This is that little piece of the Dyflinnarskiri that we always coveted and planned to have for ourselves.

Now our struggles are all over and our battles are won, we have enough wealth to get a small farm and live peacefully and well. Our people have reclaimed our lands, our birth right, here in this beautiful green and fertile land. Now it is the land of my fulfilment and eternal youth. A gentle summer breeze is blowing through the meadow, rippling the grass, and I can see my daughter Astrithr playing happily in the sunshine with her brother Thorfinn on this lovely warm summer evening. They are both teenagers now and have developed into really beautiful healthy blond children. It may not be long before they too find their future husband and wife, and then the next generation will be born, continuing the Scandinavian tradition we have established in this part of the world.

We are fortunate to have this lovely farm, the second one that I have developed extensively, and certainly the larger of the two. It is my final property as we are now back in our own homeland, I intend to stay for the rest of my life and eventually die of old age here. My wanderings are finally over; I am content with who I am, what I have and where I live.

We keep just enough cattle to pull the plough and our team of oxen are very valuable to us, our pride and joy. We have a male calf that was born in spring which will be fattened up on summer grass, before being killed in the late autumn to give us beef in the winter. We need to reserve the winter fodder for the sheep and the cattle that breed in the new year.

Our sheep have also prospered this year and produced many young, so we have a larger group than ever before, and we can put their milk into cheese making. Of course, most of their males will also be slaughtered to give us meat throughout those long dark winter months. As we are now in summer they are yielding good amounts of wool which we are collecting to be spun and then woven to keep us clothed.

The doves have also grown in number and they will be available for eating at the end of the winter when there is little other meat. The woods nearby afford us plenty of wood and twigs for our fires in the winter, and are a good place for the pigs to snuffle out nuts, acorns and berries. We are also fond of the berries in autumn if we can get there in time before the pigs take them all. It has always been important for us to work in line with the seasons, and take advantage of what nature offers when it offers it. In this happy place natural order has fallen into place to keep us always well fed and content.

The river and its many small brooks always offer fish, especially plenty of eels. The open sea is not far away and also full of all sorts of fish which are plentiful and good to eat. We were once used to eating large amounts of shell fish from the beach but we are too far inland now. Occasionally we will make the long walk to gather them as they are now a special treat, having once been every day fare.

I am fortunate to still have the assistance of Brodir, that young man who worked for me as a smith, then a moneyer. Today he is a great help in running all aspects of the farm and, of course, he still works in iron. He is far more skilled than Amleth. Brodir has been with me and the children so long that he is now one of the family.

We have several slaves working for us, captured from one of the raids on Môn; they have been with us for a few years and are progressing well in their knowledge of the Norse language. I think they are happy living with us as they do not get beaten or mistreated, as they know many others living nearby so often do. They too are almost like part of the family. It's an advantage for them to live in a household where a woman is in charge. One of them has developed a talent for bee keeping and we have seven hives which bring us all the honey we might need for sweetening and making preserves. There is a surplus to sell and it is very popular for making mead, which all Viking men love.

It is ten long years now since my husband died in combat with the Saxons, and we have had to learn to fend for ourselves. I had already done so as he was so often absent anyway that my mother and I always looked after the children and tended the farm. He had to make so many visits to negotiate and discuss great plans with important people, in addition to the actual raids and campaigns. He had no time left for the ordinary things of family life and running the farm.

When he was at home he spent most of time playing at his iron working although it was well known that he had little skill for that trade. The local smiths used to laugh about his efforts, saying the only things he could make were horse shoes. Everything else he ever made broke the first time or second time it was used. We could have been content if only he had used that time playing with his children and attending his wife.

How much happier we would all have been if he had stayed with us instead of pursuing his ambitions and engaging in great wars and adventures. When he was with us he was really a wonderful caring father, especially attentive to little Astrithr who was his real favourite. He never got to know Thorfinn, who was still a babe when he died. I am certain that his son would have benefitted greatly from his father's time and interest, and I find it difficult to keep back my tears as I think of the great opportunity that they both lost. Thorfinn has grown up in great awe of his father's reputation and treasures his legacy as a great man. All he has inherited from his father though is a black raven banner which is his most treasured possession. He was once given a broken sword handle too, but I had to take it away from him as it made me burst into tears every time I saw it.

Naturally I always hated Amleth's constant journeys away from us and was always convinced that he was not faithful to me. A Viking warrior can be many things and have great strengths, but fidelity to their wives is not one of them. They are never faithful. I do not even believe that he restricted himself to the slave girls that were captured. A successful warrior, even if he is already married, is very attractive to a certain type of Scandinavian women. Someone like Amleth was certainly wealthy enough to have several concubines. Such a role would have offered an improved life and even higher status for a poor girl, and such women gathered around him like moths around a light.

He was much more of a success in his role as counsellor to the king. Ragnald certainly valued his advice, and gave him many tasks that could only be given to his most trusted servant. He performed great deeds and had marvellous achievements but now he only exists in my memories, everyone else has forgotten him now, those great deeds and achievements are just lost forever in the mists of time.

At the end it seems that even the skill in planning battles failed him, as his final battle against the Saxons was a great disaster, a huge defeat for the Danir. So many Viking warriors were killed there, including the Kings Halfdan and Ivarr and Jarl Agmundr who was the leader of that army and, of course, his adviser and the representative of Ragnald, my own dear husband Amleth.

The story we heard later was that the Mercian Angles seem to have gained their victory by sending a great army of their own to intercept and trap the Vikings and also by gaining the co-operation of King Edward of Wessex, known as the Elder, who also sent a great Saxon army to join them. They seem to have had excellent knowledge of the movements of the Danish army and to have also moved their own armies without the Vikings ever being aware of those movements.

Even during the final battle the Anglo-Saxons managed to out manoeuvre the Scandinavians who charged the Mercian army only to find themselves out flanked by the Wessex army attacking them from behind. Most of the Vikings were slaughtered, either during the battle or in the Saxon's pursuit of them afterwards, and I am fortunate to have heard any of this account since so few survived to tell the story.

The setback was catastrophic for the Kings of Northumberland, who lost so many of their men, including their leaders, and it allowed Ragnald to depose the remaining king in Jorvik, called Eowulf, and he did so very easily. Amleth's legacy to Ragnald was a strategy that made him king of both Jorvik and Dyflinn, the two great seats of Viking power. Naturally he will always need to defend that kingdom against the Anglo-Saxons who are now stronger and more confident than ever.

So much has happened in those ten years; the Lochlain and Ragnald in particular, have grown greatly in power and strength through their dominance of these two great cities Jorvik and Dyflinn. The Lochlain lead the Danir now, even though they are so much more numerous than we are.

Although Amleth got a great deal of credit for Ragnald's early plans the king himself has really grown in power since his death. We hardly see him now since he became the king of Jorvik and he became a lot less interested in Dyflinn after he gained that crown. He has to be ever vigilant against the raids from Mercia which I believe are growing all the time. I am not sure he has ever been here since it was actually his cousin Sihtric who finally recovered it from the Irskr for the Vikings, albeit with warriors of Ragnald's army.

Ragnald has fulfilled his vow to free Dyflinn from the Irskrs but he did not do it immediately or alone. He benefitted greatly from the arrival of a large group of Viking warriors who came to this island from Frankia under another Jarl named Ottar, having first been beaten off in Wessex. They and Ragnald harried the Irskrs savagely in the south of this island and weakened them greatly so that when it then fell to Sihtric to lead the army that retook Dyflinn he did so unopposed. He was given the task by Ragnald, who then went away to busy himself fighting the Anglo-Saxons in Danelaw at the time, Jorvik already being his capital by then.

Sihtric did his job very effectively too after Ragnald's departure, following up the success of his initial raid and occupation of the city by defeating the full army of King of Leinster, and making the Dyflinnarskiri safe for us to occupy. We are still an important part of Ragnald's empire though, and his cousin is loyal and supports him with a strong fleet and supplies additions to his army when it is needed, as it so often is. There are still so many young men anxious to go to war and make their reputations and their fortunes.

Following the victory over the Irskrs we all were given the opportunity to come back here to the place where I grew up as a young girl, and there was a lot of land available to any who could take it. It was always an ambition for Amleth and I to have a small farm in the Dyflinnarskiri, and I have now had to fulfil it without him. My mother Grunhilde also made it back here with me but she died soon afterwards. We visit her grave very often, as it serves as a tribute to all of the men and women of our family who did not make it to see this beautiful little home. It is everything I ever wanted but would gladly sacrifice it all to have Amleth, Edda and my mother Grunhilde back with us.

At the time of Amleth's death and shortly afterwards Ragnald came to see me at our home on the Wirral, and at first I was touched by his sympathy and flattered by the attention of such a great man. The sympathy started to wear off quite soon, and it became obvious that his real purpose in talking to me was to gain information about the location of the buried silver hoard. He continuously and repetitiously asked me about anything that Amleth had said that might reveal the site where the hoard is buried.

In fact, my husband had talked about it quite often as it had become something of an obsession with him, and he was convinced that some day he would probably be tortured to reveal its whereabouts. In the end, it was I who was tortured by Ragnald's ceaseless pestering on the subject.

Naturally I told him all I knew, particularly of the alignment of the two oak trees at the side of the fording point, the highest navigable point on the river Ripam. It seems an obvious and clear statement and I think that even I, a mere woman, could find it from that description. I was unable to answer many of his other additional questions though. Once Ragnald returned with a new set of questions after several days on the site near Prestune, which he had obviously spent digging. He still smelt of damp earth and his finger nails were black with soil.

It seems that he had found quite a number of oak trees around that point not just two, and Amleth had not even told us which bank of the river the silver had been buried on. So much detail of its location was lost forever at the time of his death. I do not believe that Ragnald has ever found it but he has so much more wealth now that even a vast hoard like that is unlikely to matter to him anymore. He will be able concentrate on his new wealth; he now owns a great deal of gold, and can forget his old fortune in silver, just as he seems to concentrate on new kingdom of Jorvik, and forget his old kingdom of Dyflinn.

It was sad to see how much Ragnald has aged and his health deteriorated. The proud and handsome young man that fought Ivarr to gain the kingship was every woman's idea of the physically perfect man. Now he has declined into a fat balding old man with bad breath and black teeth, and no woman could find him physically attractive now. Yet they say his appetite for young girls is keener than ever before and since he gained all this wealth and power there are no shortage of young women eager to satisfy his lust.

To my mind, however, the physical changes are not as bad as the way his character has decayed. In those early days he was hot-headed and wilful but also determined and purposeful. He seems to be always genuinely concerned with the welfare of his people, a good and caring king to be admired.

Nothing could be further from the truth now, as his exposure to so many battles and so much suffering and bloodshed seems to have deprived him of any human feelings towards his fellow man. His great power seems to have gone to his head and he has become a moody and bad tempered tyrant, ruling over his people with a rod of iron, executing people for the least misdemeanour or even a misconceived slight. I confess that I was very frightened of him while he was here. I had no confidence that old friendships or even the great service my husband had given him would count for anything if he flew into a rage.

I am terribly sad for his wife and family, he treats them very badly. My husband was more kindly to me, and yet in a way he has also abandoned us. I blame him completely, there was no sensible reason to keep pushing himself forward to fight in the front line of every battle.

I will just live out my life quietly and contentedly, raising my children and developing the farm. If we ever have any problems in the future I can always fall back on the savings that Amleth left me. We had it for our old age which we planned to spend together in comfort in our small farm in the Dyflinnarskiri.

These seven bags of silver are probably more than I will ever need.

Chapter Fifteen

RAGNALD'S VOICE

The one and only thing I ever left Amleth to do on his own was to bury the silver and return with a proper description of where he buried it. Yet he has completely cocked it up, there is no sign anywhere of my treasure. May he rot forever in Niflheim! No doubt he will too, as he was a terrible excuse for a warrior and can hardly have died a good death.

In everything else he ever did I had to look over his shoulder and look after him! I always guided him and prevented him making mistakes.

Perhaps I was a fool to befriend him in the first place, but he was such a charming youth when I first met him. In those first days after we lost Dyflinn he was in complete awe of me and followed me like a puppy dog. That was very useful at times, and I especially remember how enthusiastically he ran to my red and gold banner after I had killed Ivarr at Dalkey Island, once the warriors were given permission to gather under banner of the Jarl of their choice.

He must have been so impressed by me, as I slew that useless imbecile Ivarr in single combat. At least Ivarr got a warrior's death but I am sure the Valkyrie would have turned their noses up at him after his death and refused to carry him to Valhalla. He was a fat, stupid useless bastard and I beat him so easily. It was a great laugh to cut him up and then carry off his crown, his wife and his treasure! I am sure that everyone, not just Amleth, should have thought I was the king of all kings that night. Some hesitated though.

As others hesitated Amleth ran to serve me and I am sure that he convinced many of those who were unsure to follow me. I owed him something for that action, and after that I had to raise him up in my service, although I wondered how he could ever make a warrior, when he was just that tall, slender, pretty red-headed boy?

In the end he escaped through all those battles with hardly a mark on him, no war wounds that you would notice, he only ever got the odd scratch until the Saxon caved his head in. Either he was amazingly lucky in battle or, more likely, he just kept out of the way when the real fighting started.

After that victory at Dalkey my fame as a fighter was so widespread that bad King Ottar of Vannin shit himself and just ran away when I challenged him to fight. I think he would rather have faced Tyr himself. Then the damn coward hid behind his army. It showed me how fickle Woden can be when it was I who had to leave rather than that coward Ottar.

It was not long though before I was back to get revenge, with my clever ploy to capture Ottar, right under the noses of his army, in his own castle. He underestimated my great cunning and paid the price. That time the gods backed the real winner, the man they knew deserved victory, but it taught me to make more sacrifices to the gods. They are greedy beings, and I have learnt that they love human death above all other sacrifices.

Anyway, enough of my achievements, many others will talk about them over the next few centuries, and back to Amleth. I remember how surprised and delighted he was when I first gave him a bit of responsibility, all that long time ago on the island of Môn. How his little eyes lit up when he got a few little jobs to do. The first thing he ever had to do was guard a few slave women at Maes Ofeilon but even that was beyond him. He got over excited when one of them flashed her tits and smiled at him so that he needed to drink off his anxiety in gallons of mead.

The really dreary thing about Amleth was that he was always telling us what a great and faithful husband he was, and that he never wanted any other woman but his wife Aud. I guess he was surprised at getting married to such a great looking lass and was always afraid that she would run off with someone else. In fact, she just stayed where she was and took up with Brodir, the young slave boy who worked with her. So the slave was forever ploughing her field while the farmer was away. She told Amleth that was just there to help with jobs around the house, and the stupid arsehole believed her. Now none of us are sure who the father of the little boy is.

His constant bleating about being a true and faithful husband didn't ring much truer either. He was forever trying to run off back to Môn to find that tall woman with raven black hair that he had seen on his first raid. I expect he found her and was getting his wicked way with her, not just out of sight of his wife but thinking that, even I would be fooled. I am not that gullible though. I often laughed at his stupid pretence.

I know he has told you a lot about his adventures with me, but do take care how much you believe him. Most of it exaggerates the role he played and he would miss out those parts that he didn't want you to know. I'll bet he never told you about always running off to Môn to shag that Welsc girl did he?

There was nothing funnier than his strange idea that he was a competent iron worker. I know everyone can have a hobby but it takes a real idiot to believe he has become skilled in a trade when he is totally inept. Everyone knew about his poor workmanship and returned all the broken goods to the family puppy, young Brodir, who mended all of the idiot's bad workmanship. Not just in iron working too! He repaired Amleth's bad performance in bed with his wife too.

Amleth was actually useful to me even in this issue though, not as an iron worker but as the leader of iron workers. In those early days we needed all the iron workers we could get. Every army needs weapons and the way Amleth got the few artisans we had to share their knowledge and allow others to learn their craft was hugely important. As the settlement grew and developed as our centre it was immensely beneficial to have all of those iron workers making swords, spears and battle axes. Some of them gained a really high standard of workmanship, including young Brodir.

It was not a surprise to hear that Amleth died when he trusted his own workmanship with his sword. Only a total moron would go into battle with a blade that is not made by a good artisan. It was a severe error, one of false vanity, and he deserved to die for it.

One thing I heard him say that is certainly true, that no one embodies the Viking spirit better than I do. I am sure that the name of Ragnald will be remembered throughout the centuries. My achievements will certainly be discussed in hundreds and even thousands of years time!

Sometimes he advised quite well but he also made some horrendous blunders, which I had to be very quick thinking to overcome. Maybe the worst was sending that fat, flatulent Jarl Ingamund over to the Wirral. Wirral did turn out to be the best place for us to make a settlement, at least in those early days. There was almost a disaster though as some people thought that Ingamund deserved the credit for that, and wanted him to be king. I had to slit quite a few throats of his supporters rather quietly in the middle of the night to ensure that never happened. The gods appreciated those sacrifices and that is why they favoured me.

In the end the fat bastard over reached himself too, going off to attack the Saxons. Naturally I had told him that if he failed I would slit his throat, so it was no surprise that he ran away like a coward after his failure and never came back.

Perhaps Amleth was at his best when he went off to negotiate Ottar's ransom with his wife and son. They were slippery, treacherous people and I have no doubt that they made Amleth's life a misery. I know he was hugely relived to get off that island alive, as I could see the brown stains on his trousers.

Even then he had to overcome their last efforts to cheat us out of the ransom, and he did well to get seven bags of silver out of those primitive Danes. It was a great surprise to me that they had so much silver and certainly far more than the stupid old prick was worth. I had always expected to hear that they were unable or unwilling to ransom him. I had spent quite a few happy hours with Ottar, telling him how he was going to die.

The very best advice Amleth ever gave me was to discard the Danish kings of Jorvik when they slighted me, and to set out to build up our own forces. That was really the start of our greatest successes. First Vannin and then onto Jorvik itself as the Danes threw themselves futilely onto the Saxons. Of course, these strategies were pretty obvious really and I would certainly have done them myself anyway if he had not been there, but it actually was Amleth who first suggested them.

He was really infuriating in the campaign against the Picts. First he went home to bury the silver and took forever in coming back to join us. I'm sure he went off to Môn to chase the raven haired maiden again, not that she could have been a maiden by then. Then he turned up without half of the men I gave him! He came back with some nonsense story about protecting our women from the Saxons. Even after that he spent his time riding around on horses trying to look important rather than getting on with real warrior work. All he was really doing was slowing us down; we would have been there much faster without his interference.

He did fight well in the final battle, alongside me in the middle of the shield wall where all of the real fighting takes place, man to man. Perhaps he was not a complete coward that day.

He was at the most irritating he ever got when we got back after that campaign; he was a complete old woman then! First he tried to belittle my great success in that great victory. Making out that we had lost too many men, and feeling sorry for the poor widows. Doesn't he know that it's normal to lose a few men in a war? I was very generous to the widows, allowing them to share the plunder. Not many kings would have been that generous, and the widows were very happy about it, and several of them found a suitable way to show gratitude.

Next thing, he whinged on about burying the silver hoard somewhere else. He was always shitting himself over upsetting the Angles. What problem was that? We would have just beaten them as well. Didn't he know what an invincible warrior king he was serving?

Just to make it worse Thora joined in on his side. That was when she first started to really annoy me, but it was a bit late to get rid of her then though, when she was already carrying my son, the heir to my dynasty. I had to go ahead with the wedding, as having an heir is important to a king. Especially one who is building an empire.

It was not a great problem though as after that I could spend my time in Prestune, enjoying the attention of my new woman. No need to devote all your attention to just one, when you have my power of attraction! I have to say that I had a lot of fun in Prestune. The bar maids there like to entertain their men well. Of course, I was the greatest attraction for all of them and really got well looked after. Obviously it's not often that they get the attention of such a great warrior king as me.

The one great problem with all of that was that, in the end, Amleth buried the treasure and never explained properly where he had put it. Just some silly babbling about the alignment of two oak trees. What use is that when the place is covered in oak trees?

I think he might well have planned to keep it all for himself. I still wonder if his widow knows more that she is admitting to. I never did get much sense out of her, and still wonder if she is really as stupid as she pretends. I could well see her sneaking back there with her young lover to dig up the treasure.

He certainly had started to get big ideas by then, feeling he was really important. Fancy him wanting to be made a Jarl, what a load of bollocks! He wasn't even high born. People would have laughed at me if I made someone like that into one of my Jarls.

I suppose there were just a few occasions when Amleth was useful in a man's role. He was especially useful when I used him with just a few ships as bait to lure Bardr out of his stronghold on Vannin. That was so funny! Just to make it more entertaining I left it late to attack Bardr and so gave him a fair chance of catching Amleth, and he so nearly did too. The beauty of it was that it wouldn't have mattered on either occasion if he had been caught and chopped up, there were always plenty more like Amleth. Easy to replace.

There's always another Amleth. Since he died I became not only the King of Dyflinn again but also the King of Northumberland. I did that all alone so it's now clear that I am the one who deserves to build this new empire.

The new age of Norse glory is about to begin and my dynasty will last a thousand years.